SHADOW OF A DOUBT

SHADOW OF A DOUBT

Ted Allbeury

Hodder & Stoughton

Copyright © 1998 Ted Allbeury

First published in Great Britain in 1998
by Hodder and Stoughton
A division of Hodder Headline plc

British Library Cataloguing in Publication Data

Allbeury, Ted, 1917–
Shadow of a doubt
I. Title
823.9'14 [F]

ISBN 0 340 71817 X

Typeset by Avon Dataset Ltd, Bidford-on-Avon, Warks

Printed and bound in Great Britain by
Clays Ltd, St Ives plc

Hodder and Stoughton
A division of Hodder Headline PLC
338 Euston Road
London NW1 3BH

DEDICATION

This is for Sally Maria Allbeury, also known as Sweetie-pie.
My lovely and much loved youngest daughter.

One man in his time plays many parts . . .
SHAKESPEARE: *As You Like it*

Chapter 1

Like a good many other cottages in the villages around Chichester, Sir James Frazer's house was called 'Rose Cottage'. And although it had a thatched roof it wasn't really a cottage. It had been built just before the end of the First World War for the son of the owner of the manor house. A son who never came back from the war. It was a long building of local stone with five bedrooms, three bathrooms and three reception rooms. It had a large country kitchen with the traditional cream-coloured AGA as well as an electric hob and oven. In the utility room there were the usual appliances and a large fridge-freezer by Westinghouse.

They sat in the small study facing one another across the table. Francis Healey had laid out the papers including a photocopy of the piece from the newspaper announcing the serialisation of the book. He looked across at his client and friend, James Frazer, or to be precise, Sir James Frazer.

'You've read the piece, Jamie?'

'Yeah. Several times.'

'There's no point in us putting in for an injunction, not at this stage anyway.'

'Why not?'

'First of all nothing's been published. It talks about the serialisation but the only mention of the book is that it's to be published shortly.' He paused. 'And neither of us has any idea of what's being said.'

'I have, Francis.'

'What have you seen?'

'The manuscript of the book.'

Healey looked surprised. 'Have you still got it – the manuscript?'

'Maybe.'

'Asking for an injunction will only give the book a whole heap of publicity.' Healey shrugged. 'Then they publish it in Australia or America.'

'OK. So we go for libel, for defamation.'

'I'd need to see the manuscript myself before I could advise you on that. It could be considered fair comment or in the public interest. We'll have to show that the words printed were published with malice.' He paused. 'Who is this wretched man who wrote it? I've never heard of him.'

'He's got an obsession about exposing intelligence organisations. He's an American but he spends a lot of time in this country. He's only done so-called exposé pieces in magazines and newspapers up to now. He did a book on the CIA but he couldn't get it published.'

'Why not?'

'The American publishers said it was full of libel.'

'Can you get them to confirm that?'

'I shouldn't think so.' He smiled. 'They're so scared about libel suits they'd probably think that refusing to publish might be a libel in itself.'

'Can I read the manuscript?'

'Tonight. Back in the morning?'

Healey shrugged. 'OK.'

Frazer stood up and left the room. When he came back a few minutes later he put a box-file on the table. 'There you are.'

'If I think it's actionable do you want to go ahead?'

'Definitely.'

'It's a very costly exercise you know, that's why rich men can stop people publishing information about their misdemeanours. Remember how Maxwell only had to issue a writ for books to be stopped.'

Jamie Frazer shrugged. 'So be it.' He paused. 'Are you advising me to ignore a fabrication of lies and distortion?'

'Of course I'm not. Let me read the stuff and then I'll tell you what I think. That'll be as your solicitor. Separately I'll tell you what I think as an old friend.'

Frazer smiled. 'Fair enough. Let's have a drink.'

'Fine. I'd better make mine a Coke, as I'm driving.'

When they had had their drinks, Healey picked up the box-file and

Frazer walked with him to where his car was parked.

The car was typical of the man. A Rover P5 in immaculate condition and at least thirty-five years old. Francis Healey had bought it new from the Rover dealers in Chichester. It was parked alongside Frazer's Silver Shadow Mark 1, a mere twenty-five years old but equally immaculate. There was a partly-restored Austin Healey 3000 in the double garage.

As Frazer opened the car door and tossed the file onto the back seat, Frazer said, 'No copying, Francis.'

Healey turned to look at him, surprised. 'Why not?'

'Because that was the deal I did. I gave my word.'

Healey shrugged. 'OK. If that's how you want it. If we go ahead I'll have to ask you where you got it.'

'Why?'

'So that I know that it's the real thing.'

Frazer laughed. 'Take it from me it's the real thing all right.'

It was beginning to get light when Healey finished reading the manuscript. There was no doubt that it was actionable. The piece in the newspaper was brief but the headline above was enough – '*Spy chief exposed and found guilty*'. It didn't specify what he was found guilty of but the brief text named him.

The book was a litany of unsubstantiated accusations of a wide variety of alleged misjudgments, political interference and virtual treason. Frazer was painted as a womaniser, an adulterer and a snob.

The other side would have to prove and justify the claims and that would be extremely difficult. Frazer didn't have to prove that it was untrue but the defendants would have to back up their claims and substantiate them. But for such accusations to be made against a retired Director-General of MI6 would be enough to ensure that the book would be a bestseller. He would have liked to be able to show the manuscript to a specialist libel lawyer before passing judgment but it seemed that wasn't possible at this stage. He could well understand Jamie Frazer's anger at being the victim of such venom. It wasn't the kind of thing you expected to have to face when you were in your seventies and long retired. But he would have to work out their tactics very carefully before they issued a writ.

Healey bathed and shaved, ate a plate of porridge and made himself a mug of tea before he rang Frazer.

Frazer picked up the phone on the second ring and Healey suggested they met at Rose Cottage for him to hear Healey's opinion.

The door of the cottage was wide open and Healey stood at the living-room door for a moment watching the man playing the Bluthner boudoir grand piano. Frazer was wearing a pale-blue cotton shirt and grey worsted slacks. He played by ear but unmistakably well and Healey recognised 'As time goes by', the theme tune from *Casablanca*. He walked over to the piano and when Frazer looked up and stopped playing he said, 'I guess I ought to say – "play it again Sam".'

Frazer smiled. 'Nobody ever said that in the film.'

'I know.' As Frazer finished the melody with a kind of spread-out arpeggio with the left hand, Healey said quietly, 'We'd better start work, Jamie, there's a lot to go over.'

They took their coffees into Frazer's book-lined study. It was a modest size with just a writing desk, four easy chairs and a stack of Technics hi-fi separates and a pair of speakers mounted on the wall above.

When they were settled, Healey said, 'I've read the manuscript and I can only advise you that you seem to have a very good case for a writ for libel.' He paused. 'However I do have to warn you again that libel cases are tried by juries and juries are notoriously unpredictable. I also have to warn you that the financial stakes are pretty high. Newspapers rely on their financial strength to frighten off potential litigants.' He paused again. 'I think you would have to be prepared to lose at least fifty thousand pounds one way or another. Even if you won they can drag things on at huge expense to an appeal.' He shrugged. 'It's a bit of a poker game, Jamie.'

'So when do we issue the writs?'

'You've made your mind up to go ahead?'

'I'd made my mind up before I talked to you. If you had turned me down or shown doubts I'd have found somebody else.'

'Fair enough,' Healey said, but he rather resented the tactless statement. 'Let's talk about tactics.' He paused. 'We could apply for an injunction to prevent the newspaper printing the serialisation and prevent the book being published. I think we'd get it on both counts and you could keep them on edge for months. But if we stopped publication it would weaken your case in a libel action.'

'Why?'

'Because you couldn't indicate any damage to your reputation if nobody had read the damn thing.' He paused. 'My advice would be to let both items get published. However . . .' Healey took a deep breath '. . . a word of caution and I hope you won't be offended by the question . . . Is there anything substantial in any of the comments in the book that could be used against you by their defence?'

'Like what?'

'How would we come out on the three marriages and three divorces for instance?'

Frazer smiled and waved his hand dismissively.

'That sort of crap doesn't worry me. It's the politics and the stuff about my time in SIS that angers me. Just innuendo, speculation and prejudice. It's just an attempt at character assassination relying on the fact that when creeps like this one have attacked the intelligence services in the past, they've just had to sit there and take it.' He shook his head angrily. 'But not this baby.'

'If they threw in their hand what would you settle for?'

'A grovelling apology, an admission that it's a pack of lies . . . and a lot of cash. That's what hurts those guys.'

Healey watched Frazer's face as he asked, 'How do people inside the intelligence world see you? Are they pro or anti?'

'God knows. You'd better ask 'em.'

'Who shall I ask?'

Frazer shrugged, obviously irritated. 'Try Logan or Peters. Logan's still in the business. Peters is retired. I'll give you their phone numbers.'

'Shall I mention that you suggested the contact?'

'If you want. It's up to you.'

'You'll have to get used to me asking questions, Jamie. It's all part of the process.'

Frazer reached out his hand and touched Healey's arm. 'Forgive me, old pal. It makes me terribly angry to find myself in my seventies, long retired and having to respond to some shit who wants to make his fortune out of quote exposing unquote the running of our intelligence services. We none of us ever looked for praise, not even a hint of appreciation, but, by God, a lot of good men made a lot of sacrifices; money, families, comfort, to protect this country and its people from their enemies. Domestic and foreign.'

'Have you talked with anyone at Century House?'

'No. So far as I know they haven't seen the manuscript.'

'They'll have a view on how to deal with it you know.' He paused. 'Their service is being put through the mincer as well as you personally.'

'They'll just sit tight and ignore it. Beneath their contempt. They always do that. They're a government organisation.'

'Not even when the first tricky question gets asked in the Commons?'

'We'll see.' Frazer smiled and leaned back. 'You know when I was a young man I only had one ambition and that was to either play piano in the coffee-shop of a posh West End hotel or play in a rather swish night-club. I've often thought that maybe I made the wrong choice.'

'You wouldn't have been Sir James on that route, my friend.' Healey stood up smiling, looking down at Frazer. 'D'you want to think it over or shall I just go ahead?'

'Just go ahead.' He stood up, shrugging. 'Cry havoc and unleash the dogs of war.'

'I'll speak to counsel tomorrow and I'll keep in touch. But forget the dogs of war bit, this is courts and the law, and that other favourite motto of yours was never more appropriate.'

Frazer raised his eyebrows. 'What motto was that?'

'The one you always quote. The one the army taught you – Time spent in reconnaissance is seldom wasted.'

Frazer laughed. 'You're absolutely right.' He shrugged. 'So I leave it in your safe hands.'

Healey had got the number himself and had asked the operator to put him through to the editor.

'Can I ask what it's about?'

'It's a legal matter.' Healey said quietly. 'I'm a solicitor.'

'Just a moment.'

There were a couple of minutes' silence and then the girl came back.

'He's in conference at the moment and suggests that I put you through to our legal department.'

'That's fine by me but I think you should contact him again and tell him that he'll be receiving a writ for libel against himself and the paper in the next few days. I'm only phoning as a courtesy.'

'OK. I'll see if I can contact him.'

He was treated to a jangled piece of pseudo-Bach as he waited.

Then a man's voice.

'Bowman here. What's all this nonsense about a libel writ? I'm very busy.'

'It's two writs actually. One against you, the other against your newspaper. I wanted to do you the courtesy of letting you know before it becomes public.'

'Oh for Christ's sake. What libel has somebody dreamed up now? In case you don't know – this paper's policy is to fight all libel writs all the way.'

'It's the libel that has defamed Sir James Frazer that you printed a couple of days ago. We shall be going against the author of the book jointly.'

There was a longish silence and then Bowman said, 'Are you serious?'

'Very serious, Mr Bowman. We are actually drafting the writ at the moment. I'm Sir James's solicitor.'

'Why don't we meet and see if we can't work something out?'

'I'm perfectly willing to meet you but I don't see any chance of working anything out. It's a very serious libel case. I've already had counsel's opinion.'

'Where is your place?'

Healey tried to keep the smile out of his voice as he said, 'We're at Lamb Street off Northumberland Avenue. Not too far from you.'

'When would be convenient?'

'I suggest as soon as possible. Say 11.30 here?'

'OK. I'll be bringing my own legal guy with me.'

'That's fine. I look forward to seeing you both.'

'Jamie, I won't be down in Chichester tonight but I thought I'd better put you in the picture of what's happened on day one.'

'Tell me.'

'I fired a shot over the bows of the newspaper this morning. I had a meeting in my office with the editor. Bowman. An Australian. Bright but crude and full of his own importance. Quoted the *Spycatcher* case and I pointed out that was for the book to be banned not for libel. Actually all I wanted to do was to have it on the court record that he'd had fair warning. When he left I had the feeling he was unsure what to do. Wasn't going to be stopped by anyone from publishing whatever was in the public interest – the usual guff. I asked him for a date when the serialisation was due to start. Said it wasn't yet decided. That's a lie because they have announced that they are serialising a week before the book is published and I find that the book is being published next Thursday. I'd say that he's not a happy man tonight. I've left it that I see no grounds for a further meeting. It's up to him whether he publishes or not. I'm pretty sure that all he was expecting was an attempt to stop publication and he could play the knight in shining armour exposing dirty deeds at MI6. I'm sure he's too macho to back down and when he prints we'll issue the writ.'

'Did he ask how you knew about the contents of the book?'

'No. They live themselves in a constant fog of leaks and revelations from informers for six-figure sums. I doubt if it entered his mind. If it did he'd assume we used similar methods to those he uses. Day in, day out.'

'That's good news. Thanks for calling.'

'See you, Jamie.'

As Frazer hung up he was tempted to phone Adele and ask her to come down. But old instincts die hard and he suspected that maybe they were having him watched. The newspaper would tell the TV news people so that they could start assembling outside the cottage when the first edition appeared just before midnight when they were printing the first section of the serialisation.

He switched on the satellite receiver and watched the German news programme on SAT 1 followed by a German-dubbed episode of Cagney and Lacey. He switched to CNN for the midnight news and then went to bed.

Chapter 2

When Healey had had his word with counsel it had been a hurried chat during a fortuitous lunch-time adjournment of both their cases over drinks in the Wig and Pen. Howard Rowe was usually a defence counsel and he was obviously quite pleased to be asked to handle a plaintiff's case. But he had warned Healey that all bets were off until he had not only read the book but also the serialisation. And he wanted the book highlighted by Sir James where he felt that he was being defamed. Healey was disturbed at Rowe's comment that they ought to get hold of a copy of the book as soon as they arrived at the binders. But the writ must not go in until a copy of the book had been on public offer and bought at a London bookshop. The longer the period Rowe had to read the text before it was actually distributed in finished form so much the better.

He phoned Sir James and asked him to meet him at Chichester Station that evening. On the train he put the *Evening Standard* aside and closed his eyes. The problem was the niceties of getting that early copy of the book as soon as possible. When newspapers were engaged in their so-called 'exposures', they paid an insider or, if that wasn't possible, they would have the appropriate premises broken into. He had no compunction about using similar methods but wasn't sure whether it should be his client who fixed it or would it be less illegal if he, as a lawyer, instigated the operation. He had phoned his wife before he left the office, telling her that Jamie Frazer would drive him home. He didn't need her to meet him at the station with the car.

They had gone to The Ship for a drink and a quiet talk in the residents' lounge. They were both well known at the hotel. Healey

9

explained the situation to Frazer. When Healey finished, Frazer said, 'The typesetting is already done. You've seen the pages. It went to the binders two weeks ago. They're doing ten thousand copies on the first run with the same amount in reserve in unbound pages. They could get those out in three days. They're now aiming to do the serialisation in two weeks' time. The Monday edition of the newspaper. The book will be in the shops that night. Under embargo until the Wednesday. I can get anything you want.'

'How can you be so sure, Jamie?'

Frazer smiled. 'I've done a deal.'

'What's the deal?'

'I've given an undertaking to my contact that we won't include them, the printers, in the libel writs.'

Healey was silent for a few moments and then he said, 'We're getting dangerously near walking on thin ice, Jamie.'

'What's illegal about not issuing a writ against a legitimate target?'

'Nothing I guess. But I wish you'd thought of discussing it with me before you went ahead.'

Frazer smiled. 'I did think of it but I thought you might say "no". Anyway you can always claim that you had no part in it.'

'What if the printers tip off the newspaper and the author?'

Frazer shook his head. 'They won't, Francis. They're old friends of mine. They owe me from way back.'

'Had they heard from the author or the newspaper about possible writs?'

'Not a word.' He smiled. 'That didn't endear them to their clients.'

'Their clients must be the publishers and would know that the printers would get writs too. They always do.'

'Yeah. Apparently at a meeting of all the parties concerned they were of the opinion that a private individual like me couldn't afford the financial risk of fighting a libel case in court and that we'd end up just going for trying to prevent publication. Just like with *Spycatcher*. They also said that SIS would put pressure on me not to go ahead because it would open the door for the defence to put SIS through the mincer in public. Wonderful publicity, wonderful sales and the worst that could happen would be having to shift the operation to the States or Australia. No problem.'

'Do SIS know about the book?'

'I don't know. I assume that they've read the newspaper piece about serialisation.'

'Have they contacted you?'

'You mean SIS?'

'Yes.'

Frazer smiled and shook his head slowly. 'Not a word.'

'What do you think their attitude will be to you issuing writs?'

'It'll be divided. Some will say let 'em get on with it but most of them will resent the newspaper and the publisher having one more go at SIS.'

'What are the odds on them supporting you?'

'I'm not a betting man but I'd say they'll be cool at first and then be supportive as it boils up.' He grinned. 'I'll put in my two penn'orth to make them co-operate.'

'You seem to have done quite a bit of homework on all this already.'

'I have, my friend.' He grinned. 'Time spent on reconnaissance and all that.'

James Frazer enjoyed his old-fashioned country garden but he never got involved. His man, Charlie Bates, looked after the garden, the Rolls and the cottage, and his wife, Maggie, was cook and in charge of the house. They had a small but pleasant flat over the double garage. Frazer's main interest, apart from his piano-playing, was a forty-five-foot cruiser with twin diesels moored in the old marina at Birdham. He seldom went further than the Isle of Wight or across to the French coast. From time to time he slept on the boat and from time to time he was accompanied by one of the pretty ladies who although he had known them for quite a time were still many years younger than he was. He was quite a handsome man and the grey hair suited him. Broad-shouldered and fit without doing anything about it, he just smiled when they asked him what he was going to do when he grew up.

When Frazer got the phone call a few days later he made a thermos of tea and took a slice of pork-pie from the refrigerator and headed for the car. When he got to the boat it was beginning to get dark; he ran both engines and went through his usual routine. He had a power line to a plug on the jetty and a plug-in phone. A small Sony TV and a minihi-fi stack were side by side on the mahogany structure over the companion-way down to the galley.

It was nearly two hours after he had arrived when he saw the lights of the car coming past the pond towards the mooring. It stopped as he'd instructed by the notice-board that showed photographs and details of boats for sale. When the car's lights dimmed and then went out he walked slowly towards the car. He didn't recognise the man who handed over the parcel and they exchanged no words as Frazer nodded his acknowledgement.

As he walked back to his boat he could see her lights reflected in the calm water of the marina. There were no other cars or people that he could see and no lights on any other boat.

Back in the saloon he undid the brown-paper wrapping and slit open the adhesive tape that held it together. There were six copies of the book but without their paper jackets. He took one copy and riffled through the pages as he ate his pork-pie and drank his tea. Cursing quietly as he realised that he'd forgotten the sugar. When he was folding up the brown-paper packaging he found a printed announcement that gave the date of the newspaper serialisation, put an embargo on selling copies of the book until the following day and gave a 'hot line' number for ordering further copies.

The date of the first serialisation was only four days away.

He tapped out Healey's number on his portable phone.

'Francis Healey. Can I help you?'

'It's Jamie, Francis. I've got six copies of the book. How many do you need?'

'At least three. Four if you can spare them.'

'What train are you catching in the morning?'

'The seven-fifteen.'

'I'll bring you four to the station. They'll be wrapped.' He paused. 'By the way, the first serialisation is next Monday. The books go on sale the following day.'

'The writs are all prepared. I'll have them delivered on Wednesday. But be prepared for a lot of publicity. The tabloids especially will lap it up. Even the broadsheets will get in on the act.' He paused. 'Have you got an answering machine?'

'No.'

'Well get one. Put a message on it – let me think – "Hi, this is Jamie Frazer. I'm not available at the moment. Please leave your name, number and message after the bleep." No more than that. OK?'

'OK. See you in the morning.'

After he had handed over the parcel of books to Healey, Frazer walked back into South Street and bought an answering machine. He got the shop assistant to show him how to record the tape.

Back at the cottage he made the tape and plugged the machine into the original British Telecom connection. He used his portable to ring the number and the message came over loud and clear. He got Maggie to do him a proper breakfast. Fried egg, crisp bacon and a couple of Lincolnshire sausages. As he ate he wondered if it wouldn't be a good idea to warn a few people of what was about to happen. But in the end he decided to do nothing. It would be interesting to see different people's reactions to the so-called revelations. Could be a salutary lesson one way or another.

Healey had prepared the operation meticulously. A hundred copies of the two-page spread in the newspaper. A copy of the book bought in Hatchards in Piccadilly together with a receipt. A dozen other purchases in book stores in major cities.

The writ against Sidney Bowman, the editor, was served on him personally as he was entertaining his current girl-friend at the Groucho Club. The writ against the paper itself was served and signed for in the early hours of the Wednesday morning. The writs against the publishers and the author of the book were served at the publisher's offices in Bedford Square.

Chapter 3

Bowman had sold an extra 100,000 copies of the Monday paper and now, Thursday, they were down to a mere 5,000 over the normal sales. He didn't tackle the arithmetic. He knew that he'd need to publicise the serialisation even more. That was expensive and the only prize was to maintain the 100,000 figure for every issue of the four-week Monday serialisation features. He had reluctantly agreed to the joint meeting with the publishers. They met in the palatial offices of the *Daily Bulletin* and the legal advisers of both parties were there.

The boardroom table could comfortably seat twenty-six people and the four of them looked rather odd as they took their places each side of the far end of the enormous table. There was just tea, coffee and a plate of digestive biscuits despite it being a lunch-time meeting.

It was Bowman who brought the chit-chat to an end in his own brusque Australian way.

'Well, gentlemen, it's time we looked at the situation. How about your people, Mr Keane?'

Mr Keane was the managing director of Primrose Publications plc and was used to being treated with a little more courtesy.

'Well our view is that we continue as we all originally planned,' he said rather languidly.

'That's bullshit, Mr Keane. What we all envisaged was an attempt to stop publication which would have been a boost to our circulation and your sales of the book. Even if it had taken a couple of weeks to fight it you knew you'd be selling the book all over the world. What I want to know is are your Board going to chicken out because of this bloody writ?'

'My Board have never chickened out as you put it, Mr Bowman. We have a reputation for publishing books that challenge authority and the status quo. What about your Board, Mr Bowman?'

Bowman was unused to criticism or defiance no matter how tactfully it may be delivered.

'There's one thing we didn't allow for and that was a writ for defamation. And what is virtually a joint writ with you people. And we then have to face a simple fact. If we lose, you people haven't got enough money to satisfy an unfavourable judgment. We're the guys with the big bankroll and we're the guys they'll be gunning for.'

'That was always the position, Mr Bowman. I'm sure you must have realised that.' Keane paused and then said, 'Of course an injunction to stop publication wouldn't have hurt you provided you'd got your circulation up with the initial serialisation. But it would have cost us a packet. Author's fee, editing, typesetting, printing, binding, artwork – all paid for in advance.'

'How many have you printed?'

'Ten thousand so far with sheets for another twenty thousand.'

'And how many have you sold?'

'We've supplied ten thousand and we have over-orders for another ten thousand.'

'When do you break even?'

'That's not the point, Mr Bowman. If we lose this case my company would be bankrupt.'

The red-headed man sitting alongside the publisher said, 'My name's Grimes and my partnership is acting for Primrose Publications. We seem to be ignoring the facts of life in this discussion. The plaintiff is a private individual. Do we really think he's willing to lose everything he's got by pursuing this action to the bitter end?' He shrugged. 'Has anybody checked what his financial position is?'

Bowman shook his head. 'There won't be many noughts on the end of his bank balance that's for sure. We did bear this in mind way back but you're right, we've let it get lost in the wash.'

Not to be outdone Bowman's man chipped in, 'Parsons. Acting for the newspaper group. There's good sense in what both parties are saying but the fact is that the publisher can go on recouping any financial losses from sales in other countries.' He paused. 'Couldn't we arrange some formula where the newspaper has a stake in the profits from book sales?'

Bowman looked across at Keane, eyebrows raised in query.

Keane said with a marked lack of enthusiasm, 'Would that satisfy you, Mr Bowman?'

'It evens out the stakes and rewards a little.'

'I'll talk to my Board. But it would have to be a nominal amount, say a small percentage off book sales.'

'Off the top or net?'

'It would have to be net.' He smiled without pleasure. 'We have to give our friends the booksellers a discount you know.'

'How much discount?'

'Can be up to fifty percent. Certainly not less than thirty-five.'

'It would give me a point with my Board.' Bowman changed to his macho voice again. 'So, gentlemen. Are we agreed? We aren't frightened of the writs. We'll let the legal eagles do their stuff . . .' he grinned '. . . holding things up. And we'll just carry on.' He looked across the table. Nobody spoke, neither did they nod or shake their heads. So Bowman stood up.

'You'll have to excuse me, gentlemen. I've got another meeting to attend. I think it's been a helpful discussion on the whole. Thank you.'

As he walked back to his office Bowman was in two minds about what he should do. He was a man of instinctive decision, not pussy-footing about with lawyers. He guessed that for a few thousand pounds he could print an apology, pay the money and call it a day. But it would be seen by everybody as backing down and he had built his reputation on that old Fleet Street motto, 'Publish and be damned'. He found it irksome to be in partnership with people like Keane. Weaklings, counting the pennies even if they weren't their pennies. But at least Keane was the kind of man who would accept him as the decision-maker. And as Keane could go on making a profit on the book overseas, any deal he could do to get a piece of the action would be an extra piece of insurance. He looked at his watch. He could spend a couple of hours at the Groucho playing the part of the fearless editor who reckoned it was time the public got the truth of what was going on in the corridors of power, before he had to look over tomorrow's paper. There was a note

17

on his desk to say that the paper's libel insurers would like to have a word with him before he sanctioned next Monday's serialisation.

Chapter 4

Frazer and Healey met briefly on the day after the first extract from the book appeared. Healey was wondering if his client would be a little more cautious now that the law moves had started. They had gone to Rose Cottage and Frazer poured them each a half glass of red wine.

'Have you had any reaction from other people?'

Frazer lifted his glass and smiled. 'Yes quite a lot.'

'Tell me.'

'Two calls from the BBC, four from other broadcasters. One woman saying it was time that people like me were hanged.' He paused. 'One gentleman saying much the same. And ten or so others all either supportive or neutral.' He smiled. 'I've kept the recorded tape and put a new one in. Two in fact because the damn thing is going all day.'

'What made you keep the tape?'

Frazer shrugged. 'Just old instincts.'

'A good idea all the same.' Healey paused. 'Anything from Century House?'

'Yes. Two callers.'

'For or against?'

'The D-G himself was the first one. Amiable, supportive, but suggested we meet to discuss their concerns about so-called revelations. The other was also supportive. A guy named Henman. Patrick Henman. I knew him when he was just a new-boy when I was "our man in Berlin".' Frazer smiled. 'Now *he's* "our man in Berlin". Offered any help I wanted. Said he'd been approached by the author several times. Didn't like him and led him down a few blind-alleys.' He paused. 'And

19

one lady who said she was willing to swear I was the nicest man she'd ever slept with.'

'Have you responded to any of them?'

'A couple. And the D-G. We're going to meet some time next week.'

'The attitude of SIS could make a big difference. But their support wouldn't have to be too obvious or it'll look like collusion. The old China hands ganging up against the truth.'

'They're aware of that, Francis.' Frazer smiled. 'They're not the fools that the press like to paint them.'

'I'm sure they're not.' He paused. 'Anything from the direction of ex-wives?'

Frazer laughed. 'One lady journalist said that there was great interest in something in an article she had seen way back where the author quoted some comment I was supposed to have said at some interview where I'd been asked about my former wives and I'd said "No comment except that they were all very beautiful and only one of them was a crocodile". Seems like a few people are trying to identify the crocodile.'

'Did you actually say that, Jamie? It sounds like you.'

Frazer laughed. 'It does rather, doesn't it? I don't really remember. Anyway, who cares. I heard on my grapevine that the author's coming over here in a few days' time. There was a booksigning planned at Hatchards but it's been cancelled.'

'Who cancelled it?'

'Hatchards. I understand too that they have no copies of the book on show.' He grinned. 'First blood to us.'

'Who is the present D-G of SIS?'

'His name's Platt, Sir Hugo. Got his "K" a couple of years ago. Good chap. Stands up well to the bloody politicians. Very protective of SIS. He found the book extremely offensive and I got the feeling that as they can't do anything in a court to defend themselves and expose the lies, they might see my action as partly doing their job for them.'

'You think he'll be helpful?'

'Yeah, I do. Within limits of course.'

'We're having a bit of a dinner on Thursday. We'd particularly like you to come. Informal. Seven-thirty for eight.'

Frazer smiled. 'Is this your Helen's idea to give me a bit of moral support?'

'No way. But in fact I should be surprised if the guests *weren't* interested. You've met at least half of them already.' Healey sighed and stood up. 'I'd better get going. Helen's going to her language class tonight.'

'Oh, really, what language?'

'German.'

Frazer smiled. 'She can practise on me. We Brits are always embarrassed by having to say anything in a foreign language out loud.'

Keane sent his PR girl to meet Pinto off the plane. She hadn't met him before although he had been in London several times when the book was being discussed, and she'd seen his photos on the file. He hadn't endeared himself to the publisher's staff with his petulant outbursts of bad temper and his obvious expectation that he was going to be treated like a VIP. Authors were never VIPs at Primrose Publications plc, and they saw Al Pinto as a journalist, and journalists were seen as people who would tell any lie to make a buck. Twisting what people said and quoting words out of context. But he'd been given a contract for £100,000 for world rights of his book entitled – *Who Goes There*.

By the time he was through Gatwick Immigration Control and had claimed his baggage he was an hour overdue, but Priscilla smiled as she walked towards him.

'Mr Pinto?'

'Al Pinto, yeah, that's me, where am I staying?'

'At the Park Lane Hilton.'

'I told Keane I wanted to be put up at the Connaught.'

Keane had said that the American wasn't good enough to warrant the Connaught.

'The Connaught is over-booked at the moment. They've got the builders in.' She smiled. 'Would you prefer the Cumberland, Mr Pinto?'

'No.' He shrugged. 'The Hilton'll do.'

'I'll get us a taxi.'

'When does Keane come to visit with me?'

'There's a meeting in our offices this evening at six.' She smiled. 'Gives you time for a wash and brush-up.'

'I've given 'em a bestseller and this is how I get treated. You guys are gonna have to learn to have a bit more respect.'

21

When she'd checked him in to the Hilton she wrote out the address in Bedford Square as a reminder and then left him to his own devices.

The meeting with Keane and the sales director, and Al Pinto, had been cool on both sides and Keane put the basic question, dreading the answer.

'Have you had this book read by a libel lawyer, Al?'

'What for?'

'For libel, for defamation. We've had a libel writ served on us by Sir James Frazer claiming defamation.'

'So what?'

'So if the court found against us it could cost you and us and the newspaper a lot of money. There's a writ against you too. The wording's the same as ours.'

'Keane. If anyone was gonna sue it would have to be MI6 and we all know they never go to court.'

'What about *Spycatcher*?'

'That was to stop publication. And the bastards lost even that. A government agency has to take what criticisms it gets. You can't defame a government agency or they'd be suing every day of the week.'

'But Sir James isn't a government agency, he's an individual and he's already suing us.'

'And the only way he can prove that something I've written about him is inaccurate is to get MI6 to testify on his behalf and believe me they ain't gonna do that for him nor anyone else. They'd open the door for all sorts of questions about what they're up to.'

'They could be subpoenaed by the plaintiffs.'

'And in court they'd claim they couldn't say anything because of national security.'

'You sound very confident, Al.'

'I am, old pal. I am. I've been on this roller-coaster many times. I know the rules of this game.'

'I've arranged for us to have dinner with Mr Bowman, editor of the newspaper, this evening, he'll be glad to have your reassurances.' He looked at his watch. 'It's time we were on our way.'

The meal with Bowman had been a relief to Keane. Bowman went

22

along with Al Pinto's analysis and confirmed that they would go on with the serialisation. He had also instructed the paper's lawyers to introduce as many legal delays as they could get away with to stretch out the time before a date for the hearing was decided. Bowman had invited Pinto to the Groucho Club and they were already talking like old buddies. Two go-getters who weren't frightened by a couple of writs. Two guys who were ready to take on anyone who tried to stop the public from hearing the truth about how the intelligence services broke the rules and the law.

Chapter 5

Healey's house was on the side of a hill about a mile from Lavant village. There were lights on all over the house and half a dozen cars were already parked along the lane. He locked the Rolls and walked up the shingle drive.

There were few introductions for he knew most of the guests. He was amused that they'd solved the problem of the odd man by inviting Adele, obviously to be his partner for the evening. She waved to him across the room and smiled her knowing smile but she made no move to join the group he was chatting to.

There was no attempt to pretend that they were not aware of the newspaper piece and the book. Those who mentioned it seemed genuinely angry that he could be attacked in this way. Especially as it was almost five years since he retired.

They were still on the main course when in a moment's silence in the chatter Brian Boyle said across the table, 'Jamie, I've always wondered how one got into intelligence. How's it done? How did you get in?'

Jamie Frazer smiled. 'As a matter of fact I answered a classified ad in *The Times*.'

There was some laughter and Boyle said, 'You're pulling my leg.'

'I'm not. I assure you.'

'Tell me more,' Boyle said.

'Well, in those days the classified ads in *The Times* were all on the front page. All sorts of ads, like – "Will the girl in the green hat on the five-forty train to Croydon meet the man smoking a pipe on Saturday at six under the clock at Victoria Station".' He paused, smiling. 'My ad was much less romantic. It said roughly – "linguists required for special work in Army. No promotion beyond lance-corporal. Box number something or other".'

'It's almost unbelievable. And you wrote to the box number?'

'Yes.'

'How old were you?'

'Twenty-one, twenty-two. I don't remember exactly.'

'And you were accepted?'

'Yeah. It was October 1939 and I guess they must have been desperate for recruits.'

It was Adele who said, smiling, beside him, 'He's fishing for compliments. He ended up as a lieutenant-colonel, so they weren't such bad pickers those fellows.'

The talk moved on to the train service from Chichester to London and the cost of moorings at Birdham.

Adele had asked him for a lift home to her house in Midhurst and he'd driven them back to Rose Cottage for a night-cap. He had known her for three years and he found her not only physically attractive and affectionate but good company and easy to get on with. She was forty-two and her husband, a pilot, had been killed on a training flight in Scotland five years ago. She also shared his Birmingham roots although hers were in upper-class Sutton Coldfield rather than working-class Erdington and Aston. She had bought him an Aston Villa FC scarf the first Christmas he had known her.

At the cottage he had poured her a glass of Chardonnay and made tea for himself because he would be driving. As he sat beside her on the couch sipping his tea, she turned her head to smile at him. She said quietly, 'Why don't I stay and then you can have wine too.'

He put down his mug of tea and kissed her. 'You should have been a diplomat, honey.'

'There was something odd in what you were saying at dinner tonight.'

'Must have been the company gone to my head. What was so odd?'

'You said you read the ad that recruited you in *The Times*.'

'I did, my dear, I did.'

'How many twenty-year-old boys in Brum could afford to buy *The Times*?'

He laughed. 'I read it in Erdington Library. It's a long story.'

'So tell it.'

He frowned. 'You'd be terribly bored. You really would.'

'I won't. I find it fascinating. How the hell did a boy from the back streets of Birmingham get to be a lieutenant-colonel in intelligence, let alone Director General of SIS?'

'It really is boring. But here goes. I decided in 1938 that I wanted to be a fighter pilot in the RAF. I passed all the tests but on the day before I was accepted Chamberlain declared war on Germany. I worked in a drawing-office and mine was what they called a reserved occupation. You had to stay in your job and you couldn't join the armed forces. But I went to the recruiting office in James Watt Street and told them my story. They accepted me for the army and said forget the regulations. Most people were trying to get into reserved occupations. But they were wrong. I was summonsed by the Ministry of Labour for leaving a reserved occupation without their permission. It took time to get to court and meantime I was unemployed and no dole money. I used to go to the library to keep warm.' He shrugged. 'That's how I got to read *The Times*.'

'And what happened to the summons?'

He laughed. 'I was defended by some idiot from the Judge-Advocate's department and I was fined thirty pounds. That was a lot of money in those days. The army had to pay it.' He shrugged. 'End of boring story.'

'Have you read the book?'

'Yeah. Have you?'

'Yes.'

'What did you think of it?'

'A load of crap but interesting. You've had quite a busy life, my boy.'

She stood up, reaching out her hand for his and pulling him up to face her. She slid her arms around his shoulders, her head back to look at his face as she said, 'Let's go to bed, Sunbeam.'

He looked back at her. 'Why did you call me that?'

She smiled. 'Because you once told me that your Grandma always called you Sunbeam. And I know that your Grandma was your favourite lady.'

Chapter 6

Grandma had always called him Sunbeam. She was always on his side. She and Grandpa had brought him up. He never really knew why but it had something to do with his father being killed when he was a baby. Father had been a lieutenant in the Black Watch. Nobody ever answered his questions about his father but his mother frequently said that the things he did would make his father 'turn in his grave'. It was obvious that his mother hadn't liked his father. She didn't like her son either. She was a very pretty woman and there had been a lot of men who would have liked to marry her, but she had no liking for any man. From time to time he had to live for a few weeks at his mother's house. He didn't know what prompted these visits but he hated and feared them, listening to a litany of his faults and shortcomings. He was never quite sure what his faults were but he got the general message. He was no good.

His mother's verdict seemed to be confirmed by the interview with his headmaster at King Edward's Grammar School. 'Mrs Frazer,' he said, 'Your son is on the dust-heap of the school and will be on the dust-heap of life.'

Grandma had spoken to a man in the next road who was a foreman at Number One foundry at the local iron-foundry. A week later Jamie Frazer was, at the age of fifteen, working in the foundry as a moulder's labourer. The tough moulders took the boy who had no father under their wing and despite the terrible conditions when working with molten iron, Jamie Frazer thrived. He got on well with the men and they liked him too. He found it strange to be liked and praised. After two years on the foundry floor he was moved up to do the blueprints in the drawing-office. It was about that time that Helen Lockhart told him that he had lovely blue eyes. It was the first nice thing that anyone had ever said to him and he fell instantly in love. He never mentioned it to her of course but nothing ever gave him such pleasure until the day many years later when he was promoted to major.

When he was eighteen he moved to another company which paid an extra ten shillings a week. He had been there nearly two years before it became too boring to endure any longer. It was then that he applied to join the RAF on a short-service commission as a fighter pilot.

Chapter 7

The next morning there was a problem. There was a crowd of news people in front of the cottage. Crews with TV cameras, a dozen microphones in outstretched hands and countless people with small recording machines. He walked back into the bedroom and stroked Adele's forehead until she woke.

'Hi, honey. There's a great gaggle of journalists outside the cottage. How about I phone Maggie Bates and get her to come over and do us breakfasts. You get dressed. Keep away from the windows and I'll go down and see if I can send them on their way.'

She pushed back a long strand of hair and reached for his bathrobe lying across the foot of the bed.

'Just tell 'em to go to hell, Jamie.'

The journalists shouted to Maggie Bates as she let herself into the cottage but she ignored them. But a few minutes later Frazer, in a pale-blue cotton shirt, chinos and sandals walked down the drive to where the journalists were waiting.

'Good morning. Because I have issued a writ for libel, the book and newspaper thing is *sub judice*. So I can't answer questions on the subject. If there's a couple of non-related questions I'll try and answer them.'

'Sir James . . .' the girl thrust a microphone towards him '. . . Sir James – when do you expect to be in court?'

He shook his head. 'I've no idea. You'd better speak to my lawyer.' He smiled. 'He's given me strict orders not to talk.' He paused, still smiling. 'And the older ones among you will know that I always obey orders.' It was a clear reference to the fact that he had a reputation for always ignoring any orders when he was in the army if they didn't suit him.

There were a few more questions which he diplomatically swept aside and finally he said, 'My housekeeper, Maggie, is making up a couple of thermos flasks of tea for you. Ah, here she is. Thank you all for coming.'

Fifteen minutes later the journalists had left and Jamie Frazer had endeared himself to twenty more people. When the case got to court it would probably be on the front pages every day. But right now it would barely make a couple of lines on page five.

Chapter 8

Sir Hugo had taken a private room at the Travellers' Club, a favourite place for SIS people, and the waiter had brought in cold cuts, vegetables and crème caramel for dessert. There was a silver-coloured thermos for coffee and another for tea.

'I know you don't like tarted-up food, Jamie, so I got them to give us things we could help ourselves to.'

They took what they fancied and settled back in the large leather club armchairs. As Sir Hugo wiped his lips with a paper napkin, he looked across at his predecessor. He hadn't followed Jamie as D-G. There had been a military man for a few years in between in the hope of him taming some of the wilder elements of SIS. But it hadn't worked.

'How's this wretched business affecting you, Jamie?'

Frazer shrugged. 'I'm just leaving it to my legal guy. His name's Francis Healey and his number's in the book.'

'Was he ever in our business?'

'No. I thought it was better to have an outsider.'

'Good thinking. This scumbag Pinto or whatever his name is. You ever come across him before?'

'Not in person . . . but I spoke to an old friend of mine in Washington when the paper first said it was serialising some book about me. The paper said the author was an American named Al Pinto. I asked if my friend had heard of the guy and why he was picking on me.

'He told me that Pinto was one of those sleazebags who goes around trying to dig up dirt and scandal about politicians and public figures. He calls himself an "investigative journalist" but he's just a creep who's happy to turn off his probing for a bag of dollars.'

'So where do you come in?'

'Ah, yes.' Frazer laughed. 'The old ceremony again. Why pick on me?' He paused, collecting his facts. 'You remember that chap George Blake, yes?'

Sir Hugo shifted in his chair as if the name made him uncomfortable. 'Too bloody true I remember him . . . go on.'

'Well it seems like somebody at Doubleday, the New York publishers, got a manuscript about Blake making him look like a hero. They asked me to look it over unofficially. The writer talked about his several, very long interviews with Blake when he was in the slammer. I did a bit of checking against my memory and it turned out that the writer had never met Blake. In fact the date of one supposed interview was six months before we rumbled Blake. The publishers not only rejected the manuscript but put the word around to other publishing houses. The book never saw the light of day.' He paused. 'The author was Al Pinto. My Washington friend said he thought that was the motivation for this stuff about me.'

Sir Hugo nodded. 'We've done a bit of ferreting about ourselves. It might be useful if your chap Healey got in touch with me. One of our researchers has found over forty factual errors in the text.' He shrugged. 'Anyway, does no harm to get together and see if there are areas where we can help.'

Frazer smiled. 'What's the official view about the book?'

'The official view is that we haven't read it and it's nothing to do with us.'

'And unofficially?'

'They're worried that this little bastard wants to make SIS look like a bunch of criminals and traitors.'

'What if they call somebody from SIS as a witness?'

'We shall take every step we can to claim that we have nothing to say and claim exemption from appearing on grounds of national security.'

'What do they feel about me issuing a libel writ?'

'Supportive, but a bit worried.'

'Why worried?'

Sir Hugo shrugged. 'Just worried about the defendants thrashing about on our patch.'

'Will they assist me if necessary?'

34

Sir Hugo smiled and winked. 'Of course not. We are strictly neutral.' He shrugged. 'Of course, if your chap Healey was to need some basic information I guess we'd have to fulfil our legal obligations.'

As Frazer had to be in London for his meeting with Sir Hugo, Healey had made an appointment for Frazer to meet his counsel. Howard Rowe QC specialised in libel and was always concerned that his clients were told that in his opinion libel and defamation were the most uncertain areas of the law. He was big-built and had been a lock-forward for both the Oxford University rugby fifteen and later for the Wasps. He showed signs in his face and waistline that he still enjoyed an aftergame beer or two even if he was only refereeing these days.

'Before we discuss my opinion, let me outline what the law says on defamation.' He paused. 'The law says that a statement about a person is defamatory of him if it tends to do any one of the following:

a) expose him to hatred, ridicule, or contempt;
b) cause him to be shunned or avoided;
c) lower him in the estimation of right-thinking members of society generally; or
d) disparage him in his business, trade, office, or profession.'

He paused and then went on. 'In my opinion I am quite satisfied that the defendants have offended on at least three of those categories. Maybe all four.' Rowe paused and looked at Sir James, taking his time as he said slowly and carefully, 'And now, Sir James. I've got to warn you that libel cases are the most unpredictable cases in the whole of the law. Divorces, murder, theft, assault and commercial fraud are paradise compared with the libel courts. A libel case is decided not just on facts but on impressions. Impressions of the witnesses, even of counsel. And then we have our twelve just men and true. Only the good Lord knows how *they* reach their decisions. I don't, and half the time I don't think they do either.

'And of course there's the money aspect. Huge sums of money can be awarded. Amounts far beyond what the offence deserves. And the private person like your good self who launches an action against the money-bags, be they individual or commercial, is taking the risk that if he or she loses it could, repeat could, cost you every cent you've got. Money, property – even your home.' He paused. 'So I want to stop there and ask you – Sir James, do you realise the risks involved?'

'Yes. But I'd like to hear your opinion.'

Howard Rowe briefly touched his copy of the book, pages flagged by blue, red and green tabs. Then he opened the file on the desk in front of him.

He looked across at Frazer. 'Before I give you my thoughts, why are you so sure that you are prepared to run the risks involved?'

'Mr Rowe. I'm a single man. I've no dependants. Why the hell should I let some villain get away with a scurrilous and false attack on my character and my career?'

Rowe nodded. 'Good enough. So down to business.' He smiled at Healey and Frazer in turn and then said, 'I've studied the book and particularly the pieces you have highlighted and . . .' he paused and looked at Healey '. . . I think it's just a question of *quantum.*' He turned to look at Frazer. 'I think this is as good a case as I've ever seen from either side of the fence. I think it's just a question of how much damages we get.' He paused for several moments and then said, 'However . . . and I always hate lawyers and judges who preface their remarks by saying "however"? But I need to say it in this instance. So here goes. However, this case is going to give the defendants a perfect stage for painting a picture of you as a philanderer, an adulterer, an incompetent who probably cost people their lives and – to round things off – a snob.' He paused again, looking at Frazer. 'Which of those items worries you most?'

Sir James shook his head. 'None.'

'What about the ex-wives?'

Sir James smiled. 'I'm sure that anything they could say unfavourably about me was said at the time of the divorces.'

Rowe nodded. 'This fellow paints you as a hard leftie bordering on communist if not actually a secret member of the Party.'

Sir James sighed. 'I voted Labour in 1945 but so did most servicemen. And I voted Labour again in the next election. I've voted Liberal a couple of times and Tory, I suppose, five or six times.'

'As a matter of interest to me, what made you change from Labour?'

'The Labour Party under Attlee said what they were going to do to put the country right. In their first five years they did all the things they said they'd do. But when it came to the second time around they'd done it all. They had no idea what to do from then on. They were pathetic.'

'And the Liberals?'

'I voted Liberal because I admired Jo Grimond. When he retired from politics they didn't seem the same.'

There was a long pause and then Rowe said quietly, 'Did anyone ever lose his life because of decisions you made?'

It was long moments before Sir James responded and then he said quietly, 'You can never be sure but I'd think the answer is probably yes.'

'Anything you'd like to ask me?' Rowe said as he closed the file in front of him.

'Yes. How long before it gets into court?'

Rowe looked at Healey who turned to look at Sir James. 'I'm recommending that we put in an injunction to stop further serialisation and further sales and distribution of the book.' Healey looked back at Rowe. 'I wanted to give them time to withdraw or publish so that we could establish deliberation and maybe malice. We've established that, so now let's annoy them with a stopper.'

Rowe nodded. 'I doubt if a court would let them go on when there's a writ outstanding. So to answer Sir James, what do you think? I'd guess we won't be in court inside a couple of months at least.'

Healey nodded. 'I agree.'

Rowe looked at Sir James. 'Is that OK?'

Sir James shrugged. 'Suits me whenever it is. I'm glad you think you can stop more publishing.'

Rowe stood up, holding out his hand. 'Glad to have met you at last, Sir James.'

Healey was having a meal with a friend at the Law Society so Frazer took a taxi to Victoria Station and caught the next train to Chichester. He took a first-class single and found an empty compartment. He looked briefly at the *Evening Standard* and then tossed it onto the seat opposite. They had those things on the headrest that Grandma called antimacassars. They were supposed to keep men's hair oil off the upholstery. He leaned back his head, adjusting the rest and then, closing his eyes, he slept.

Chapter 9

Adele had phoned and suggested that she came down and they could go to the matinee at the Memorial Theatre. He'd traded that for going down to the boat and then having lunch at the Yacht Club. She'd parked her car at the cottage and they'd gone down to Birdham in the Silver Shadow.

The marina at Birdham was old and much loved but it had few facilities. At one time there had been a marine store but that was now an artist's studio although he had never seen anyone there. They had to go round the long way so that he could park alongside the boat. The MV *Aquila* was on the first mooring with a wooden finger boardwalk on the far side. He cleared off the canvas cover from the wheelhouse and instinctively checked the engines, warming them up before he turned the two switches. They responded instantly and he left them running, then he leaned heavily over the rail and reached out for her. He smiled as he saw that she was standing barefoot with her shoes in her hand.

When he had made her comfortable in the saloon, he did his routine check of the electrics and the instruments. Radar, depth gauge, rev counters, voltmeter, twin thermometers, fuel gauge and security system. He switched the radio to Channel 16 but there was no traffic.

He walked her up the lane and across the lock-gates to the main Chichester Marina and through to the clubhouse.

They had the standard fry-up of sausages, bacon and two fried eggs with tomatoes followed by apple tart with Häagen Dazs.

When they got back to the boat it was warm enough to sit on deck and he opened a bottle of Paul Masson Cabernet Sauvignon.

'How long have you had your mooring here? They're terribly hard to get.'

He shrugged. 'About fifteen years. It was half-empty in those days.'

'Did you already have the cottage?'

'Yes. But I had a place in London as well. I gave that up when I retired.'

'Why did you settle in Chichester?'

'When I joined the Intelligence Corps in the first days of the war, the Army said we were a disgrace to the military.' He laughed. 'Saluting with the wrong hand and answering back to officers. That sort of thing. So they decided that we all had to have three months basic infantry training. And I was sent down here to do my training at the Royal Sussex barracks.' He smiled. 'I loved it. All of it. Friends, and what to me was freedom. A lovely city and the thing that made you a real man in those days – battledress. Nobody boned their boots or polished their brass as enthusiastically as I did. And suddenly I had a virtue. I wasn't a conscript, I was a volunteer – had given up a reserved job to get into the Army.'

'What did you do at the barracks?'

'There was a squad of us I Corps chaps and we did drill . . . square-bashing, Bren guns, .303 rifle, gym, map-reading . . .' he shrugged '. . . the usual infantry recruit stuff.' He smiled. 'The regiment used to march with the band playing "Sussex by the Sea" to the cathedral on Sunday mornings. I loved it. I read the lesson in the cathedral one Sunday morning and in the afternoon I won the doughnut-eating contest at the Women's Institute canteen.' He grinned. 'What more could a fellow want?'

'You're a strange man, Jamie Frazer. You really are. Looking so cool and laid-back and the self-assured veteran of a war, and then going back to civvy street and finding it boring, so you go back into that strange world you'd abandoned. What on earth was the attraction?'

He looked away from her across the water towards the lock to the channel. It was a long time before he looked back at her and said, 'It was home, honey. The only one I knew. It was the place where I knew the ground-rules. And I was valued there. Europe was in turmoil and by then I knew a lot about Europe.' He shrugged. 'The army and the war

40

were my university. I had no qualifications that interested civilians.' He smiled. 'I can still remember the words of my demobilisation reference. It said that Lt.-Colonel Frazer had a wide knowledge of the German intelligence organisations and of the Nazi party. It added that my judgment was respected by the German authorities, Military Government and MI6. You can imagine the reaction to that of some personnel manager at Marks and Spencer or the GEC.'

She felt that there was nothing she could say. She found it sad, but he wouldn't have agreed with her. Despite her feelings, there was no doubt that he was always the right man for the job. Definitely a round peg in a round hole. But a mask all the same.

She looked back at his face and said, 'You'd have done well whatever you tackled.' She paused. 'I saw in this morning's paper that you're thinking of asking the High Court for an injunction against the author of the book and the newspaper. How's the legal stuff going?'

'It's going to plan. Francis Healey is a wily old bird. He laid out his tactics before we went in and he's won every point so far. It's the Queen's Bench Division that hears an application for an injunction and our application goes in tomorrow.'

'Will you get it?'

'Francis thinks we will.'

The application was heard in chambers. It was heard ex-parte as the defendants had not put in an appearance. Howard Rowe had presented the facts and the application had been granted. With the proviso that the defendants could oppose the injunction provided they did so within twenty-four hours.

They entered an appearance late that afternoon. It was not well-presented and the judge claimed that as there was already a writ for libel and defamation in process it would be merely adding to the alleged defamation if publication was continued.

Bowman was fuming as counsel explained to him in the corridor after the hearing that there were no further grounds for an appeal.

'So what if we go ahead anyway?'

'Mr Bowman, if you went ahead after this hearing you would end up in jail within an hour of it appearing. Not a member of your staff. But you personally. I strongly advise you to follow the court's ruling. I shall put that advice in writing to you and fax it to you and your legal department within the hour.'

As Bowman turned away angrily and walked towards the journalists at the foot of the wide stone steps, his counsel whispered to his junior to go with Bowman and prevent him from adding slander to libel.

In response to the first question Bowman shrugged. 'We shall obey the court's ruling but the public can see one more flagrant example of how the establishment protects its own. We now have the judiciary as a tool of the intelligence establishment which is anxious to protect its own.'

'Protect who?' A voice called out.

'The man, the people, who are trying to stop the public learning the truth about the dirty tricks and . . .'

Junior counsel relied on his gown for status and interrupted. 'Mr Bowman has to go to a meeting, gentlemen. Just one last question.'

A woman reporter held out a microphone. 'Do you wish you hadn't published this serialisation?'

'Never. Never. They are not going to be allowed to strangle and suppress the free press of this country. Our action is a clarion call to all those who – like us – want the truth to be told.'

Junior counsel edged Bowman to a waiting taxi and bundled him inside. He stood watching as the taxi drove off. What hypocrites these media people were. Digging around in the gutter while claiming the moral heights. Echoes of Shakespeare and Macbeth – *'False face must hide what the false heart doth know'*.

Chapter 10

The phone rang about 10 p.m. and James picked it up still looking at the news on CNN.

'Frazer.'

'Hello, Jamie. How are you?'

'I'm fine thank you. I know the voice but I can't quite place it.'

'It's Laura. I'm phoning from Edinburgh. I was contacted by the newspaper you're suing. They wanted me to say what a bad husband you were. Beating me up, and that sort of crap.'

'I'm sorry about that. Unfortunately I can't stop them but I'm sure you dealt with them suitably. How's Joe by the way?'

'Joe. Who's Joe?'

'The guy. The golf-professional wasn't he?'

'Oh God. That Joe. That was fifteen years ago. There have been several Joes since then.'

He laughed softly. 'I hope one of 'em improved your swing and that tendency to slice.'

'Don't be a pig. I saw a picture of you in *The Times* about this libel thing. I must say you looked even more handsome than I remember.'

'It was probably out of focus.' He paused. 'What sort of questions did the creeps from the newspaper ask you?'

'There were two of them. A girl reporter and the fellow was some sort of legal type. All they wanted was anything unfavourable about you. Were you violent, what were you like in bed, why did we divorce? The usual stuff that tabloids go in for. I was obviously a great disappointment. But I thought I should warn you.'

'I appreciate it, honey. I really do. What are you doing in Edinburgh?'

'I'm running a bistro with a couple of friends. Boring, but it's a reasonable living.' She laughed. 'And my golf's improved up here.' She paused. 'Well. All the best with the legal stuff. Take care.'

'And you, my dear. Thanks for ringing me.'

As he hung up he wondered who else they were pursuing to try to justify that wretched book. He phoned Francis Healey and told him what his ex-wife had said.

'Unfortunately there's nothing we can do to stop that sort of thing. That's why there was a legal chap there, to see that the girl didn't go too far and we could claim that it was harassment. Anyway it was nice that she obviously didn't fall for them.'

'She isn't that kind of a gal. They picked the wrong one there.'

'What about the other two?'

'Joanna's in a nursing home in Switzerland, and Patsy's dead. Died ten years ago.'

'Fair enough. I had a call as I was leaving the office tonight from your colleague Hugo Platt. He suggested that he and I meet. What do you feel about that?'

'Up to you, Francis. No problem my end.'

'OK. I'll contact him tomorrow.'

Sir Hugo paid off the cab and checked the address on the slip of paper. Healey and Partners' offices were in an old building off Northumberland Avenue, but inside it was bright and modern, and Francis Healey came out into reception to welcome his visitor.

When Sir Hugo had settled himself in one of the chairs across from Francis Healey, he said, 'Have you heard anything from the other side about Jamie's business?'

'Nothing except the normal drift of paper between opposing sides.'

'Tell me. What would you say to them if they threw in their hands?'

'I'd say they were very wise but it would cost them at least half a million plus legal costs of both sides.' He paused. 'Why do you ask?'

Sir Hugo shrugged. 'I heard a very faint whisper of problems on the other side.'

'Tell me more.'

'Just a vague indication that the author and publisher and the newspaper don't see eye to eye about how to proceed.' He held up a cautionary hand. 'But remember it could be exaggerated or just not true.'

'Could I ask what your source is?'

'I'm sorry. I didn't hear what you said.'

Healey opened his mouth to repeat his question and then realised that he'd already been answered. He felt slightly embarrassed at being so naive in asking the question in the first place.

'Do your colleagues know about this?'

'Of course. We have an interest in the case because the book paints a totally distorted picture of our organisation and its work. As you know we have no standing in the matter, the author pins all his criticisms on one man rather than the organisation. We should have liked the injunction to prevent publishing to have gone in before publication of either the book or the serialisation but we understand why that didn't happen until later.'

Healey paused for a moment and then said, 'I've got the feeling that there's another reason why you're telling me this, Sir Hugo. Am I right?'

'Yes.'

'Can I ask what it is?'

'The way this information came to me suggests that at some stage the other side, or at least one of them, let's say the newspaper, might approach us, and I mean SIS, to do a deal.' He paused. 'It might be sensible to discuss that possibility with your client and see what his reactions would be.'

'He wants his day in court, Sir Hugo.'

'More like two months in court if everyone wants to play silly buggers.'

'Do SIS have an attitude on such an approach?'

'Certainly not.' Sir Hugo stood up slowly. 'I do hope I haven't confused the issue.'

'You certainly haven't done that. I'm grateful to you and your colleagues for keeping me informed.'

'Just me, Mr Healey, not my colleagues.'

When Sir Hugo had left, Healey sat at his desk, thinking. He felt that there had been some message apart from the words that had been said. But he wasn't sure what the message was. Maybe Jamie would recognise it. Maybe it wasn't a message but a warning. He phoned

Frazer but his telephone was on the answering-machine.

It was later that evening that he saw Jamie Frazer in the bar in the interval at the Chichester theatre. When he had told him about Sir Hugo's visit, Frazer had smiled. 'No it wasn't a warning but it *was* a message. A rather devious one that could be indignantly denied if you pressed the point.'

'What *was* the message then, Jamie?'

'They're worried about what might come out in court. They've looked at all the items where they can claim national security but a lot of them won't stick because they're too far in the past to affect current security. I'd also say that their information was deliberately leaked by the defendants. Somebody there would like to back out, or at least do a deal.'

'Who?'

'I suspect the newspaper. It's their money that's funding the defence.'

'Sir Hugo didn't blink when I said you'd want at least half a million and all the trimmings. Abject apologies and all that.'

'I'm not interested, Francis.'

'Why so sure?'

'Because when these things are settled out of court the mud still sticks. The apology in the newspaper is drawn up by bloody lawyers and is just a formula. But what the public remembers is the accusations. I'd still be an adulterer, a fornicator, a womaniser. Not to mention a traitor, careless with other people's lives and politically biased. No way, Francis. No way do I do a deal with those bastards. And I want you to pass that on to Hugo from me. I want blood as well as a hell of a lot of money and abject apologies on all counts. Not just some routine piece that is virtually saying – we have to do this but we don't mean it. It's just a legal thing.'

For the first time Healey realised what anger and frustration his client had managed to control and conceal over the past weeks.

'All right, Jamie. Leave it to me. I'll pass a discreet word to Sir Hugo so there's no doubt in their minds about what you want.' He smiled. 'Where's Adele?'

Jamie Frazer laughed. 'My guest tonight is Maggie Bates not Adele. I discovered that Maggie's never been to a theatre before in her life so I thought I'd better give her a whirl.'

As Healey drove home he realised why there had always been such loyalty to Jamie Frazer from his men. It must have been easy to end up hero-worshipping the man. He'd make a good witness.

The following day he received a notification from the defendants that they would have separate representation in court. He was surprised when he read that Sir Graham Pollock QC would appear for the newspaper. Counsel named for the author and the publisher was not a specialist in libel and normally worked in the divorce courts. But Sir Graham Pollock QC was probably the most famous libel lawyer in the country. Even in defamation cases he was always polite to his victims and avoided theatrical gestures, but his preparation was thorough and his tactics were carefully worked out to drive home point after point to a jury. He looked, and in fact was, a perfect gentleman. Juries felt that it would be almost a kind of *lèse-majesté* not to accept his arguments.

When Healey phoned Howard Rowe with the news it turned out that he already knew. Sir Graham's clerk had sent him a courtesy copy.

'What do you think it means, Howard?'

'First of all I think they're shit-scared of what they've got themselves into. They're quarrelling about responsibility and they don't share the same defence any longer. Every man for himself. Pollock will go over it and my guess is that he'll come back with an offer.'

'Jamie won't accept an offer. I've already discussed it with him.'

'I know. You told me.' He paused. 'Let's be patient and wait and see.'

Chapter 11

It was a week before the offer to settle came with a call from Pollock suggesting a meeting with Healey at the Law Society. There was no beating around the bush and Pollock said, 'I've a mind to recommend that my client settles – with a financial settlement and an agreed apology. What do you think?'

'I had more or less anticipated the possibility and I have already discussed it with my client. But he is adamant about going ahead. He feels that unless the public know that the book, and therefore the serialisation, were both untrue and malicious the mud will stick.'

'I can understand that but it's up to you and me as officers of the court to bring this wretched business to an end.' He paused. 'There are two aspects that you need to consider regarding your client, who I might say I feel is a first-class chap in every way, and the first is to point out that unless you claim that he's a latter-day saint there's going to be some item that comes up in court that he doesn't like. There always is something.'

Sir Graham paused but Healey didn't respond.

'The second point is that once the case is on I shall have to do my best to show that not only Sir James but the organisation he worked for and eventually headed, have a lot of skeletons in their cupboards. I'm going to have to be very critical of a lot of people and a lot of operations that could well be considered as both illegal and immoral.'

Healey nodded. 'I'd expect nothing but a rough ride from you, Sir Graham. But I have to carry out my client's instructions. Howard Rowe is out of the country at the moment or I should have asked him to meet you instead of me.'

49

'I understand you are an old friend of the plaintiff.'

'Yes. We've known one another for years.'

Sir Graham reached for his brief case and pulled out a single foolscap sheet.

'Just for the record this is my proposal.'

Healey glanced at it quickly and noted that the damages offered were £100,000 and plaintiff's legal costs. The proposed apology was, as Frazer had forecast, the usual formula that apologises with legal tongue very visibly in cheek.

He folded the sheet and looked at Sir Graham.

'I'll put it to my client again but don't expect a change of mind.'

'I gather that SIS are not too happy about being filleted in public.'

Healey smiled. 'I've no idea, but they're entitled to be angry at having to answer unfounded allegations by a virtually unknown scribbler trying to look like an historian.'

Pollock sighed and shrugged. 'You're right. But who are we to criticise?'

Two days later Healey was able to contact Howard Rowe who wanted them to keep to protocol and submit the out-of-court settlement offer to Sir James. When Sir James had refused to accept it, Howard Rowe moved on and prepared a series of questions for Sir James to answer. They covered the kind of questions that he might be asked in court.

When Francis Healey took them across to Rose Cottage at the weekend he found Jamie at the piano playing for Adele. When he stopped playing and looked across to where Healey was standing, Adele looked too and said, 'This man is so lucky or so talented. I don't know which. Whether he's playing Gershwin or just talking – you've got to listen.'

Healey laughed. 'It's the audience that counts.' He paused and sat down beside Adele, looking at Jamie Frazer.

'I've got some questions from counsel. He'd like your answers in about ten days. He says they could be on tape if that makes it easier.' He stood up and put the paper on top of the piano. Frazer nodded and smiled.

'I never play for you, Francis. Tell me something you'd like.'

Healey thought for a moment and then said, 'I'd like Lara's theme from *Zhivago*.'

Frazer looked suddenly interested. 'Why that?'

Healey shrugged. 'I've no idea, I just like it.'

Frazer played the Lara tune and melded it into '*All I ask of you*' from Lloyd Webber's *Phantom*.

When he closed the keyboard-lid he smiled as Healey said, 'That's Helen's favourite piece, the second one you played.'

Jamie laughed. 'You're a couple of closet romantics. All cool and calm on the surface but hearts on sleeves in private.' He paused. 'And very nice too. Maybe that's as revealing a psychological test as any other. Ask people what their favourite piece of music is. You could divide the world between Chopin and Rachmaninov.' He laughed. 'Or Bing Crosby and Frankie Sinatra.'

Adele had poured them drinks and discovered some sausage rolls and they had sat in the spring sun in the garden and chatted for almost an hour. Healey was aware as he left that Jamie Frazer hadn't even looked at the paper on top of the piano.

Jamie took Adele to the boat in the afternoon. There were no particular reasons for going but she knew that the boat was a kind of retreat from the world for Jamie Frazer. A man who normally looked the world in its face and didn't give a damn.

Later that evening Frazer phoned Francis Healey.

'About these questions, Francis. What are my answers supposed to do? Do I give the answers I'd give if asked these questions in court?'

'No. That's not the purpose, Jamie. Howard Rowe has gone through the book as if he were on the other side. The questions are those he would ask if he were defending. He doesn't want formal replies, he wants the background about whatever the subject is so that when he puts rebuttal questions to you on those items he knows what it was all about. That's why he suggested you taped the answers so that you can recollect the circumstances and describe what it was all about.'

'Does this mean he has doubts about those items?'

'No way. It's nothing like that.' He paused. 'It's your old army saying again – "Time spent in reconnaissance" et cetera, et cetera.'

Jamie Frazer laughed. 'You're a cunning old bastard, Francis, under that avuncular appearance of yours. OK. I'll get on with it. How long have I got?'

'The indication from the court is that it will be heard in about a couple of months. He'd like your answers inside a couple of weeks. But that's a guess, an informal guess, but not an actual date.'

'By the way, what order shall I do them in, they're not set out chronologically?'

'Any order you like. Howard can shuffle them around himself later. Try to knock it off in a couple of weeks or so.'

'Will do.'

Chapter 12

From: H. ROWE QC
            28 Pryke's Court, NW1

To: Sir James Frazer
            Rose Cottage
            The Mile, Nr. Chichester, Sussex.

STRICTLY CONFIDENTIAL

Subject: Book entitled *Who Goes There?* Author Al Pinto,
              published by Primrose Publications plc

Questions for Sir James Frazer to consider.

Chapter references.
1. In chapter 2 it refers to your 'penetration' of the Oxford Group/ Buchmanites and unfavourable comments on your reports.
2. Officer Selection Board – why did you not go to OCTU?
3. What were circumstances of your sudden promotion from WO2 to Captain?
4. In chapter 5 it claims that you were 'thrown out' on orders of the Emperor for favouring Italian prisoners-of-war?
5. Chapter 6 mentions unauthorised actions in Rome concerning Capitano Simonetti.
6. Why were you brought up by your grandparents, not your mother?

7. What were your relationships with left-wing organisations? *Chapter 12.*
8. Why did you vote for Labour in 1945? *Chapter 13.*
9. What were your duties after being 'thrown out' of Ethiopia?
10. What were your relationships with 21 Army Group in 1946/7? *Chapter 15.*
11. Why did you leave SIS?
12. What did you do in civilian life?
13. Why did you go back to SIS?
14. Unsuccessful marriages. Why?
15. Relationships with Russians. London/Berlin.
16. It is claimed in Chapter 17 that you 'went missing' for 2 years about 1950–52. What were you doing?'
17. This question is not related to the book text: Have you ever done anything in your military/intelligence career that you are ashamed of?
18. Have you ever met, talked to, or corresponded with, the author, Al Pinto?
19. In chapter 23 it is claimed that when you were D-G you were investigated by a committee because of doubts about your loyalty. Is this true, and if it is, what was the outcome? The book implies that you were found guilty and given the chance to resign and this was why you left SIS.

Chapter 13

The move from the infantry training with the Royal Sussex took place on a Saturday morning. The new location was the depot of the Intelligence Corps in what had been a theological college in Winchester. The permanent staff who administered and ran the military aspects of the depot were ex-guardsmen who brought the petty discipline of the Brigade of Guards that decreed that it was an offence for a private soldier to look an officer in the eye, and that in the Commandant's office a private soldier had to salute the Commandant's empty chair if he wasn't there himself. Inevitably they were ridiculed and despised by the Intelligence Corps training staff and their trainees. There were some who said later that it was at least good training for life in intelligence by learning how to beat the military at their own game. But the military staff and its foibles weren't a problem for James Frazer. He didn't realise it at the time but he was a born soldier and he responded enthusiastically. It was even suggested to him by the Commandant that if he transferred to the Brigade of Guards he would have immediate promotion to sergeant. He actually considered it but the senior Intelligence Corps officer had got wind of the proposition and immediately raised hell with the War Office.

Frazer's problem was his I Corps colleagues. They were friendly enough but they were middle-class, better educated and entirely self-confident. He felt that their amiability with him was rather like the friendly but patronising attitude that the gentry had to their faithful family servants. In fact, Frazer's colleagues were not all that different from him, they were just more sophisticated. They came from families who had interests beyond the home. Interests in the arts and politics that made the humdrum lives of his grandparents seem virtuous and kindly but incredibly restricted. His grandparents had not only never travelled in their own country, but had not even explored most of the city in which they lived. They saw no reason to travel, and were satisfied with their routine daily lives. They were typical of most working-class families in those days. Even after the war they had refused the offer of electric supply to the house despite it being installed free of charge. It was Grandma's view that gaslight was better for reading. For some years their home was the only one in the city still without electricity.

There was an old army motto that said 'Never volunteer for anything'. But Jamie Frazer volunteered for everything; a special rough-riding course on motor-cycles, a week at a deep-interrogation centre, a week's solo survival test on a Scottish moor and a refresher course in German. The army saw the enthusiasm and recognised one of their own, and the I Corps had shrewd head-hunters who knew how to choose men whose vices could be as useful as their virtues.

The intelligence training was modular and trainees were diverted at different stages to what could be their special functions. Fluent linguists who were not built for physical efforts were diverted to deep-interrogation camps, mathematicians and champion chess-players were posted to the code-breaking unit at Bletchley Park, successful survivors of unarmed combat training were sent to special active units and some, like Frazer, carried on with more complex intelligence training at a hotel that had been taken over in Matlock, a quiet and picturesque town in the Derbyshire hills. From that point onwards Jamie Frazer, although he didn't know it, was a marked man. The basic shrewdness and the energy and enthusiasm, were seen as the seed-bed for a very versatile character.

They were sitting on the bench alongside the pool watching the goldfish nosing at the water-plants. It was the first time that year that the fishes had been visible. They had spent the winter deep in the darkness of the pond.

'Is it the sun that has brought them out?' she said as she leaned forward to look at the fish.

'I think it's because the days are getting longer. Most wild things, especially birds, don't respond to the sun as we do, but they begin to pair up and nest as the days get longer.'

'By the way, I meant to ask you. What on earth is a Buchmanite?'

He looked puzzled. 'What made you ask that?'

'It was one of the items on your lawyer's list of questions. Talks about you penetrating the group whatever that means, and unfavourable comments on your reports.'

He laughed and was obviously amused. 'When we had finished our training we had to do an actual job. I was given the choice of infiltrating either Jehovah's Witnesses or the so-called Oxford Group.'

'What had they done?'

'Nothing. But we were interested in any organisation that was controlled from outside the UK. Jehovah's Witnesses were controlled from the USA and the Oxford Group was controlled from somewhere in Switzerland. We wanted to know what they were up to.'

'And Buchmanites?'

'That's what the Oxford Group was called originally. After its founder Frank Buchman.'

'So why Oxford?'

Frazer shrugged. 'It sounds intellectual. You could think it was connected to the university but it wasn't.'

'So what did they do?'

'It was a semi-religious outfit. Repentant sinners. All will be forgiven. That sort of stuff. Quite nice people actually. Meant well and it lasted until some years after the war.'

'And your reports?'

He grinned. 'At the first four meetings I attended there were several pretty girls all confessing what wicked lives they had lived before they joined the Group. I just reported the routines and some names but I added what I thought was a touch of humour and said how disappointing not to have known the pretty girls before they joined the Group. It came back with a handwritten note scrawled all over it by a senior staff officer who said something like "This stuff is fit only for the *Daily Express*." ' Frazer laughed. 'And I was so bloody naive I thought it was a compliment. I kept showing it around. Fame at last.'

She shook her head. 'And the creep who wrote the wretched book makes it sound like you'd been found guilty of some terrible military disaster.'

'It shows he doesn't have any first-hand knowledge of what I was up to in the war. He's just a rogue trying to make a buck.'

'What happened after the Oxford Group thing?'

'I was posted to port security in a small port outside Edinburgh called Methil. It was the collecting point for all the big convoys. I was under-cover acting as a clerk to a big outfit of ships' suppliers called Salvesan. Only one man there knew what I was really doing.'

'And what were you doing?'

'A lot of boats were sailing under neutral flags and they could have crew members who were pro-Axis.'

'What could they do?'

'Minor information gathering when they came ashore. Pursuing information on troops and defences. Stuff that was easy to pick up in pubs. They could just disappear and act as full-time spies. I had lists of suspect men and it was my job to go out to all the neutral boats and check their crew-lists and manifests. If I found a naughty boy I'd arrest him and bring him back. There were a lot of German spies being landed on the Fife coast at that time.'

'How long did you do that?'

'About six months and then my cover was blown and I was withdrawn.'

'How did that happen?'

'I had lodgings at a small house in Leven. As a civilian of course. My landlady said it was her daughter's birthday the next Saturday and her daughter was in the Women's RAF, a WAAF. She asked me if I'd like to go to the party and I said yes, of course. She mentioned that they were going to have a spey-wife.' He looked at her, smiling. 'Do you know what a spey-wife is?'

'No. I've never heard of such a thing.'

'Neither had I. Well a spey-wife is a kind of fortune-teller. Reads palms and tea-leaves and cards and tells you what she sees. She did me last because I was the only English person there. She just held my hands in hers, palms up and without even looking up she said I wasn't a clerk but something to do with spies. By the time she'd said her piece my cover was blown and you can imagine what it was like. The room was silent. Some embarrassed and some shocked.'

'What on earth did you do?'

'I laughed and said it was a great story. Then I went down the street and phoned Scottish Command who told me not to go back to the house and they would have me picked up at the dock gates. I was taken back to Edinburgh and de-briefed. But I never found out what happened to the spey-wife. Or who blew my cover.'

'Did they blame you for it?'

'No. They were Scots and they understood these things. I went back to my Field Security Section and the following week I went to Edinburgh for an Officers' Selection Board.'

She was silent for several moments and then she shivered and said, 'Let's go inside, it's getting cold.'

As they walked into the cottage the phone was ringing. Frazer listened to the recorded message and then a man's voice said, 'It's Peters, Jamie. Joe Peters. You've got my number, can you give me a call about a chap named Healey . . .' Frazer interrupted the voice and said, '. . . I'm on the line, Joe. How are you?'

There was the usual confusion on the other end that happens when taped messages are cut short. 'I'm OK. This chap Healey says he wants to have a chat with me about the old days. Says you gave him my number but I thought I'd better check with you.'

'He's OK, Joe. He's my lawyer in this libel case. You've probably read about it.'

'Yeah. It's time somebody hit back at these bastards who get away with their phoney revelations time and again. And we never go for 'em. You can rely on me. Any help you want.'

'Thanks, Joe. I think my guy just wants background material on my wicked past. And speaking of the past, how's the pretty Susie?'

'She's fine. Sends her love. So do my three daughters – your local fan club.'

Frazer laughed. 'That's my just reward for teaching them unarmed combat.'

'No way. It's those blue eyes of yours. Anyway. Call me if you need me.'

'I will. And thanks.'

Chapter 14

Of the two names that Frazer had given him Healey decided to make his first contact with Joe Peters who was retired from SIS rather than Logan who was still with the organisation. Logan would be more useful when he needed to gauge what the internal arguments about SIS's attitude had concluded.

Joe Peters had a small antiques business in the Pantiles in Tunbridge Wells and when Healey arrived, Peters closed the shop, and they drove up to the Spa Hotel at the top of the hill. They made themselves comfortable in armchairs near the french windows and when they had ordered sandwiches and drinks Peters held up his glass.

'Here's to our mutual friend.'

Healey raised his glass too, sipped the whisky and as he put the glass back on the low table he said, 'It was good of you to see me Mr Peters . . .'

'Joe – for God's sake. And I'll be glad to help the old bastard any way I can. How's he holding up under the strain?' He laughed. 'As if I need to ask. He'll be ice-cold and waiting for the right moment to kick 'em in the groin.' He laughed. 'But I guess that's your job.'

Healey smiled. 'I suppose it is.' He paused. 'If you were asked to describe Jamie to a stranger – what would you say?'

'Work or play?'

'Both.'

'OK. Work. Bags of guts. But not a rusher-in. Looks at what's going on before he jumps in. The best interrogator we ever had when he was in the field. Almost like he could read people's minds. Sometimes he'd look at you quite casually as if he knew something about you that you didn't know yourself. He cared totally about anyone involved in any of his operations. The top brass recognised his dedication and efficiency and that meant that he got all the shitty operations.

'Mind you, underneath that toughness was a streak of softness for losers. He was very aware of people's personalities and how best to motivate them. Especially women.' He paused. 'He had a rather old-fashioned view of women. Was against them being used in active operations that could involve them in unnecessary risks. Women loved him of course. So did most men for that matter.'

'How was he as Director-General?'

Joe Peters shrugged. 'First-class field officers seldom get the chance of D-G or even Deputy. Their virtues don't work when politics are involved. But Jamie took it all in his stride. When he fought with the Foreign Office they listened, which wasn't their usual attitude. And they gave him what he wanted more often than not.'

'What sort of things did he fight about?'

Peters thought for a few moments. 'I guess his biggest row, or at least the most important one, was about the funds for GCHQ. The funds for GCHQ and SIS were out of the same budget and Jamie thought that SIS should have a larger budget for HUMINT.'

'What's HUMINT?'

'HUMINT is intelligence from human sources, contacts, informants, networks and penetration. GCHQ is SIGINT, intelligence gathered by radio and electronics. Interception, cryptography and code-breaking. Jamie's view was that GCHQ were doing a first-rate job on their existing funds and that HUMINT was going to be more important in future.'

'Did he win?'

'No. At least he didn't win that argument. They overrode him but as things turned out Jamie was proved right. There ain't no SIGINT where the IRA is concerned. Anything we get is HUMINT. And the Foreign Office view was shot down in flames when Saddam invaded Kuwait last year. Neither GCHQ nor their US counterparts NSA gave even a vague hint that it was going to happen. Despite weeks of warnings of something going on from HUMINT sources.'

'How did the Foreign Office see him?'

'The politicians, the top brass liked him and respected his views but the understrappers saw him as a dilettante.'

'Why, for heaven's sake?'

Peters smiled and shrugged. 'They didn't think that a D-G should be sitting down at a piano in the Soviet Embassy, or the French Embassy for that matter, playing *In the Mood*. They even had the brass neck to tell him so.'

'What was his response?'

'Told 'em to get stuffed.'

'What do you think SIS's attitude will be to Jamie's libel case?'

'They'll stay on the sidelines until the other side ask some questions that they wouldn't want answering. They'll have an observer counsel in court and he'll jump in if they ask touchy questions.'

'What if we subpoena SIS people to give evidence in Jamie's favour?'

'I'd guess that they'd play ball. Cagey replies but supportive of Jamie.' He looked at Healey. 'There'll be a lot of serving officers watching what goes on. They'll be rooting for Jamie and they'll be drawing conclusions about what their bosses' attitudes would be if they themselves were ever done over.'

'If you *had* to find a fault with Jamie, what would it be?'

Peters thought for a long time. 'I don't really know. Maybe his attitude to women.'

'In what way?'

'He falls for them too easily and then when he eventually rumbles them he's too rough and ready.' He shrugged. 'But always that last bit of himself not handed over. I'm sure that's why he never had any children. I've seen him with kids and he's great. But I know that he feels that having a child could tie him permanently to someone he doesn't trust any more.' He looked at his watch. 'I'd better get back and open the shop if you've finished with me.'

'I'll run you back. And you've been a great help. Much food for thought.'

Jamie and Adele had walked from Rose Cottage to the pub and had sat outside in the spring sunshine with a glass of beer between them. A number of people had come up to them to speak to Jamie, and eventually they were persuaded inside for a drink with his obvious supporters.

They stayed for an hour but were careful to drink very little.

As they strolled back to the cottage the sun was going down and he slid his jacket around her shoulders.

'The pub landlord was obviously a fan of yours. Free rounds on the house and all that.'

He laughed softly. 'He's no fan of mine, honey.'

'What makes you think that?'

'He used to claim that he had been a major in SAS. Majors in the SAS are pretty thin on the ground and I did a bit of checking. He was a civilian barman in an officers' mess at an infantry depot at Catterick in Yorkshire. He was thrown out for putting his hand in the till.'

'Did you tell him you knew?'

'No. Why should I?'

'Because he's a liar and a phoney.'

He laughed. 'Everybody tells lies. Most of them are harmless attempts to seem more than they are. Brave, rich, good – whatever. But he'll know by instinct that I know about him. Knowing what he tells lies about is all that matters.'

'Do you tell lies?'

'Sure. Mainly social lies to seem agreeable.'

'Do I?'

He smiled. 'No comment.'

'You beast. You should have said that I'm the exception.'

'You're not only the most honest person I know but you're the least vain. You're very beautiful but I have never seen you take a sly glance at yourself in a mirror. Most pretty women do that. But not the really beautiful ones.' As they got to the cottage gate he said, 'Let's go to the Ship for dinner.'

They had taken their coffee at the table and because he seemed relaxed she risked going back to the subject of lies.

'Do you check everybody for lies?'

'It was part of our training that everyone tells lies about something or other. Finding out what they tell lies about might save your life some day or save an operation from going down the pan.'

'So how do you find out what they lie about?'

He shrugged. 'Again, that's part of the training. You dig little holes and wait to see which one they fall into.'

'And you do this to everybody you meet?'

'More or less. It becomes instinctive. In most cases it's not significant.' He smiled. 'Of course it doesn't endear you to your wife or girl-friend but our people give you a warning lesson on how not to treat your nearest and dearest as if she was a member of the Gestapo.'

'Do you tell them what you find out?'

'Of course not.' He paused. 'And of course it can sometimes disadvantage the agent concerned.'

'How?'

'Well. You get an instinct for when people are lying. Little bells ring and red lights blink and when you get back to civilian life they don't necessarily stop. So some guys ignore the lights and the bells and they behave more gullibly than a normal guy would do.'

She looked at him, shaking her head slowly. 'What a mess you men make of things.'

He smiled but didn't respond. That too was part of the process.

He poured her another coffee from the pot and as he passed across the cream he said quietly, 'What are you doing next Tuesday?'

She looked surprised. 'Next Tuesday? What . . .' and then she closed her eyes. When she opened them she looked at his face. 'I didn't think you'd remember. I was going to say that I was going up to London.'

'And be unhappy on your own at home?'

'I guess so.'

'Does no harm to be unhappy once in a while but in this case it's destructive.' He paused. 'In my opinion.'

'So what should I do?'

'You and I will fly up to Glasgow and put some flowers on Tim's grave. And think about him. And then we'll fly to Berlin. Stay at Kempinski's. Look around the new Berlin for a couple of days. Then on to Amsterdam for a day and back to Gatwick and the car.'

'What made you remember?'

'He was a large part of your life. He's still part of it. If something affects you then it matters to me.'

She reached across the table and put her hand on his. She looked at his face for long moments and then said quietly, 'You really are something special, Jamie Frazer. Thanks for remembering and we'll do what you said.'

Chapter 15

It had been intended as just a meeting to review the state of the game of the several libel defences, but Sidney Bowman had got the feeling that all was not going to plan. He sat with his hands pressed palms down on the polished mahogany table as if he were steadying the proceedings, as Sir Graham Pollock QC gave them what he called an oversight of the situation.

'My instructions from my client, Mr Bowman, have not been changed. However, I have talked with counsel representing Mr Keane and Primrose Publications plc and I gather that they are relying on Mr Pinto who has chosen to defend himself in person.' He paused and looked at Al Pinto. 'Am I right, Mr Pinto?'

'Sounds OK to me.'

Sir Graham nodded and turned to Keane. 'So I have to ask you, Mr Keane. Would you let me have sight of your libel lawyer's report?'

Keane shuffled his papers around and avoiding Sir Graham's eyes said, 'The libel clause in the contract puts the responsibility on the author not on us.'

'I see. So you are relying on the libel lawyer's report that was commissioned by the author, Mr Pinto here.' He paused, smiling. 'So Mr Pinto, could I see your libel lawyer's report on the book?'

'I already told you guys. I don't believe in lawyers or spending money on them. I don't need a report, I use my experience on these matters.'

'Could you enlighten us about your experience in this particular matter?'

'Yeah,' Pinto said, leaning back in his chair. 'There's been at least twenty books written taking the piss out of the CIA, MI6 and MI5. All of them claiming waste of public funds, abuses of civil rights and political bias.' He paused for effect. 'None of 'em sued anybody for anything. They just leak a few unfavourable stories about the writer and that's it.' He shrugged dismissively. 'They'll set the IRS on you for back taxes and you'll have your phone bugged until they get tired of it.' He shrugged again. 'That's it. That's my experience. Not guessing. Not surmise. But fact. They won't do a thing.'

There was a brief silence while he let Pinto's statement sink in and then Sir Graham said, 'We're not talking about MI6 in this case, Mr Pinto. You're being sued by an individual for libel.'

'Makes no difference, pal. They won't let him go ahead. They'll stop him. If it goes to court they'll throw in their hands the first time you ask a question about clandestine operations.' He grinned. 'Will you please tell the court the names and addresses of all those people whose telephones, homes and offices are being subjected to MI6 surveillance? National security? But that's what my book says is all wrong. Rights of privacy. Constitutional rights. I rest my case my Lord.'

There was another silence and then Sir Graham said with obvious disbelief in what he was saying, 'You could be right of course, Mr Pinto. Meantime can we take it that in fact no libel lawyer read this book of yours before it was published? Everyone was relying on everyone else for having taken that rather elementary precaution.'

'Don't ask me, mister. Ask them.' And Pinto waved his hand dismissively around the group.

Sir Graham went on. 'You suggest that there are questions that could be asked that would damage SIS.'

'Yeah.'

'Could you give me an example?'

Al Pinto smiled, a knowing smile. 'I'll tell you when you need it, mister.'

Sir Graham turned to Sidney Bowman. 'I think you and I should have a little talk, Mr Bowman. I expect our friends here have other things to do.'

Sir Graham led Bowman into his own office and pointed to a chair.

'Mr Bowman. I think it's time that you faced the facts. So far as the libel is concerned, it is my opinion that you and the others will be found guilty. The publishers have nothing to say but there is no way we can prevent Al Pinto from putting on his act in court. Despite the difficulty of predicting how even a normal libel case will turn out, I can tell you categorically that you have no chance of winning. Also I think that the damages awarded will be considerable. And the fact that neither you nor the others took the elementary precaution of having the text read by a libel lawyer is going to be taken as almost incredible. Careless to say the least. And totally irresponsible, if not devious.'

'D'you want me to find another lawyer, Sir Graham?'

'You are free to do so but I should be adding fuel to the fire if I withdrew at this stage. The only consolation I can offer is to do my best in court to present the carelessness as ignorance rather than disrespect for the law, and hope that the damages would be within reason. But I do warn you that the damages will be considerable.'

'What about Pinto's theory that he can provide you with questions that could make SIS do some deal to stop the proceedings?'

Sir Graham half-smiled. 'Mr Bowman, we are both men of the world, we have to deal with reality. I fear that the Pintos of this world live in a fantasy world.' He paused. 'They would probably claim that it was part of being creative. To answer your question, I doubt if Mr Pinto knows anything about SIS that would worry them for a moment. They are used to dealing with people like Pinto.' He paused. 'Remember – Pinto is a foreign national who isn't much liked in his own country. He's a very vulnerable man.' He diplomatically looked at his watch. 'Anyway. Call me if I can help in any way. And remember that despite what I've told you, it is my job to defend you when we get into court. And I shall do that to the best of my ability.'

Chapter 16

Frazer had booked them a suite at The Central Hotel and they'd gone up overnight by train. They had breakfast the next morning in the hotel. As the old railway terminal hotel, the Central was not Glasgow's most sophisticated hotel. But it was comfortable with good food and old-fashioned service.

He hired a car and drove her out to the cemetery at Bearsden. He had bought some small plants and a trowel while she was freshening-up in their suite. Later he had planted the primroses and polyanthus in the turf that covered the grave while she took a photograph of the grave and the polished headstone. They stayed for about half an hour and he took her hand as they walked back to the road and the car. When she noticed that he was driving past the hotel she said, 'Where are we going?'

'A place called Gourock. Not a beauty-spot, but I last saw it in 1940 or 41.'

When they were on the M8 she said, 'What made you think of the trowel for the plants on Tim's grave?'

He smiled. 'Every Saturday afternoon Grandma would take me to the big cemetery at Witton. She'd have a bag with a fork and trowel and a watering-can. We'd do up Auntie Louie's grave and any other nearby that looked as if it wasn't being properly cared for. We'd leave the house and at the bottom of the hill was Brookvale Park, and there we turned right to go to the cemetery. But once a year we'd turn left and that meant we were going to the cinema. To the Star. Laurel and Hardy or Rin-Tin-Tin.'

'Was it always a surprise?'

'No. Not really because I always carried the bag with the trowel but on the Star day there wasn't a bag.' He laughed. 'But I used to pretend it was a surprise.'

'How old were you then?'

'Seven or eight.'

She smiled. 'And already beginning to be a bit devious.'

He smiled. 'You've got to remember that my life was controlled by women. Grandma, my mother, aunts and cousins. I've always said that if as a small boy you grow up coping with a posse of women and survive, then dealing with the Gestapo is easy.' He pointed to the right. 'Those are the Gourock docks over there.' He threaded his way down narrow cobbled streets between huge warehouses and machinery and stopped the car right at the edge of the dock.

'When my Field Security Section went overseas we went on board the boat at this dock. She was called the *Highland Princess* and she had previously been used as a refrigerated meat-ship. A big ship but very primitive. Designed for sides of Argentine beef, not for people. There were well over a thousand soldiers crammed onto that boat. We had no idea where we were going. After about four hours loading, the Merchant Navy crew went on strike because of the conditions. Things got really bad and in the end they brought in the redcaps and about a hundred infantry. They trained machine guns on all the gangways until the ship was away from the dock. So that nobody could leave the boat. It was my first taste of what it was like when authority was agin you. I stood at the rails and watched as the ship moved out into the Clyde. It seemed terribly sad to be sailing away with your own people's guns aimed at you. A terrible farewell when you didn't know when you'd be back. Or even if you would be back at all.

'And then we turned at the headland and on the other shore just below Dunoon I saw the sun shining on a group of very young school-children. They were cheering and waving to us as they walked in line along the path at the top of the headland. And for me it wiped out all the bad part.' He smiled at her. 'I always told myself I'd come back up here some day. But I never did until now.'

'Where did you actually go to?'

He laughed. 'Well there were thirteen of us and between us we could speak almost every European language there is. So. Being the army they posted us to Kenya where our languages were virtually useless.'

'So what did they do with you all?'

'They sent me on a crash course in Swahili at Makerere College.' He laughed. 'Came out speaking better Swahili than most Africans.' He looked at his watch. 'We'd better go back to the hotel and get on our way to the airport. Our flight to Berlin is just a stopover at Glasgow from New York to Berlin. Most of the seats will be already occupied.'

'Why did you choose to go to Berlin?'

'It was part of my life for so long. Germany in general and especially Berlin. I haven't seen it since the wall came down.'

In fact the plane had been half empty. A lot of passengers got off at Glasgow. She sat in the window seat and he'd translated the front-page pieces for her from the *Frankfurter Allgemeine*. There were strikes in Minsk demanding Gorbachev's resignation, the US were starting the withdrawal of their troops from Kuwait and in London the hated Poll Tax had become the Council Tax, and Helmut Kohl was giving a speech hinting that unless there were monetary and political union in the EU there could be war.

As they lost height just before landing at Tegel he was able to point out the Brandenburger Tor and the lights of Unter den Linden.

It was midnight when they ate in the restaurant at Kempinski's and when they had finished he walked her out into the fresh air on the Ku-damm, looking in the shop windows of Berlin's rival to Bond Street and the Champs Elysées. They walked up to the ruins of the cathedral and there were still people around, skate-boarding, buying roast potatoes in foil and the usual drunks and furtive drug-pushers.

He woke early next morning and by 6 a.m. he had shaved and dressed and scribbled a note for her to say that he had gone out for a stroll and would be back about 7.30 for breakfast.

He had walked up Fasanenstrasse to Kant Strasse and along to Savigny Platz. He walked slowly around the square and hesitated at the corner of Grolman strasse. Finally he had walked up Grolman strasse until he saw the building. It was an artist's materials shop now at street level but the three storeys above were much the same. The same windows, the same curtains and the same plastered wall, painted with just a touch of pink in the whiteness.

So many times he had stood where he was standing now in the shadow of the bookshop behind him. Waiting for the lace curtain on the middle window to be pulled aside. It seemed such a long time ago. It *was* a long time ago. Must be nearly thirty years ago but even now he half waited for her to put the vase in the window. Letting himself in. Walking up the narrow stairs and she'd be there on the main landing. Blonde hair flying, arms outstretched as she ran towards him. So loving, so excited to be with him. Nothing else mattered to her. Nor to him.

Suddenly he felt tired and sad. He knew then that he shouldn't have come to Berlin. There were too many ghosts. They had been the happiest two years of his life and he hadn't even thought of it ending. The other women had talked of love but it had never been her kind of love. Admiration maybe, a liking, even affection for him. But with her it had never been just words. It had been total love to the exclusion of all else. Nothing else, and nobody else, mattered. And she was so beautiful. He had seen priests turn to have another look at her as they walked together in the sunshine. The sun had always seemed to be shining in those days. He stood for several more minutes looking towards the building. But he didn't see it. Then he turned and walked back to the hotel. She was still sleeping when he got up to their room. He switched the TV to radio and tuned to DLR Köln which was playing the Glazunov violin concerto. He drew up a chair as she started to stir and waited for her to wake up. He wished with all his heart that he was back in Rose Cottage.

He took her to see the remnants of Check-point Charlie, Alexander Platz and the tower, they went inside the new cathedral building, the old Reichstag building and in the afternoon he took her to the Tiergarten and the Bertolt Brecht Museum. He had arranged that they moved on to Amsterdam the next morning and they landed at Schiphol mid-afternoon.

They booked in at the Krasnapolsky and then did the canal boat trip. After dinner that night he'd walked her through the red-light district to the Leidseplein and a basement with a sign that said 'Jambo Club'. At the bottom of the stone steps a large black man asked Frazer for some ID. Frazer had smiled and said, 'Is Thys here?'

'Yeah.'

'Would you tell him Jamie Frazer's at the door with a lovely lady.'

A few moments later a grey-haired man came hurrying to the door, arms wide open. 'Jamie. Jamie. Come on in.'

Frazer introduced Adele. 'This old guy is Thys van Acker. A good friend from the old days. The bad old days.'

Van Acker kissed her on both cheeks and led them through a bar to another dimly-lit room where a five-piece outfit was playing 'Blues in my heart'.

'Who are they, Thys? They're great.'

'All old has-beens who kinda drifted in and made themselves at home. After eleven you can't get in the place.' He waved his hand. 'This is my table. Make yourselves comfortable.'

The band had moved on to 'Old-fashioned love' and Frazer said, 'Why nobody on the piano?'

'Never found one who fitted in. Tried several but they didn't like any of 'em.' He smiled. 'Squeezed 'em out.' He laughed. 'You know how they are.' He paused. 'How about you have a go after their break?'

'I haven't played with other guys for fifteen years, Thys.'

'So what. A piano's still a piano.' Van Acker turned to Adele. 'Make him play, kid. He's good.'

It was well after midnight when she and van Acker sat listening as Jamie did a wonderful Art Tatum style 'My blue heaven'. Van Acker turned to her and said quietly, 'Ain't that something? The whole place is silent. Just listening. These people know the real thing when they hear it.' He paused. 'He should have had those fingers fixed long ago.'

'I don't understand.'

'He can't use the little fingers on both hands and listen how he stretches into those stride chords.'

'Why can't he use those fingers?'

Van Acker turned to look at her. 'He ain't ever told you about that?'

'No.'

'D'he ever talk about Magdeburg?'

'No. He's never talked about the past.'

'Don't tell him I said anything about his fingers or Magdeburg. I was part of his network in those days. A line-crossing outfit going over the border into the Russian Zone.' He paused and sighed. 'I'd better shut up. Just keep it in mind. When the KGB caught him they did him over. When he escaped and got back they should have given him a decoration. Instead they just threw him away. And in the end they were desperate to have him back.'

'Have you heard about the libel case?'

'No. What is it?'

She told him briefly and he said, 'I can't believe it. It's crazy. If he wants a witness or anything you just let me know. There's plenty of others too.' He banged his fist on the table. 'The bastards. All of 'em.'

'Don't mention it unless he does, will you?'

'No. But I know him, he won't mention it. Too bloody independent.'

It was 4 a.m. when they walked through the still busy streets to the hotel. They were catching the mid-day plane to Gatwick and Charlie was meeting them with the car.

Chapter 17

Question 2   **Why did you not go to OCTU?**
Question 3   **What were the circumstances of your sudden promotion from WO2 to Captain?**

The *Highland Princess* and the rest of convoy 137 had been attacked by U-boats lying in wait on the route to the South Atlantic. Seven troopships and two ships were sunk before the convoy discipline broke down. For a week the *Highland Princess* lay off the coast of South America and from then on ration cigarettes had borne legends in Portuguese.

The remnants of the convoy dropped anchor off Mombasa and its weary passengers were ferried ashore on the tugs and drifters that serviced the big boats.

Frazer's unit of thirteen men and one officer were directed by redcaps to a lorry that took them down the coast to Kilindini where they spent the night sleeping on the sandy beach.

The train journey to Nairobi had taken two days with a night spent in tents at the station at Simba. At Nairobi an intelligence officer had arranged transport for them to a military encampment outside the town.

On the morning of the third day an Intelligence Corps lieutenant had asked for Sergeant-Major Frazer and told him that he would be taking him for an interview at East Africa Command HQ in Nairobi. He had been ordered to take his personal kit as he may be kept overnight.

At Nairobi he had been marched in to a small office in an annexe where a major with I Corps badges sat at an army-issue wooden table. Frazer guessed he must be in his mid-forties.

He went through the depot drill, stamped his boots, saluted and said, 'Warrant Officer Two. Frazer, James. 10350556, sir.'

The major nodded and pointed to a chair in front of his desk.

'We don't go in for that depot bullshit except on state occasions. Do sit down.'

When Frazer was sitting, with his kit at the side of the chair, the major said, 'My name's Lucas. George Lucas and I do liaison with our mutual friends in Winchester and London.' He paused. 'I was looking at your AB64 and I notice you went to the WOSBI in Edinburgh. Yes?'

'Yes, sir.'

'You were recommended for sending immediately to an OCTU.' He paused. 'Why didn't you go?'

'The section was mobilised for overseas while I was away at the War Office Selection Board. Sir.'

'Why didn't your CO get a replacement for you?'

'I don't know, sir.'

'One of those traditional little birds tells me that you and your CO are not on speaking terms. Is that so?'

Frazer hesitated for a moment and then said, 'He leaves me to get on with it, sir.'

Major Lucas smiled but very slightly. 'OK. We know where we stand.' He paused. 'General Platt has told your CO personally that we noticed and don't like it. He's being posted away from the section to a staff job.'

Frazer said nothing and after a pause Major Lucas carried on. 'We're sending you on a crash course in Swahili at Makerere College in Uganda. After that you'll be going to the Battle School at Nakuru where, if you make the grade, you'll be commissioned. Any problems?'

'No, sir.'

'Right. Report here at noon and you'll be driven up to Makerere.' He stood up and held out his hand. 'Best of luck, young man.'

Swahili is not the spoken language of any African tribe or country. So, lacking in background, literature and history, its only appeal is that it is both easy to learn and a lingua-franca over almost all of Africa. Students emerging from the college had only one problem – they spoke better Swahili, with a wider vocabulary, than most Africans did.

Jamie Frazer, with his natural ear for a foreign language, came out speaking good Swahili but with an active dislike of the arrogant Kenya 'settler' who considered learning an African language made you a white-nigger. He found it strange too that these 'settlers' resented even more those black Africans who, having been to Oxford or Cambridge, spoke better English than they did.

Back in Nairobi he was given three days' leave before heading for the Battle School at Nakuru. The school had a reputation for providing three months of hell under the guise of being a specialist training unit for jungle-warfare. A newly coined description anticipating service in Burma and the 14th Army. Unlike normal OCTUs Nakuru used live ammunition on its training operations. Another lesson that he learned was that the Kenya 'settlers' he so disliked were the stars of the Battle School and won all the awards on the punishing programme.

He arrived at Nakuru on the Saturday afternoon and was shown to his quarters in a tented area. Only the permanent staff were housed in the wooden accommodation. On the Sunday the Camp Commandant, a Brigadier-General, gave them an uncompromising talk on the rigours that lay ahead for them. Yes, he confirmed to a question, they did use live ammunition. He pointed out unsmiling that the Italians and Japanese also used live ammunition. He wished them luck but without any sign of genuine encouragement, and pointed out that no matter whether they were privates or sergeant-majors they would all be addressed by the permanent staff as 'sir'. He warned that it could be disadvantageous to believe they meant it.

Frazer was woken at 04.30 hours and told to report to the Camp Commandant's Office complete with his kit in fifteen minutes. And then a Scots Guards Captain gave him the good news. They had received a signal from Command. He was to be commissioned on the spot and trucked back to Nairobi immediately. His hand had been shaken and they had even found a pair of shoulder pips with green Intelligence Corps cloth backing to be sewn on his shoulder straps. A sandwich and a thermos with tea was handed over and he was taken to a 3-ton lorry for the long dusty journey to Nairobi. He slept most of the way.

At the guard-room in Nairobi he was checked and told that the Duty I.O. was expecting him. He was told that the DDMI, the Deputy Director of Military Intelligence wanted to see him at 10.00 hours. He was also told that he was improperly dressed. The Intelligence Corps didn't go in for second-lieutenants. He was a lieutenant and was given an extra pair of green stars to go on his shirt flaps. He was given a camp-bed in one of the annexes and one of the 'boys' would sew on his extra stars for the morning.

Brigadier Lawrence, the DDMI, was not an I Corps officer but an ex-gunner who was expected to keep his body of wayward and sometimes eccentric I Corps officers moderately military. No long hair, no silk neck-scarves and no beards unless required in the line of duty. He likened his task to running a circus, but he was quite fond of his charges. Like most real army people he saw the army as a family and his chaps were his family. To be praised or kicked up the arse as circumstances called for.

After the stamping and saluting Lieutenant Frazer was sitting on the visitor's chair.

'You realise, Frazer, that you're improperly dressed?'

Was he being tested to see if he blamed others for his mistakes? He decided on discretion.

'No, sir. I didn't realise that.'

The Brig looked at him. 'Has nobody told you of your new posting?'

'No, sir.'

'Right,' the Brig said as if that solved the problem. 'What do you know about MI6?'

'Only what we were taught at the depot, sir. At Winchester and Matlock.'

'Well. Our people in MI6 have got a file on you as a possible recruit and they've got a job they want you to do. First of all your new posting is a captain's posting with effect from today. Congratulations.' He paused but not long enough for a response. 'Your appointment will be as Military Liaison Officer to HRH Haile Selassie. You'll go in with our troops under General Platt and Wingate and in the meantime we want you to look after the old boy. Keep him happy. Find out what he's up to – if anything. But that's only your cover. What we really want is for you to tell us after we've got him back in power what's going on in Addis Ababa. The politics, the graft, who's who, the Ethiopian army and all that sort of stuff. We'll be having reports from the Minister in

Addis and the Head of the Mission but we want an independent view. No diplomacy. No covering up. And all the gossip.' He paused. 'Who do you bank with?'

'I don't have a bank account, sir?'

He had the feeling that the DDMI knew already that he didn't have a bank account. Anywhere.

'That's OK. Open one locally. Try Barclays. You won't be getting your normal pay slip. Your pay will go to your bank direct and it won't be from the War Office. It'll be from one of the merchant banks. And you'll be glad to know that while you're working for MI6 you don't pay Income Tax. We don't want those bastards building up a list of who's working for SIS.' He leaned back in his chair. 'You'll get a proper briefing from Holroyd on your new posting in the two weeks before we mount our offensive.' He put his hands on the table. 'Any more questions for me?'

Only a moment's hesitation. 'No, sir. Thank you, sir.'

The Brig walked with him to the door. 'Best of luck.' He shook Frazer's hand and then turned back to his desk.

Captain Holroyd was waiting for Frazer outside the DDMI's office. His greeting was a handshake as he said, 'You jammy bastard.'

Jamie Frazer had been amused that having sent him on a crash course to speak Swahili they now posted him to the one country that didn't use Swahili. It had its own ancient language – Amharic. But in his contacts with the Emperor they both spoke English or, when the Emperor wanted to be formal, they spoke French. Frazer could vaguely remember seeing pictures of the Emperor appealing for help from the League of Nations way back in 1935 when the Italians had invaded his country. Nobody offered even token help and the Emperor had become an exile in England with his family. The League of Nations was more concerned with pacifying Mussolini than coming to the aid of one of its members.

The campaign to free Ethiopia wasn't particularly difficult. The Italians had already been thrown out of Somalia by the same troops. But once the army had occupied Addis Ababa, Frazer's problems really began. The occupying British army mission obviously had had wind of his real work and they refused to give him accommodation at the British army's cantonment. There was no ambassador appointed, just a Minister who operated from a closed estate. Frazer was told quite openly by the Minister that he was *persona non grata* and was banned from any contact with the diplomatic mission.

London, through Nairobi, told him to find his own accommodation in the city. He was told that he could spend whatever was necessary to be independent and to pay whatever was needed for information and informants. He found himself a small house in a mainly Italian quarter of Addis. Most Italians had been repatriated to Italy and Italian prisoners-of-war were in camps down in Kenya or Magadiscio.

It was obvious that the Italians had been good colonisers once the war against the Abyssinians was over. Superb roads and beautiful public buildings had obviously cost countless millions of lire. The Italians had clearly not gained any economic benefits from the conquest. The other thing that seemed strange to Jamie Frazer was the easygoing relationship between the Italians and the Abyssinians. Most of the Italian immigrants were artisans and they got on well with the locals. The mixing was undoubtedly helped by the fact that Abyssinian women were probably the most beautiful in the world. Italian men married local girls and even more had girl-friends and mistresses. There was no evidence of hatred or even dislike between the two communities. It looked as if it had been Rome's policy to allow only a very limited number of Italian women immigrants. Whether by accident or design it seemed to have worked.

When the army took over enemy or occupied territory from the Italians, Rome left behind an organisation to go underground to engage in sabotage and political subversion and it was to penetrate the stay-behind organisations in Addis that London wanted him to initiate if possible. His task was not made easier by the Emperor sponsoring Italians who could provide the palace with services like repairing radios, domestic equipment and cars. A further disadvantage was that the Abyssinians were only too happy to hide and protect escaped POWs and friends. Both the palace and the general population virtually ignored the British garrison. Nobody was particularly grateful for having been liberated. Life went on much as it always had done.

His first reliable informer was Borinski, a Pole who had lived for twenty years in Addis and Harar. He spoke English, Polish, Italian and Amharic.

Hans Borinski worked at the Bank of Ethiopia and handled the paperwork of the merchants who dealt in commodities like grain, coffee, leather and precious metals. There was not much going on in the market that he didn't know about. The bank was run under a British civilian appointed by the Consulate and with a banker's background he declined to give any banking or trading information to the British. But Borinski had taken an instant liking to the young officer who came into the bank to discuss opening an account. He had advised against such an action and put Frazer in touch with a friend in the Banque de Grece.

Borinski had found three servants to run Frazer's house and a driver for the Lancia Aprillia he had bought. A cook and a youth who acted as a gardener and security man for the house. They had all been vetted and hand-picked by Borinski himself, but with the warning that Frazer should never trust anyone in Addis. Borinski had the theory that the reason why Ethiopians and Italians got on so well together was because they were all the same. Dishonest, feckless, liars and wastrels.

The training back at Matlock on how to run an informant network was not only very primitive but totally inappropriate to the chaos that reigned in Addis. The citizens of the capital city of Ethiopia were quite openly venal, greedy and immoral. Somebody had once said that 'while we all know what went on at Sodom, nobody knew for certain what went on in Gomorrah'. But whatever it was it was certain that you could do it in Addis Ababa. However, Hans Borinski was an exception. Upright, honest and a good husband. Aged about fifty he had one of those Roman emperor faces. Big features, darkish skin and black, curly hair. Despite his inside knowledge he lived on his salary and the money that Frazer paid him merely met his expenses.

At the end of his first month in Addis Frazer had a network of informants covering the stay-behind Italians, the men who ran the black-market, the leaders of the Ethiopian Army and in the Imperial Guard. The Italians obviously had no intention of causing trouble to the occupying forces or anyone else. All they wanted was to live and work in their shacks in the market with their pretty girl-friends.

It was Borinski who came up with information that really mattered. It was estimated that a Greek, George Synodinos, was the richest man in Addis. He had franchises all over the Middle East for world-famous trademarks but he never left Ethiopia apart from a monthly trip to

Djibouti. It was the trips to Djibouti that interested Frazer. The Red Sea
port was still in the hands of the Vichy French but Frazer's local
informers reported that he stayed at a villa he owned and that his visitors
were locals and not French. When Frazer's third report on the Greek
went to London he received an urgent request to put a major effort into
finding out what Synodinos was up to. Did he have any close relationship with the Emperor? Frazer's investigations showed that Synodinos
was visiting the Emperor several times a week. What was also
interesting was that a young Greek woman who owned a night-club in
Addis was at some of the meetings. She was an extremely attractive
young woman and the night-club was very profitable. It was assumed
at first that she was either the Emperor's mistress or the Greek's
mistress.

Frazer started going every night to Kathi Kathikis's night-club and
inevitably his good looks and friendliness attracted the girl. She started
inviting him to tea. Somebody had told her about traditional English
teas and there were cucumber sandwiches cut in neat triangles with the
crusts removed. And genuine Ty-phoo tea bought on the black-market
and wildly expensive. She was five or six years older than he was but
when she first invited him to stay the night he was happy to conform.
The more he saw of her the more he liked her and although she had
other relationships from the past it was obvious that she was rather
more than fond of him. The young Englishman in his captain's uniform
dancing nightly with the attractive young Greek girl were seen by the
regulars as rather romantic, and the club band always played '*Parla mi
d'amore*' when they first went on the floor each evening. Borinski said
nothing on the subject but he definitely didn't approve. He saw it as
typical Italian behaviour, not the kind of behaviour expected from an
Englishman. Especially an officer. But Borinski admired his Englishman and if that was how he wanted to go on – then, so be it. The girl
herself was too shrewd and experienced a local not to realise that
Captain Frazer was more than just the Military Liaison Officer to the
Emperor. But she was too used to the intrigues of Addis Ababa to ever
raise the question of why he was there. And Captain Frazer was equally
diplomatic about not asking what her relationship was with the King of
Kings and Lion of Judah.

It was Kathi herself who raised it as they had breakfast together on a Sunday morning after he had stayed overnight.

'How do you get on with HRH?'

Frazer shrugged. 'He's OK. No trouble at all.'

She smiled. 'Go on. Ask me how I get on with him.'

He looked at her, smiling as he said, 'I'm sure he's crazy about you, sweetheart. And that's all that matters.'

'If I say I've never been to bed with him, would you believe me?'

'Sure I would.'

'Nobody else would believe me.'

'So what?' He shrugged angrily. 'To hell with 'em.'

'How much money have you got in the bank?'

'I've only recently had a bank account. About a hundred pounds.'

'You don't sound very interested in money.'

He laughed. 'I haven't got enough to make it interesting.'

'You could earn a lot of money here in Addis.'

'For what?'

'Doing favours. Not noticing what's going on. When you've got some money I could tell you how to make it a lot more.' She smiled. 'That's what I do for the Emperor.'

'I thought he was very rich.'

'He's as poor as the beggars in the market.' She paused. 'That's why he's so close to Synodinos. And when HRH nods his head in one direction or another he makes a lot of money.' She paused. 'I don't mean thousands. I mean hundreds of thousands. Not banknotes, my love. The real thing. Gold. You can trace banknotes but you can't trace gold.'

And suddenly the bells rang. He couldn't wait to talk to Borinski but he took her first for a swim and dinner at Lake Biscioftu and went straight to Borinski on his way home. He was led into the dimly-lit front room.

'Tell me about the gold coins in the market, Hans.'

Borinski smiled. 'You didn't seem interested when I told you.'

Frazer shrugged. 'I wasn't, but I am now.'

'There's a lot happened since we talked about it.'

'Tell me.'

'The gold wasn't the usual small piece, it was shaped and there were some faint markings on it. The man who had it took it to a goldsmith in the *gebbi* to check that it really was gold. That turned out to be a fatal mistake. The goldsmith recognised what it was. It was an antique Japanese coin from a special collection that was supposed to have disappeared in a terrible earthquake in Tokyo in 1923. He said it was worth about a hundred and fifty thousand US dollars. Maybe more.'

'Can we talk to the chap who got it and find out where it came from?'

Borinski shook his head. 'A senior officer from the Imperial Guard arrested him and took him away. About an hour later the same officer arrested the goldsmith. Already there were rumours that the gold had come from the palace itself. That it had been stolen without the thief knowing how valuable it was.' Borinski paused and then said, 'What made you so suddenly interested in the gold?'

'We were talking about money and Kathi said that gold was safer because it couldn't be identified.' He paused. 'Will there be a chance to talk to the goldsmith when he's released?'

'He won't be released, captain. I'd guess that they are both dead by now. This was obviously a theft from inside the palace. We ought to be thinking about how Japanese treasures got there. I understand that the original collection was the most important in the world.'

'Are there theories about this in the Japanese community here?'

'Yes. They're very frightened.'

'Why should they be affected by this?'

'They're afraid that the Emperor is doing favours for the Japanese. Either him direct or through Synodinos.'

'What kind of favours?'

'Naphtha for the Japanese mother-ships that service the Japanese warships in the Indian Ocean. The coast near Djibouti would make a good transfer point.'

'Why should HRH do this?'

'Because he's penniless. Ask Kathi Kathikis.'

'She said that too. That he's broke.' He sighed. 'I can't believe he'd do that but I'd better tell London.'

Frazer spent the rest of the night writing out his report and then encoding it. The only help that he got from the Military Mission had come from a high-powered order from London that the Military Mission's Royal Corps of Signals unit would be at his disposal with top priority for all his traffic to and from London. He telephoned the Signals Captain for his message to be picked up and dispatched immediately. The Signals people were always obliging and took no part in his being ostracised by the Mission and the Consulate.

Five hours later London responded. He was to drop everything else and concentrate on Synodinos. His information fitted in with information from other sources. The Royal Navy had been trying to find out how the Japanese mother-ships in the Indian Ocean were able to operate for so long without returning to base for refuelling. They were now convinced that his theory was correct. But they pointed out that before they could move on the Greek they would need evidence that would stand up in court. And they emphasised that Synodinos had real influence at high levels, including London. A specialist numismatist had confirmed that the gold piece was almost certainly a piece from the lost Fujii collection.

With an urgent need to employ more informants Frazer had another problem. Ethiopian informants would not accept payment in banknotes, no matter whether they were pounds, dollars or lire, and had to be paid in coins of small denominations which meant that he needed a dozen sackfuls of Kenyan currency every week. He used the Signals unit to send an urgent message to Nairobi asking them to make a £1000 deposit at the Banque de Grece that could be converted to East African coins. The informants were paid by weight on a pair of kitchen scales. But the network was beginning to pay off after a couple of weeks. Most days he had to go through the charade of being Military Liaison Officer to the Emperor. Aware now that HRH was as deceitful as he was himself. The Emperor's list of protected Italian POWs who were useful to the palace came to several hundred names. Frazer had to protect them from arrest by the Military Mission and in turn the Mission's staff made Frazer's life as difficult as possible. They withdrew his facility to draw petrol from army stores and held back his private mail and his pay cheques. It seemed crazy that he had to buy his petrol from a garage owned by Synodinos.

The information he was passing to London was not much more than a diary of Synodinos's movements and visitors day by day, but London seemed satisfied.

It was in the fourth week of the surveillance when the car arrived at

Frazer's house and a Somali youth handed him a note. It was a hand-written note from Synodinos asking him to do him the favour of coming back to the Greek's place with the car. Just for a friendly chat, the message said.

Frazer took his house-boy with him and Jamu waited for him in the car when they arrived at the Greek's villa near the palace. The Greek was waiting for him, smiling and friendly as they shook hands and made themselves comfortable around a low coffee table. Synodinos was a good-looking man in his fifties. Casually dressed and speaking good English he talked about his garden and the problem of getting a really good cook. And then, almost as if he were still talking about his domestic problems, he said, very quietly, 'I thought I ought to warn you that you're getting into rather stormy waters, Captain Frazer.'

When Frazer didn't respond Synodinos went on, 'I'd like to avoid having to take more drastic measures so I thought it best I told you face to face that you would be wise to stop playing games with your little men. You're out of your depth and you're getting to be a nuisance.' He paused. 'Don't force me to take more drastic action, please.'

For a few moments Frazer didn't respond and then he stood up. 'It's been nice meeting you, Mr Synodinos, at long last. I understand your threats but I have to remind you that you too could have problems if you are not very careful.'

The Greek stood up too, facing him. 'Tell your people in London about our meeting today.' He looked away and following the look Frazer saw a young girl coming into the room. She was smiling, holding out a bunch of wild flowers. As she looked at Frazer the Greek said, 'My daughter Aliki. Capitano Frazer.' Frazer ignored the mild insult of the 'capitano' and said, '*Kalamera tee kauafe.*'

She laughed. '*Kala efkhareesto.*'

Looking at her father she said, 'I'll put the flowers in a vase. Don't let me interrupt.' She smiled at Frazer as she turned away. '*Tha ta ksanapoome.*'

When she had left, Synodinos seemed less aggressive as he said, 'She's the image of her mother. So beautiful.'

'She must give you a lot of pleasure. That lovely smile and those beautiful eyes.'

Synodinos looked at Frazer in silence for long moments and then said, 'No wonder my countrywoman, Kathi Kathikis, speaks so fondly of you.'

Synodinos walked with Frazer to the door and out into the sunshine of the garden. As they stood at the gate Synodinos said, 'Are you married, Captain?'

Frazer smiled. 'Maybe when the war's over. Now's not the right time.' He smiled. 'It could take my mind off my job.'

Synodinos smiled. 'Take care, young man, and don't ignore what I said to you. Things aren't always what they seem.'

As Frazer drove back to his place, Jamu, the house-boy, said, '*Habari gani?*'

Frazer shrugged. '*M'zuri tu.*'

A week later he had his regular formal meeting with the Emperor. As usual it was uneventful apart from a complaint from HRH about a letter from Pickfords in Bath threatening that unless the long overdue amount for storing the Royal household goods was paid they would be sold to defray expenses.

Frazer made sympathetic noises but suggested that the complaint should be made to the Consulate as a civilian matter.

As he was walking across the palace parade-ground to his car he was stopped by Ras Mulagueta, the CO of the Imperial Guard. He escorted Frazer to the stable block where the polo ponies were kept. Half-way down the row of stables Mulagueta opened the bottom section of a half-door and pointed to a figure lying in the straw in the empty stable. Frazer walked over slowly, already knowing who it was. It was Jamu who was supposed to be on weekend leave. On his black skin the bruises were hard to identify but the broken skin, broken legs and the blood were enough. He was dead.

He looked at Mulagueta. 'Who did this?'

'No idea, capitano. No idea. Maybe he had enemies.'

Mulagueta was tall. Well over six foot. A Danakil from the north. And ugly with it.

'I'll arrange for him to have a funeral and be buried tomorrow.'

'Is not possible, capitano. I believe this man was a criminal and I will have him disposed of in the correct way.'

'What way is that?'

Ted Allbeury

'Burning, capitano, burning.'

'I'll speak to HRH about it.'

Mulagueta smiled. 'It is I who decide these things, not Ras Tafari our little prince.'

Frazer looked for long moments at Mulagueta's face and then said softly, 'Mulagueta, you're a shit and you'll pay for murdering that young man.'

Mulagueta laughed. 'Who will do it, capitano?'

Frazer turned and walked away. He notified London about what had happened but they made no comment.

Borinski had been waiting for him at his house and had already heard on the grapevine that Jamu had been found dead and he had warned Frazer that he too could be a target. A week after the visit to the palace stables, his house-servants had all disappeared and it was Kathi Kathikis who told him that they had been scared away by Mulagueta's people. She had found replacements for them who were loyal to her and not afraid of Mulagueta or his men. Kathi was more important to the Emperor than Mulagueta and they knew it.

He had no meetings with HRH for ten days. They had all been cancelled by the palace. London were still pressing for information on Synodinos and Borinski had passed him details of Synodinos's transactions through his bank that showed movements of large amounts of money for transactions covering hides and coffee.

It was almost a month after Jamu's murder that Kathi had come to his house. The first time she had ever been there. She was obviously agitated and said she had come to warn him that he was in danger.

'Have you had a letter from the palace?'

'No. He's dodged meeting me for over a month. Why should he write to me?'

'I can't tell you.' She shrugged. 'They made me swear I wouldn't.'

'Don't tell me then. I can look after myself, honey, and if they killed me there'd be a big row. The little man wouldn't get his funds from London if he misbehaves. That was part of our deal.'

'They can make it look like an accident or somebody drunk. There's a dozen ways they could do it.'

He smiled. 'Let me make you a cup of real English tea. My Grandma always used to say that there's nothing so bad that a good cup of tea won't help.'

She shook her head. 'I can't stay. But promise me that if you're in trouble you'll come to me? Not even the little man in the palace would dare play games with me.'

'OK. I promise.'

'How could you get out of the country if you had to and you were in a hurry?'

He shrugged. 'I'd leave it to London.'

She shook her head in disbelief, tears in her eyes, as she said, 'I'll have to go.'

She almost ran to the car that had been waiting for her.

The letter from the palace was delivered early that evening. It was formal. Notifying him that he was *'persona non grata'* and must leave the country within the next forty-eight hours. It went on to point out that he no longer had diplomatic privileges. It took him an hour to destroy his papers and collect his few personal belongings.

He phoned the Consulate and the Minister told him that he could not be accommodated on the Mission cantonment. As a formality he phoned the British Military Mission where the Military-Secretary made clear that they did not consider him as being a British officer and he would not be welcome at the mission encampment. He contacted the Signals unit and dictated a message for London that ended by saying he could only be contacted through Borinski. By the time he got to Borinski's house Borinski had already been contacted by London. They wanted him to destroy all his official documents and to avoid involving Borinski by moving elsewhere. Notifying them where he could be contacted. A plane would be sent from Aden to pick him up from the Addis Ababa airstrip at 20.00 hours the following day. A replacement as Military Liaison Officer would be on the plane to take over. London would accept calls from Borinski's telephone number to Nairobi HQ. He phoned Nairobi immediately and the Duty Int. Officer took the call and was given the phone number where he could be contacted.

Borinski shook his head. 'Why go to Kathi Kathikis? Stay here. To hell with your people in London.'

Frazer sighed. 'She'll look after me, Hans. Don't worry.' He paused. 'Will you phone her and tell her I'm on my way?' He hugged the old man. 'Thanks for all your help. I shan't forget it. I've left the sacks of coins at the house. Just give it to the informants as you think fit.'

91

Borinski nodded. Too overcome to speak.

They sat on the balcony of her apartment on top of the club building. The sun was setting and the sky was the inevitable velvet blue that offset so perfectly the waves of bougainvillaea that flowed across the roof.

'Are you sorry to be leaving, Jamie?'

He smiled. 'Sorry to be leaving you – yes. Not sorry to be leaving Addis. I shall miss you.'

'What will you miss? Sleeping with me or what?'

'I'll certainly miss that, but I'll miss you yourself. Talking with you. Dancing with you. Just knowing that you're here.'

'Do you trust your people in London?'

He shrugged. 'I take 'em as I find 'em. It doesn't involve trust.'

'Do you trust me?'

'Absolutely.'

'What did you think of Synodinos?'

'Charming, sophisticated and a real bastard.'

She smiled. 'Not bad. Not bad. You must have feminine intuition. Most people see him as all good or all bad.'

'And you? How do you find him?'

'He was the first man I ever slept with. He helped me a lot. That's how I got this club. I was only sixteen when I first knew him. He didn't pretend. I was his mistress and that was all. But he was generous with money and I think his wife knew about me.' She smiled. 'And of course he was Greek too and little Greek girls are brought up not to trust their countrymen when they come bearing gifts.'

'Will you drive me to the airstrip tomorrow evening?'

'Yes. But I won't wait. That would make me too sad.'

'Let's go and dance.'

She laughed. 'Why not?'

It was beginning to get light when they went to bed. It was June 22 and although they didn't know it the German tanks and artillery were pounding their way at that moment across the frontier of their erstwhile allies, the Russians. It caused little comment the next day, for most inhabitants of Addis Ababa would have had difficulty in explaining who was at war with whom. None could have given even a vague suggestion as to what the war was all about.

They spent Jamie Frazer's last day in Addis at their favourite place just outside the town at the Italian restaurant at Lake Biscioftu. The restaurant was still run by Italians. Frazer and Kathi both knew them well from previous visits, Signor and Signora Baffi were on the Emperor's list of 'essential' Italians.

Although he normally wore civilian clothes, Frazer had polished the buttons and belt of his uniform but kept to his soft desert boots instead of his army shoes.

When he was ready to go she sat on the bed looking at him. She had seldom seen him in uniform but she decided that he looked rather smart in his captain's outfit. She had found one of her waiters who had a camera and made him take a few photographs of Captain Jamie Frazer.

As she edged her car through the double gates in the wall around the club she said quietly, 'Don't look now but the green Fiat is tailing us. It's one of the Imperial Guards' vehicles.' She paused. 'You heard about Mulagueta?'

'What about him?'

'Somebody shot him in the back. Died instantly.' She smiled. 'Your account's squared now. I got the money from Borinski but didn't tell him what it was for.'

At the airstrip she parked beside the wooden buildings that housed the primitive equipment for controlling take-offs and landings. There was a captain there from the Military Mission who bowed and scraped to Kathi Kathikis and pointedly ignored Frazer.

She said softly, 'Let's go outside. He says the plane is due in ten minutes.'

Outside she stood looking up at his face. 'It's a funny word – love. And I'm not sure what it really means but I think I love you – and I know I'll miss you, Jamie Frazer.' She paused. 'And I know I'll never forget you.' She sighed. 'Don't say goodbye, just kiss me and I'll go.'

He put his arm round her and kissed her gently for long moments until she pushed him away, turning and walking slowly to her car. She didn't look back.

Chapter 18

When, after four weeks, the publishers stopped paying for his accommodation at the Hilton, Al Pinto moved to a low-cost room in the backstreets of Bayswater. As he paid off his taxi Sidney Bowman wondered if it was the right address. But the handwritten card under one of the bells confirmed that this was Pinto's new address. Meetings were no longer at the coffee shop at the Hilton.

Pinto's place was one room, fair-sized with a fold-up settee bed and some oddments of furniture. There was a toilet and a shower behind a curtain in one corner.

'So,' Bowman said as he settled himself in the only comfortable chair. 'It's time for a little chat, my friend.'

Pinto raised his eyebrows but said nothing, so Bowman launched himself into his piece. He had a little more sympathy for the American than the publishers had. Pinto was a freelance journalist and Bowman knew the problems. The need to get a story and not enough time to check the facts in case some other hack beat you to it. Or the facts could spoil a good story.

'I think you've got to realise, old chap, that the buck stops with you. They're still going to drag us into court. All of us, but you're the one at the top of the heap. It's your bloody book, mate, and you've got to take the responsibility for what's in it.' He paused. 'You do understand that, don't you?'

Pinto shrugged. 'I've still got my passport, old pal. If they, or you, try to pin it on me . . .' he shrugged '. . . I'll just take the next flight to New York.'

'That wouldn't be a good move for you, Al. You've got to remember my newspaper's got all the dough it needs to go to law and if you did a moonlight flit we'd go after you in the States for damages.'

'Damages for what?'

'Breach of contract.'

'What contract? I've got no contract with you. My contract's with the publishers.'

'And they've got a contract with us. They're all hooked up together but the buck stops with you.'

'So what do you want me to do?'

'First of all to recognise that yours is the prime responsibility for landing us in all this shit.'

'You should have checked the book before you serialised it. So should the publishers.'

'You're absolutely right, my friend. We should have. We were careless. But we acted in good faith. And those contracts put the responsibility for what's in your book right on your plate. And you bloody well know it.'

'So you were too goddamned careless to check the book yourselves and now you'd like to make me the fall-guy. What's new?'

'What's new is that you start taking some responsibility for the mess we're all in because you sold us a book that was full of libels.'

'I don't understand. How do I start taking responsibility? You, Mr Bowman, have been laying down the law on what we do. Not me.'

Bowman settled himself back in his chair and looked across at Pinto.

'Way back I remember you hinting that if there were problems with the libel action you knew things that could make the other side back off.' He paused. 'Can you do this or was it just bluffing?'

'I can find people who'll show that this guy Frazer is incompetent, immoral and a traitor to his country.' He shrugged. 'Their people may try to make him look like a cross between Mother Teresa and Shirley Temple but the simple fact is that he ain't.'

'They don't have to prove or disprove anything. We have to prove that what you wrote is fact.'

Pinto waved an arm dismissively. 'Look, Bowman, I've been around the spook world for a long time. If you want me to find witnesses to his failings I'll do it.'

Bowman said quietly, 'I leave it to you, Al. Just don't do anything to make it worse.'

As Bowman stood up to leave, Pinto said, 'You want to throw your hand in don't you?'

'Too bloody true I do. If I could back out for a hundred grand and costs I'd consider myself lucky.'

'So why don't you do that?'

'Our lawyer tried it weeks ago. They wouldn't play.' He looked at his watch. 'Got to go. Keep in touch.'

Pinto didn't get up and Bowman let himself out.

Al Pinto sat with his eyes closed and wondered why he'd never learn. When people challenged him, especially Brits, he was always tempted into making some even more unlikely boast about what he could do. It wasn't his fault, it was their fault for tempting him. He decided that a visit to the Groucho was the best cure for his problems. Bowman had got him a temporary membership of the Groucho and he felt at home there. All those Brit bullshitters reminded him of home.

As he ordered his first drink he saw that Bowman was there, laughing uproariously with a group of men who were standing around him as he told them the latest inside story on the Royal Family. He saw Bowman glance towards him and then look away as if he didn't recognise him.

Al Pinto was on his fourth Bell's when a man strolled over and moved in beside him at the bar. He was grey-haired, tall and rather dignified, wearing what had obviously once been a very expensive tweed suit. As Pinto put his empty glass on the bar top the man said, 'Somebody told me that you were the American who's involved in the libel case. He didn't mention your name. My name's Davies. Owen Davies.'

He looked expectantly at Pinto who said, 'Yeah. My name's Pinto. Al Pinto.'

'Pleased to meet you. What're you drinking?'

'Bell's, no ice.'

Owen Davies called to the barman for two Bell's and turned back to Pinto.

'It's time somebody did a bit of digging around in SIS. Pity it had to be a Yank who did it. Should have been one of us.'

'You mean a Brit should have done it? But they don't know what goes on. And if they did, they'd be scared to say it.'

97

'You're right of course. But when I said one of us I meant somebody who'd been in the racket himself.'

'For Chrissake, are you telling me you were one of 'em?'

Owen Davies smiled a quiet, modest smile as he shrugged his shoulders, careful not to spill his drink. 'Used to be, Mr Pinto. But not now. I retired a few years ago.'

'Were you there when this chap Frazer was there?'

'I was around at the time.'

'You actually knew him?'

'Kind of. Unfortunately.'

'Why unfortunately?'

'We didn't like one another and he was, after all, an influential man.'

'Why didn't you like him?'

'I thought he was a phoney, and anyway he lacked the class, the status. A kind of inverted snob. If you'd been to Oxford or Cambridge you were a suspect. Another Kim Philby.' He paused. 'Not the lily-white hero that some make him out to be.'

Pinto hesitated for a moment and then said, 'Why don't we go somewhere and have a bite of lunch?'

'Why not? I might be able to help you.'

Pinto paid the bill and turned to Davies. 'There's a little Italian place in Newport Street, it's OK and quiet.'

Al Pinto had learned that when you had a working meal with Brits they didn't get down to business until the coffee. He'd asked Keane why this was and Keane had looked shocked and said that 'it wasn't the done thing to talk business when you were eating'. But he found that Owen Davies wasn't like that, although he was obviously a man who came from that sort of background. As soon as the *minestrone* came, Davies launched into his attack on the hypocrisy of the clique that ran SIS.

'But you said that Frazer wasn't one of those people.'

'That's what his front was. Used to call himself working-class, whatever that means these days. But he was one of 'em all the same, strong against the Labour Party as much as against the Commies. Turned a blind eye to what a few of them were trying to do to bring down Harold Wilson. But in the end he sold us down the river.'

'You say "*us*", does that mean you were one of them?'

'Let's say I was on the inside track of intelligence.'

'Could you prove any of this?'

'I could give chapter and verse of the things they did, that he didn't stop.'

'What kind of things?'

'Bugging their phones. Breaking in and going over their files. Planting rumours with the media. The usual stuff.'

'And you say he was suspected of having contact with KGB people at their embassy here?'

'Yeah. There were pointers that way.'

Pinto hesitated for a moment before he took the plunge and then, looking at Davies's face, he said, 'Would you testify in court about this stuff for my defence?'

'I couldn't afford to, Al. I've got a part-time job as security adviser to a merchant bank. They'd give me the boot and I need the extra money.'

'How much do they pay you?'

'Ten grand.'

'D'you have a contract?'

'No. It's just word of mouth. They'd use some excuse, nothing to do with me giving evidence. They'd say I was falling down on the job or they were taking on somebody in-house and full-time. They'd have some excuse.'

'How about you gave me all the details? Everything you can remember. You don't give evidence. You're just acting as my researcher, my consultant and nobody knows about it. How about that?'

'That could work, Al. Just as long as nobody knows.'

'Let's think about twenty grand. In cash. Would that be OK?'

'Sounds OK to me, Al.'

'Give me a couple of days and I'll come back to you. Give me your address and phone number.'

Pinto wrote the details on the back of the typewritten menu and slipped it into his jacket pocket. 'Tell me,' he said, 'How do I know you're genuine?'

Davies shrugged. 'You don't. It's up to you, old chap. You must have contacts. Your pals at the newspaper can soon do a check. Or . . .' he smiled and shrugged '. . . or we can just forget it. Like I said, it's up to you.'

Al Pinto's current experiences told him not to go it alone.

'I'll get back to you in a couple of days. Is that OK?'

'Anytime you want, my friend.'

Bowman looked at the reverse side of the menu and then reached for the internal phone. He pressed four numbers and waited.

'Security.'

'Is that Jackie?'

'Yes, sir.'

'How'd you know it was me?'

'The gravelly voice.'

Bowman laughed. Jackie was very pretty.

'Something urgent. I want you to do a general check on a guy named Davies. Owen Davies. Claims to have been a spook with British intelligence. His address is Flat B, 27 Covington Road . . . it's somewhere in Pimlico.'

'Is he still in the services?'

'No. Must have retired some years back.'

'How urgent is it?'

'I could wait until we go to press tonight.'

He heard her laugh and then she hung up.

Bowman looked at Pinto. 'Phone me back about six. OK?'

'I'd risk it if it were up to me.'

'I know you would. That's why we're in the shit right now.'

The message from Security came back in two hours. Yes. Owen Davies had been an officer in intelligence for fifteen years. He was retired early. Nobody knew why but the story was that he was too political. He now had a part-time job as a security consultant and was paid £5,000 a year.

Bowman started with the Groucho, trying to contact Pinto, but eventually gave up the chase. Pinto phoned in himself at 6 p.m. Bowman arranged to meet him at the Groucho later that evening.

After a few drinks at the club, Bowman moved them back to his own 'hospitality' suite at the newspaper where they talked over the meal.

Bowman was in two minds about getting involved any deeper. Some of his editor acquaintances obviously thought he'd just been caught

100

with his pants down, but a number had said they were sure that he would have some rabbit he'd bring out of the hat when it got to court. It was the latter rôle that appealed to him but there was another rôle that he wanted to preserve. The rôle that portrayed him as a frantically busy editor who had been grossly let down by others who ought to have known better. If they were going to use this chap Davies then it had better be at arm's length so far as he was concerned. He knew he should consult their lawyer but he equally knew that so far as the law was concerned they would be walking on the thin legal ice of 'payment or inducements to witnesses'. He could just bounce the evidence from Davies onto Pollock QC at the last minute.

Bowman dipped into the *crème brulée* in its little pot and said, 'So what have you got in mind, Al?'

'We offer him five grand and another five when he produces the goods.'

'How much are you chipping in?'

'Don't try and smart-arse me, Bowman. You asked me to get some counter-evidence and I've got it. If you don't want it – too bad, I'll forget it.'

'Have you mentioned this to your publishers?'

'No.' Pinto looked surprised at the question.

'I heard that Keane's board are going to give him the chop when the case is over.'

'Does he know that?'

'I've no idea. I couldn't care less. He's just a wimp.' He paused. 'Back to the washing-up. OK. We'll finance it but you've got to supervise him. We don't want a lot of waffle. It's facts, dates, names, we need from him. D'you think you could do that?'

'Yeah. Leave it to me. We'll have to pay him in cash . . .'

Bowman interrupted. 'Come in tomorrow morning and I'll have it for you. Keep me in touch every day about what he's giving you but I don't want anything in writing. And not a word to anyone else. This is just between you and me. I don't want to end up in the slammer for bribing a witness.'

Pinto shrugged. 'Me too neither, old pal.'

Chapter 19

The plane had taken him from Addis to Nairobi where, as the duty Int. Officer explained, he was to have a couple of days' leave while they 'sorted out what to do with him'. The problem was, he said, that Frazer was now partly controlled by SIS in London.

Nairobi decided in the end that he should be posted to 14th Army in Burma who needed people with experience of running informant networks.

The Short Sunderland flying-boat took off from Mombasa for the refuelling stop in Ceylon. At Colombo the local Int. Officer was waiting for him as he got ashore.

'Captain Frazer?'

'That's me.'

'Do you speak Italian?'

'I get by, yes.'

'We've had a signal from London that seems to require you to be sent back to London because of a need for Italian speakers. But it was so mangled we've had to ask them for a repeat. There's a tent over there where you can get tea and a sandwich and I'll hold the plane until we're clear what London want.'

There were at least a dozen American officers in uniform in the big EPIP refreshment tent and the talk was all about the difference it would make now that the Japanese had attacked Pearl Harbour and the United States was officially in the war. Two Field Security Officers had noticed the green flashes on his shirt and had come over and introduced themselves. But Frazer's thoughts were on that signal from London. The possibility of being posted back to London or somewhere in Europe was too good to think about. But almost immediately the duty Int. Officer had come back. The message had been repeated. It said he was to be given a top travel priority and sent straight back to the UK.

The IO said, 'I've had your kit taken off the plane and put on another Sunderland that leaves for Alexandria in an hour. Cairo have been notified by us and by London of your priority but Omega House is full of high-priority bodies.' He shrugged. 'You'll have to keep hassling them or you'll be downgraded.'

Frazer smiled. 'I'll do that.'

'You can pick up your cigarette rations and then we'll go down to the docks.'

Flying on a Short Sunderland was a privilege in itself. Luxurious seats and even in wartime there were curtains at the windows and a hibiscus flower in a funnel-shaped vase above the window.

The plane had already landed at Alex before Frazer woke when the hygiene crews came bustling on board to spray passengers and the plane's interior. Against what, nobody knew.

A staff car took him to the hotel that had been taken over as the HQ of Middle East Command's Intelligence. Frazer was not surprised when nobody had heard of him or his travel priority. He hung on to his Movement Control Order issued to him at Colombo. Colombo may be the HQ of SEAC, South East Asia Command, but neither the war against the Japanese nor Colombo carried any weight in Cairo. He was given a room in an adjoining hotel that had been taken over as a transit camp.

By the third day they had at least found his paperwork. Brushing aside a travel priority issued by some other command, they told him that he could expect to wait another ten days, but he had to be ready to move at an hour's notice. Three days later he had been called for interview by an I Corps lieutenant-colonel who questioned him thoroughly about Synodinos. He gathered from the conversation that London were hoping to get together enough evidence to arrest the Greek. The colonel smiled as he said, 'But knowing London and the convoluted games they play, I doubt if they'll make a move against him. He's got too much influence.' He laughed. 'Probably more than SIS have themselves.' He paused. 'Who's your controller at SIS?'

Frazer shrugged. 'I've no idea.'

'Who recruited you?'

'I was just told by the DDMI in Nairobi that I was to be Liaison Officer to the Emperor but that I was to follow a brief concerning Italian stay-behind organisations.'

'No special training or briefing?'

'Just Winchester and Matlock.'

The colonel shook his head slowly. 'Just remember. There's a war on. So truth and honour don't matter any more. From what I hear London are pleased with your time in Addis. But remember, when the chips are on the table you're on your own. Always. Never kid yourself that you're special to them. Or anybody else.'

For some moments Frazer sat there in silence, expecting more but the colonel nodded towards the door.

Frazer saluted and as he turned away he saw the faint knowing smile on the colonel's face. An officer doesn't salute when he isn't wearing his cap.

Four days later he was woken in the early hours of the morning and an hour later was on the tarmac at one of the airstrips. He had a place on a Dakota flying to the UK via Gibraltar. In fact he would be the only passenger. It was an RAF plane taking engines back to the UK for servicing.

As one of the crew led him back through the piles of equipment, he was shown his place. It was a pile of tarpaulins on the floor between two engines. There was no heating and only a small light at the crew end of the plane. At Gibraltar he was given a mug of tea from a thermos as he stood on the tarmac waiting for the plane to be refuelled.

The rest of the journey was a nightmare of shivering cold and constant sudden lurches of height and direction to avoid enemy fighters as they crossed the Bay of Biscay. They landed at Hurn airstrip and he was given a travel voucher to Wentworth Woodhouse in Yorkshire which was the new Intelligence Corps depot. But Frazer had been a soldier long enough to suspect that nobody would even be aware of it if he took a couple of days in Birmingham before reporting.

There was already an air-raid warning on when he arrived at his grandparents' home. His small room at the back of the house was still there, kept waiting for him to come back. They were delighted to see him but he had seen enough of the bombed houses and buildings on the way from Snow Hill Station to realise that life must be very grim for the elderly couple.

The bombers came over soon after dark and he put on his helmet and stood at the front door watching the searchlights and the noise from the anti-aircraft battery in Brookvale Park. When a bomb demolished a house at the bottom of the hill he went back inside and persuaded Grandma that she must go into the air-raid shelter across the road. There was no point in trying to persuade Grandpa to go. He wouldn't leave the house no matter what happened.

Grandma had said she had to change, and ten minutes later she appeared in her best silk coat and her big toque hat with the artificial cherries. He found it angered him intensely, the sight of this old lady in her Sunday best stumbling into the mud of the shelter. She had never been in a shelter in any of the previous air-raids but his tin helmet and his uniform made him into somebody who had to be obeyed.

Back at the house he sat with his Grandfather who sat at the table with the evening paper spread out in front of him. As another plane droned over, the old man said, in a quavering voice. 'That's one of ours, lad.' The explosion a few moments later had to compete with the sound of the old man's tears dripping onto the *Birmingham Mail*. And Jamie Frazer realised then that he was now older than his grandparents.

Two days later he took the train to Sheffield and a taxi to Wentworth Woodhouse. The taxi driver wouldn't let him pay the fare.

At the depot nobody had any idea as to why he was there or what to do with him.

The intelligence services always took over superb buildings as their depôts or headquarters, and Wentworth Woodhouse was no exception. About four miles from the town of Rotherham it was a great eighteenth-century mansion with a 600-foot frontage, and the Intelligence Corps treated it with due respect. Music at dinner in the officers' mess was likely to be provided by top performers like Hepzibah Menuhin and Myra Hess. Captain Frazer preferred to catch the tram into Rotherham and do the Rotherham Glide at the local dance-hall. Otherwise he stayed on the tram all the way to Sheffield and danced with the local girls in the basement of the famous Cutler's Hall. Sheffield made almost all the cutlery for the whole of the country and the countries marked in pink on school atlases. He kept his evening trips to himself. The permanent staff at the depôt were still the military types and Frazer knew well that they would consider his jaunts as being not suitable behaviour for an officer and a gentleman. But he was amused to find that when he played jazz on the beautiful Bechstein in the mess, he had a bigger audience than the concert pianists had. He played most nights after he got back from Sheffield or Rotherham and people stayed up late just to hear him play. He saw it as a kind of insurance against the military types.

He had been at the depôt for almost a month before he was summoned for an interview in London. The interview was in a room at St Ermine's Hotel and the man who was waiting for him was wearing civilian clothes. Frazer guessed he was in his late forties. The man pointed at the armchairs.

'Make yourself comfortable. My name's Scott. Tom Scott.' He smiled. 'I've been reading about you. We seem to have kept you pretty busy one way and another. Any comments?'

Frazer shook his head. 'No, sir.'

'Just Tom, please.' He paused. 'What did they tell you when you were called back to London?'

'Not a thing apart from London looking for Italian speakers.'

Scott smiled. 'Somebody was being cautious, it's nothing to do with Italy at this stage.' He paused. 'Have you done a parachute course at Ringway?'

'No.'

'A radio course?'

'No.'

'Well. Back to the Italians in Addis. Were they a real problem from a military point of view?'

'No. Not the slightest, but the people who ran them in Rome were very professional. The problem for them was that the people on the ground had no incentives for making trouble. They were happy as they were.'

'What did Rome want?'

'Sabotage of power plants and the telephone system. Harassment of British occupation troops and propaganda against the Emperor and the Imperial Guard.' Frazer smiled. 'It was all completely ignored.'

'Who was the brains in Rome?'

107

'A chap named Simonini.'

'Civilian or army?'

'Neither. He was OVRA, the Italian version of the Gestapo.'

'I know from your file that you seem to have a real aptitude for languages. Swahili, Italian and some French and German. Quite a mixture. How good are your French and German?'

'Fluent but not perfect grammar.'

'How come so many languages? When did you learn them?'

Frazer shrugged. 'I just pick them up easily. Mainly self-taught.'

'I've fixed you a small flat in Sloane Street and you'll have a couple of days to move in before you go to Ringway and then on your radio course here in London.' He paused. 'By the way, have you any emotional commitments? Fiancée, girl-friend or whatever?'

Frazer smiled. 'Several whatevers but nothing serious.'

'You realise that you're full-time SIS now don't you?'

'Nobody told me but I got the impression that nobody was sure where I belonged.'

Scott stood up. 'You're SIS now. Full-time.' He smiled. 'Let me take you to see your new place and hand over the key. Have you got a rail warrant to go back to Sheffield to get your kit?'

'I brought my kit with me. I don't need to go back.'

'OK. Let's go.'

The place in Sloane Street was virtually just one fair-sized room plus a bathroom and kitchenette. It was simply furnished and a cleaning woman with security clearance would come in three times a week and clean up.

When he was about to leave, Scott asked, 'Have you ever been to SIS HQ?'

'No. I don't even know where it is.'

'Come and see me there tomorrow. The address is 54 Broadway, just off Parliament Square. We're on the third and fourth floors. Don't be deceived by the various name-plates. You'll see signs for the British and Foreign Bible Society, the British Empire Service League and the Broadway Press. And you'll find a uniformed commissionaire at the door. You just ask for me. Another chap will escort you to a small annexe where they'll check your identity, and check with me. When they're satisfied they'll bring you up to my office.'

'What ID do I use?'

'Just your I Corps ID will be fine.' He paused. 'That brings me to another point. In SIS you'll meet a lot of different sorts of people. Some will be, like you, I Corps officers, some will be from other regiments, some will be professors of one thing or another. Some you'll find less endearing than others but as time goes on you'll see that all of them have qualities, some apparent and some less obvious. So a word of warning. Don't jump to conclusions until you've been around for a bit.' He smiled. 'Time spent in reconnaissance and all that nonsense. I'll expect you about 11 a.m. tomorrow. Meantime take some pleasure from having been chosen to join what is a very élite community. A community that will certainly make a new and significant change in your life. One way or another.'

Chapter 20

She sat in the canvas chair watching him as he looked up at the sky, shading his eyes from the sun with his hands.

'What can you see, Jamie? There's nothing there. It's just blue sky, not even a cloud.'

He turned to look at her, smiling as he said, 'I was just thinking about when I first came to Chichester to do my training.' He shrugged. 'Seems a long time ago.'

'What's the sky got to do with it?'

'Because in those days you couldn't look up at the sky that summer without seeing a Spitfire or a Hurricane. Or maybe a Messerschmitt.' He waved his arms. 'This was where the Battle of Britain was fought. Sussex and Kent. Dog-fighting up there every day. Nobody remembers it these days. Except old fogies like me.'

'You're fishing for compliments. You want me to say you don't look a day over fifty.'

He smiled. 'What we have in our memories is the whole of our lives. Remember the hotel we stayed in in Berlin, Kempinski's?'

'Of course.'

'Remember the main road it was on? The Ku-damm?'

'Yes.'

'Well, the first time I saw that hotel was on May 8 1945. The day the war with Germany officially ended. Berlin had been taken by the Russians and it was just a heap of rubble. Right outside Kempinski's was a great big hole in the Ku-damm. And down in that hole was a German Tiger tank with just its gun sticking up into the road. I stood looking at the place where the tank had been when I went out for that early morning stroll. There were other things that reminded me of the past. And when I got back to Kempinski's from my walk there was a title of a German film on a poster in the lounge. It said, "*Das leben ist eine baustelle*", in English – "*Life is a building site*". It's so true. All the bits and pieces that make up our lives. Not days or dates but people and events and music.'

He stood there looking at her expectantly but all she said quietly was, 'You never cease to amaze me, Jamie Frazer.'

'In what way?'

'There are so many Jamie Frazers and I sometimes feel I only know half of them.' She paused. 'Can I ask you a personal question?'

'Try.'

'Didn't any of your wives want children?'

He shrugged. 'I wouldn't have married anyone who wanted children.'

'Why not? I've seen you with kids. They love being with you.'

'If an agent has children they're his Achilles heel. Pressure points. If you cared for children that much you shouldn't take on the kind of work I had.'

'Was it worth the sacrifice?'

He shrugged. 'Who knows?'

She sensed that he was annoyed by the question and she stood up. 'Let me treat you to lunch at the pub in Bosham.'

'I think I'll call it a day, my dear.' He smiled but it was a wan smile. 'Rest the old bones.'

As he drove her back to Rose Cottage and her car he was unusually silent and unresponsive.

'What are you thinking about, Jamie?'

'About Berlin.'

'What about it? The tank in the street?'

'No. I was thinking about a place I often visited when I lived in Berlin. A kind of old-fashioned square called Savigny Platz.'

'And it's made you sad?'

'A little, but I'll get over it.'

Chapter 21

The RAF organised and ran the parachute training school at Ringway, but there were not many army officers being trained for parachute jumps in 1942. There were only two other army officers on his course, the rest were RAF and Royal Marines. He wondered why Marines needed parachutes, but chatting about backgrounds was discouraged.

Two days were spent in the gym learning how to fall without injuring himself. Forward rolls, backward rolls, and swinging from ropes. They were shown how to pack a parachute but strongly advised never to do it. It was a job for trained personnel. All parachutes were checked and packed by RAF girls who were the centre of conflicting rumours. One rumour said that if you made a pass at the girls you could end up with a tangled parachute harness. The other rumour said that could happen if you *didn't* make a pass at one of the WRAF girls.

Learning how to swing in a harness from the roof of a large barn was supposed to teach you how to control the last hundred feet of your parachute drop.

The first jumps were from the wicker basket of a captive balloon that swung in a sickening pendulum movement that made the jump itself a positive relief. The sergeant-instructor was armed with all those ghastly juvenile jokes that had never amused anybody. His standard commentary when a trainee was sitting at the edge of the hole he was to launch from was – 'Remember what your mother told you. Keep your legs closed all the way down'. A few creeps conjured up a dutiful chuckle but most trainees groaned.

Frazer had completed all his aircraft drops in ten days including a drop into water at night and on the last day he had been given his cloth parachute to be sewn over his left-hand breast-pocket.

Back in London Tom Scott had met him at the station and gone with him to his place in Sloane Street. There was an envelope with mail that had arrived for him and he opened it as the taxi made its way from Kings Cross to Chelsea.

There were two letters from the Military Secretary. The first contained a two-inch strip of the Africa Star for his battledress and barathea jackets. The second letter from the Mil Sec was just a terse extract from Part Two Orders that told him that his rank of Captain in Addis Ababa was only a local rank and the Military Mission in Addis were not prepared to take him on their strength. He now reverted to his substantive rank of lieutenant.

He showed the letter to Scott, who read it, and passed it back, shrugging as he said, 'Typical bloody army. But take no notice. Your army rank doesn't count one way or another in SIS. And most of the time you won't be in uniform.' He had the consolation too that his pay from SIS was not subject to tax.

Scott was standing at the window looking at the traffic in Sloane Street. Without turning he said, 'You start your radio course tomorrow. When you've finished that you'll be going on a crash course at Oriel College. A language course.'

'Is this Italian?'

'No. It's French.'

'I don't understand. Why French?'

'Have you heard anything about an outfit called SOE? Special Operations Executive?'

'I've heard gossip about it. Something to do with the *maquis*.'

'That's part of what they do. The Free French look after that side. Our side, the London side, is more concerned with gathering intelligence about German troops in France and sabotage of communications. Rail, roads, electricity and telephones. That's where we want to use you.'

'Doing what?'

Scott smiled. 'All in good time, Jamie. Do the radio bit and the language bit first and then we'll talk about your rôle.'

The top floor of the Peter Robinson department store at Oxford Circus housed a number of secret operations. With its constant flow in and out of shoppers the store provided the people involved on the top floor with a perfect cover for their comings and goings. The course in using Morse code was intensive and the Royal Corps of Signals girls were very efficient. When it was possible the trainee was paired with the Signals girl who would take his Morse messages when the trainee was operative in an occupied or enemy country, so that she could recognise his manner of using the Morse key.

For once Jamie Frazer didn't shine at his work. He learnt the code quickly enough but his transmissions were erratic. On the last day of training his instructor had left the small cubicle where they worked for a few moments and had left his file on the desk beside the headphones. He had a quick look at her report on him. The last question said, 'Describe the transmission pattern when the trainee operates under pressure.' In her neat, rounded schoolgirl-writing she had written, 'This officer always transmits as if he's under pressure.' There was much discussion by the training staff on his performance but the officer in charge guessed that Frazer would have a radio operator who was competent and would only transmit himself in some dire situation.

Jamie Frazer had taken his Signals girl to Hammersmith Palais that last night to celebrate scraping through the course. She was obviously much impressed by his parachute badge. Lieutenant Frazer had made a considerable impression on the female training staff.

It was a Sunday when Frazer took the train to Oxford. It was a long journey. In wartime trains stopped at almost every station.

He wondered what it would be like at a university. It seemed a long way from old Manton's office at school and him saying that 'he was on the dust-heap of the school and would inevitably end up on the dust-heap of life'. Maybe he'd send him a postcard with the Oxford postmark on it. He still felt a twinge of anger whenever he thought about the incident. The indifference to what the effect might be on a boy's life. The arrogance of a man who could decide young people's fates. He'd show the bastards.

Despite the sunshine the station at Oxford looked grim and un-inviting but there was a taxi on the forecourt. As he walked through the ticket barrier, a girl walked up to him. 'Are you Lieutenant Frazer?' She smiled. 'I guess you must be. Tommy told me about you being a parachutist.'

'Who are you?' He said, smiling. 'And who is Tommy?'

She looked surprised. 'Tommy Scott, he saw you onto the train. I'm your contact here in Oxford. I've bagged the taxi for us. And my name's Sabine. Sabine Fleury. My parents are French.'

When he had paid off the taxi driver, she led him through an archway to the college. 'Don't look at this part, it's very dull. We go through here, the library and after that you can look around and enjoy it. This is the view you will have from your room. And this is St Mary's Quad. I love it. Tommy Scott used his influence to get you a room in college. You're really rather lucky.'

Frazer laughed. 'I'm sure that I'll enjoy it here. You can't be on the course. You must be bilingual with French parents. Are you at the college yourself?'

'Oh,' she said, shrugging her shoulders. 'I just do odd jobs for SIS.' She smiled at him. 'Sorting things out when they don't work very well. Stroking ruffled feathers or being a bit cross with inflated egos.'

'Does that mean you're actually in SIS?'

'Yes. I'm afraid so. But I'm really more SOE.' She smiled. 'That's where my heart is.'

When she said that they were standing by the window in his room and he looked at her face. She was very pretty but it was more than that.

'Why?'

'Why what?'

'Why is your heart with SOE?'

'Because I want France to be free again and I want to help make it happen.' She paused. 'My father's in SOE. The French bit. RF Section.' She smiled. 'The lot that your side of SOE dislike so much.'

'What does he do?'

She shook her head, still smiling. 'You mustn't ever ask people in SOE what they do.' She turned to look at the room. 'Well, Lieutenant Frazer, this is going to be your home for a few weeks. I hope you enjoy it.'

'I'm sure I will.'

She noticed that he didn't even glance around the room. Still went

116

on looking at her. She hoped he wasn't going to be a nuisance. But he was rather attractive. Maybe he'd be a rather nice nuisance.

'I've left your course programme in the packet on your bed. They work you really hard but you'll find yourself speaking current colloquial French and you'll have a good idea of what it's like in Occupied France.'

'Is your mother SOE?'

For a moment she hesitated and then she said, 'Yes', very quietly, and he knew that he shouldn't pursue it.

He put his kit on the bed and then as he turned to speak to her he saw the tears in her eyes.

'What's the matter?'

She shook her head and wiped her eyes with the back of her hand. 'Nothing.'

'I'm sorry if something I said upset you.'

She sighed, looked towards the window and then back at his face. 'It wasn't you. It was me. I told you a lie. My mother isn't in SOE, she's in a Nazi concentration camp. She's Jewish and political. She was an early target. My father was away when they picked her up and he came for me and brought me here to England.' She shrugged. 'It's a stupid lie but I pretend it's for real. She would be SOE if she had the chance.'

'Meantime you stand in for her.'

'Yes. I pretend I'm her.'

'How about we go and have a meal in town?'

She hesitated for a moment and then said, 'OK. Let's do that.'

He carefully avoided any personal questions as they ate at a local cafe and their talk was all of the course and its success.

It was strictly forbidden to speak anything but French. The French daily papers, two days old, were brought over from Lisbon, the films they were shown were all French and the small radio in his room was locked on to a French transmitter. Lectures were given on living conditions in both zones of France, the German intelligence services, the Abwehr, Sicherheitsdienst and the Gestapo. The new rules and documentation ordered by the German Kommandatura in Paris and some indication of French politics under the occupation.

In the third week of the course Scott had come up to Oxford to see him. After some chat about the course, Scott had got down to business.

'Before I go into what we want you to do let me explain about SIS and SOE. Right from its formation SOE was made part of SIS. It seemed a sensible thing to do. SIS's long experience of clandestine intelligence was there to be used. But in fact it hasn't worked out that well. The function of SIS agents in occupied France was, and still is, to gather intelligence. Information on German troop dispositions, the possibility of the Germans invading Britain, French internal politics, collaboration and so on. The function of SOE was laid down by Winston Churchill himself – "set Europe ablaze" was his edict. So SOE is involved in sabotage and disruption. Sabotage of German installations, communications, manufacture and to encourage the French population to resist the occupiers.

'As you might guess, those two functions are in total conflict. SIS want peace and quiet for their work and SOE and their activities make it much more difficult for the traditional SIS agent to operate. The Germans are constantly on the alert against any kind of resistance or opposition. Then, inside SOE we have another problem. RF Section. RF Section was forced on us by de Gaulle who threatened to wreck the whole idea unless the Free French could control SOE. In the end they were forced to compromise and have their own separate organisation run by the French and virtually out of our control.

'The reason they wanted this was nothing to do with winning the war but controlling French politics when the war was over. De Gaulle is an ambitious man and he wants to make sure that he's France's leader when peace comes. On the ground it's the communists who organise underground politics in France today and they want to control post-war France.' He smiled and shrugged. 'Sorry about the lecture but it's all part of the picture. It's not quite so cut and dried as I've described but the essence is there and you need to be aware of it.' He paused. 'Any questions?'

Frazer said quietly, 'It sounds as though you're planning to send me there for some particular reason.'

'How would you feel about that?'

Frazer shrugged. 'I'll do whatever your people want me to do.' He paused. 'Can I ask, why me?'

'Oh, a whole mixture of reasons. I won't go into them but we're satisfied that if anyone can do this particular job it's you.'

'And what's the job.'

'We want you to go over there and look at both operations and give us an unbiased report on their effectiveness. The essence being – is either of them doing any good and what would be the consequences of closing down RF Section completely.'

'Is that what SIS want – to close down RF Section?'

'Let's say that there are some – only some – senior people in SIS who have been against SOE right from the start. Some for practical and legitimate reasons and others from prejudice. If someone – you – can provide us with an unbiased picture of the situation on the ground it could help us make the right decision.'

'When do I go?'

'In about a month.' He paused. 'How do you get on with Sabine Fleury?'

'She's been a great help. I like her. She's very committed to SOE.' He smiled. 'And she's very pretty.'

'And she's a first-class radio operator too.' He paused. 'I was thinking of sending her with you as your radio operator. What do you think?' He added, 'She's done all the standard SOE training courses and done well. And of course she knows France and the French because of her parents.'

'Tell me about her mother.'

'When you've answered my question I will.'

'My instincts about having her with me are divided. On the one hand I'd find it a disadvantage to be responsible for someone I rather liked and admired. And on the other I have to accept that I would not be particularly welcome in the networks who knew that I was assessing their value, so it would be good to have someone I value to share my isolation.'

Scott smiled. 'A good assessment. And speaking of you being isolated reminds me of your time in Addis where that applied. Which leads me to have the pleasure to inform you that your reinstatement as captain in the I Corps is in this week's Part 2 Orders. Congratulations.'

Frazer smiled. 'I ought not to care but thanks. I'm pleased.'

'And now, Sabine Fleury?'

'I'm torn. I'll do whatever you think best.'

'I think she'll be ideal in most ways. She knows it's a possibility that she'll be sent to France. Maybe you'd like to be the one to tell her.'

'OK. I'll do that. But I shall make clear that if she doesn't want to then it won't affect her position in SIS. OK?'

'Of course. The same applies to you. If you chose not to do this it wouldn't be a mark against you on your record.'

'So tell me about her mother.'

Scott leaned back in his chair, folding his arms across his chest.

'Right. Rosa Fleury was born Rosa Beckmann, her father was a lecturer at the Sorbonne. Political history. Rosa was academically very bright. Studied law and became a lawyer. Extremely left-wing like her old man, but she went further. A convinced and convincing Communist. Member of the Party. Served on God knows how many committees. Vitriolic about the establishment and bankers and politicians and big business. The usual stuff. Except that Rosa Beckmann made a case for Communism. She was good-looking but not a beauty and she met a writer. A novelist. And she fell for him like a ton of bricks and he for her. They adored one another. They married. The war came. Then the surrender. Theo Fleury was in Lille when the Gestapo picked Rosa up in Paris about two weeks after they marched in. By the time he knew, she was already on her way to a camp. Ravensbruck. He smuggled Sabine out to England. He's in his fifties and he writes stuff for BBC French broadcasts and *France Libre*. We suspect that Rosa will be dead by now and he's a lost soul. Sabine is his only reason for staying alive. She's besotted about France and he – he's like I said – a lost soul.'

'I'll need to have a long talk with her before I decide. Are there any alternatives?'

'Yes. At least three, but technically not as good as she is.'

'What next for me?'

'Another week here so long as they pass you and then a complete briefing on the SOE networks in France. That will be in London. You'll also pay visits to SOE establishments here. Beaulieu and Wanborough and a few other smaller outfits.'

Frazer had spent two days talking to the girl. She knew the risks she would run and the responsibility she would have in being virtually their sole contact with London. He was both pleased and irritated that she had checked him out with girl-friends in the Signals training unit and learned that he had barely passed the tests. At least she had shown some initiative. Right from the start of their talks she had made clear her eagerness to go. And she pointed out quite correctly that if he didn't take her one of the networks would be delighted to have her. Good radio operators were in short supply. She had answered responsibly all the questions he had put to her and the more he learned the more he realised that Tom Scott had not picked her out without a great deal of thought. Their personalities and characters were different but they made a good combination. He finally made her the offer on the evening of the second day of talking with her and when she accepted he realised for the first time that she too must have been looking him over in the weeks he had been on the course.

They had a meal together later that evening and it had been her turn to quiz him. About the crash French course. She recognised that he was a natural linguist but had only a rather primitive understanding of grammar. His test was – does it sound right when you say it. But he showed that he analysed instinctively those oddities of the language that seemed strange to a foreigner.

'Tell me something that you find strange or inexplicable.'

He thought for several moments and then said, 'OK. *Venir* – to come. *Je viens, tu viens*, et cetera. But you use it in a strange way by putting *de* on to it.'

She frowned. 'I don't understand.'

'*Je viens de boire*. Looks like "I have come from drinking". But that isn't what it means. In French it means I have *just been* drinking. Crazy. How do you explain that?'

She smiled. 'I've no idea. It's just idiom.' She laughed. 'I shall always see you from now on as a man wiping his mouth with the back of his hand and saying "*Je viens de boire*".'

He smiled. 'Can you be ready to move to London on Saturday?'

'Yes. Of course.'

'I'll phone Scott and let him know. Where will you stay?'

'With my father. He's got rooms near Victoria Station.'

'Will it upset him that you're going on active service?'

'No. It was he who got me the introduction to Tommy Scott.' She paused. 'By the way, how did you learn Italian and Swahili?'

Chapter 22

Bowman sat at his desk turning back a few pages of the sheets that were stapled together. He read through the last four pages again and then pushed the papers aside and looked at Al Pinto.

'Will he sign this crap?'

'If we pay him he will.'

'This stuff about bugging Harold Wilson's phones. D'you believe it?'

'No reason why not. It's the kind of things they do. And he gives the dates.'

'And the stuff about Frazer staying in the building after everyone's left except the duty people? Is that kosher d'you think?'

'There'll be log-books and registers we can subpoena.'

'I wanna meet him. How soon can you fix it?'

'Where d'you want to meet him, here?'

'There's a pub in Kings Road called The Fisherman's Arms or The Angler, something like that. I'll see you both there any time he can make it. Sooner the better.'

'You going to go with it?'

'Not till I've talked to him.'

'Why isn't this enough?'

'I want to know the motive.'

Al Pinto shrugged. 'It's the dough. He needs it.'

'No way. There's more than that. I wanna know what it is. Like I said, if he's kosher we'll do a deal.'

Chapter 23

Frazer had spent nearly three weeks reading through the records of seven SOE networks in France. Two in Paris, the rest in Occupied France. He had talked with the SOE staff who controlled them and read their personal files. Tom Scott had introduced him as an historian reporting to the Prime Minister personally on whether there was enough material to warrant starting an official history of SOE before the papers were mislaid or destroyed. He had given Sabine Fleury the task of reading and commenting on the radio traffic from the seven networks.

The meeting with Tom Scott was at 54 Broadway and the three of them sat around a table in a small office on the fourth floor.

Tom Scott looked across at Frazer. 'Tell me what you think?'

'How long will I have over there?'

'Ideally three months but we could go to four if it really mattered.' He paused. 'Which network do you want as your base?'

'Brantôme.'

'Why there?'

'The most active of the seven you picked out with the possible exception of Paris Two. But I couldn't do the job from Paris. They'd get me in weeks.' He paused. 'Brantôme are well-organised. They don't try and cover up their blunders and they follow out Baker Street's instructions whenever possible.'

'What did you think of Nantes?'

Frazer shrugged. 'There's something wrong there. I'm not sure what it is.'

'What do you think it might be?'

'My guess is that it's something political. Somebody who maybe should be in RF rather than with us.'

'Have you got enough information to do the job?'

'Not really but I've got all that can come from just reading words on paper and a few people's opinion.'

'How did Baker Street treat you?'

Frazer laughed. 'Let's say I think they were a bit suspicious. Polite but formal and trying to find out what I'd been doing before this job. But they got used to me in the end and were quite friendly.'

'I don't want you to use the SOE codewords for the networks or your traffic could get confused with theirs. They won't be able to decrypt you at Baker Street because you'll be issued with one-time pads.' He paused and slid a sheet of notepaper across the table. 'How about that for your codewords?'

Frazer looked at the paper; smiled and passed it to the girl, who read it and shook her head.

The list was just a codeword for each network.

sita	Brantôme.	tisa	Chartres.
saba	Clermont.	kumi	Paris One.
nane	Nantes.	tatu	Paris Two.

She frowned and looked from Scott to Frazer and it was Frazer who enlightened her.

'A touch of humour from 54 Broadway. The codewords are the Swahili words for the numbers from six to eleven.'

She was obviously not impressed.

Scott said quietly, 'The Met people say that there will almost certainly be two suitable nights in two weeks' time. Does that suit you both?'

Sabine said sharply, 'It suits me. I'm ready to go.'

Frazer said, 'It's OK for me too but there's a point I want to raise regarding my cover. I don't want any suggestion that I'm in charge or that I'm sitting in judgment on them. We've agreed that my cover will be that I'm there to see what help they need. Agreed?'

Scott nodded. 'Of course.'

'So I want some assurances that when a network really has need of something London will do something about it.'

'Within reason, Jamie. I'll supervise it myself.'

Frazer nodded. 'The word will get around if my calls for help are ignored.'

'Just keep their requests reasonable.'

'No. That makes me involved in their operations. I'm just an on-looker and a messenger-boy.'

'Fair enough, Jamie. Fair enough.' He nodded his approval. 'Good thinking.'

Scott pushed back his chair and stood up. 'Let's see if we can get ourselves a sandwich across the road at the pub.'

The night before they were due to be dropped, Frazer took the girl to a jazz club in Soho where he sometimes played. She had already heard that he was a piano-player but she hadn't realised how talented he was. Always the small band left him plenty of space for solo breaks especially when they were going through all the classic rags like 'Tiger Rag' and 'Canadian Capers'. It was already 2 a.m. on the morning of their drop when he joined her at the table in the alcove.

'Don't you think we ought to be getting some sleep, Jamie? It's going to be a long day.'

He smiled. 'Are you bored?'

'No. But it's not my kind of music.'

'What's your kind of music?'

She laughed softly. ' "Parlez-moi d'amour" and "j'attendrai".'

'It's a deal. I'll play those for you and then we'll go.'

'Why are the men in the band all so old? Is it because of the war?'

He laughed. 'No. Most jazz musicians have been doing it for a long time and most of them aren't as old as they look. They live pretty crazy lives.'

'I hope you don't get like them?'

'I hope I end up playing as well as they do.' He stood up. 'Let me play your pieces for you.'

She saw him speak to the band who put their instruments aside as they looked across at her. He didn't jazz her pieces up and he'd finished up with 'J'ai deux amours' before he came back to collect her and find her a taxi home. They were to meet at 11 a.m. later that day for their final check-up and clearance.

* * *

Tom Scott sat in the front passenger seat with Frazer and Sabine Fleury on the back seat. It was getting dark as they passed through St Albans. Scott had been through this ritual of the journey to a drop many times. Sometimes the agent was silent for the whole journey as his mind was already on what would happen in a few hours' time. Sometimes the passenger couldn't stop talking. Scott had done the trip too many times to draw any conclusions about the state of mind of the agent who was going to be dropped. It was tough enough leaving behind people you loved. Not knowing when you would see them again. Not even knowing that you would see them again. And all the pre-drop planning and preparation couldn't disguise the fact that you didn't know who would be waiting for you – people from the network or the Gestapo. And after months of danger and harassment there was always the thought that it all might turn out to be a total waste of time. Once they got to the airfield at Tempsford they would be kept busy on final checks and some of the tension would go in the routine.

As the staff car pulled up at the guard-house they were all checked carefully and then directed to the main building. When they got through the elaborate black-out precautions, an RAF Squadron Leader was waiting for them. In the reception area Scott was pleased to notice that SOE had sent one of its own officers as a courtesy to mark the co-operation of SOE and SIS.

Frazer's clothes had been bought from a French refugee who had passed through Wandsworth interrogation centre and Sabine Fleury's clothes were French anyway. Their documents were given a final check and a Met officer said that the weather was fine for a drop.

An hour later they walked across the tarmac to the Dakota that was taking them. A final handshake from Tom Scott and they clambered up the metal steps into the aircraft. An RAF sergeant fastened them into their seats for take-off and checked their parachute harnesses.

Half an hour after take-off, the sergeant had brought them each a mug of hot tea and confirmed that the weather conditions were ideal.

The Tempsford Dakotas, Whitleys and Stirlings had been converted to make parachute jumps easier and it meant avoiding the open door in the fuselage and the inevitable rush of wind and turbulence.

The girl was sitting with her eyes closed and he reached out and took her hand. It was icy cold.

The sergeant came back again. It was time for them to prepare for the jump and they watched him pull back the lever that would release the cover of the hole through which they would jump. The navigator came back and said they could see the lights and the reception party had given the correct password with the torch.

Frazer said to the girl, 'I'll go first. See you down on the ground.'

As the cover came back there was the rush of cold air and the red light came on. He scrambled into the sitting position and jumped on the green light.

The ground came up with a rush and the surface wind dragged his canopy so that he lost his footing. He heard footsteps running and hands pulling off his harness and collapsing the 'chute and there was moonlight enough for him to see the other 'chute at the far side of the field.

A voice said, '*Bienvenue*' and he felt himself being hurried to the shelter of a hedge. The girl was already being pushed into the back of a farm cart as he arrived and as he clambered up inside he saw her smiling through the tears on her face. And as he heard the clatter of the farm-horse's hooves on the metalled road it reminded him of the noise when he was a small boy and the milkman drove up in his cart to deliver Grandma's milk. He closed his eyes and wished he was back in that small bedroom at Mere Road.

Chapter 24

Bowman knew as he talked to Owen Davies that what he was giving them wouldn't stop them from losing the libel case. But played carefully it might get them some mileage out of persuading SIS to think it worthwhile putting some pressure on Frazer to do a deal. He wasn't sure how to go about it and decided to think about it for a couple of days which was not a typical Bowman reaction. As he closed the slim file and pushed it into his desk-drawer his internal phone rang.

'Bowman.'

'It's Jackie. I've got the financial report on the Frazer guy you wanted. Shall I bring it over?'

'Yeah.' He hung up and walked over to the window. All those little model cars down in the street, rain on the windows and the distant dome of St Paul's barely visible in the summer mist. He'd been a taxi-driver himself for three months in Sydney when he lost his job at the newspaper. With considerable exaggeration he always described it as the happiest time in his life. No responsibilities, lots of fresh air and good mates to have a laugh with.

With a knock on the door and his brusque 'Come in,' he turned to look at the girl. She was very young for the job and she was very pretty. And best of all she was always cheerful. Always a smile. He liked people who smiled.

As she handed him the two typed sheets he pointed to the nearest chair and put the report on his desk in front of him. He read it slowly and then read it again before he looked across at the girl.

'Are you sure about this?'

'Yeah. It's all on the record, one place or another. The amounts might vary a bit by a couple of thousands but the shares and bonds are up to date.'

'And this figure for total convertible assets, that's accurate too?'

'Yeah.' She smiled. 'I got that off his tax returns.'

'How did you get those?'

She grinned. 'Don't ask me.'

'So at any time he could lay his hands on about ten million quid without any problems?'

'More like twelve than ten.'

'Jesus. No wonder the bastard comes on with this shit or bust attitude.' He sighed. 'Can I keep this stuff?'

'Yeah. It's the only copy remember. I don't want it to go in the filing system.'

'Neither do I.' He shrugged. 'Food for thought. Food for a lot of bloody thought.'

When the girl had left, Bowman had another look at the figures and details of the report. There was no way they were going to be able to frighten the bastard because of him running out of money.

All day he kept thinking about the figures. How the hell did a civil servant accumulate that kind of money? But from the information it looked as though the money had been around for a long time. There was nothing adventurous or risky about the investments. Stocks, bonds, shares and a lot of property. Just what an accountant would advise.

As usual he spent the early hours of the evening at the Groucho and it was in the taxi on the way back to the office to see the first edition through that he realised that the information from Owen Davies about Frazer was the only card he had left to play. He'd got to make Frazer accept an out-of-court settlement. The lawyers wouldn't play ball so it meant looking at the only other player in the game. SIS itself. But they were more spectators than players. And they weren't his kind of people. He'd have to do it himself. Direct. Face to face. But who? And was it legal? They weren't involved in the case. They weren't witnesses. He sighed as he paid the cabbie and walked into the newspaper's reception area. They wouldn't have much liked the things that Al Pinto had said about their organisation. But the bastards must be used to it by now. He'd sleep on it and maybe do something about it tomorrow.

* * *

He was playing the piano and she was reading the newspapers. He had two or three delivered daily since the case started. She looked up when she realised that he was playing 'Manhattan' and walked over to lean on the piano watching his face as he played. When he had finished he closed the lid gently and smiled up at her.

'Why so serious?'

She shrugged. 'I was angry at that piece about you in the tabloid that quotes from that wretched book.'

He laughed. 'The bit about the man who pretends to be working-class but rides around in a white Rolls Royce?'

'Yes.'

He shrugged. 'Just ignorance. Being working-class has nothing to do with money.'

'So what makes somebody working-class?'

He smiled. 'Making sure nobody leaves the lights on in a room when there's nobody in it.'

'But surely money matters?'

He was silent, thinking, for several moments. 'Money only matters in a negative way. When you don't have quite enough to get by. When you have money beyond what you need for a roof over your head and daily living, money only has one value.' He paused. 'And that's the independence to be able to tell 'em to get stuffed when you want to.'

'Wouldn't that make someone aggressive or at least arrogant?'

'No. Because for some crazy reason, when you know you can tell 'em to go to hell you don't do it. You don't need to. You know they can't touch you.' He smiled at her. 'Let's go to the Ship and have lunch.'

'Are you rich enough to tell them to go to hell?'

He laughed and stood up. 'Just rich enough to buy us a meal at the Ship.' He paused. 'And by the way, my Rolls cost me less than a Ford Escort would cost today.' He smiled. 'But you couldn't love an Escort.'

Inevitably, after they had eaten, he had taken her down to the boat. She had slept on the double bed in the big aft cabin and he had carried out his usual checks of the equipment. She heard him humming to himself contentedly as he checked the gauges and indicators and was faintly resentful that he seemed to find more peace from the boat than he did from her. He had never said that he loved her, not even when they were making love. But she knew that whatever affection he had for a human being he had for her. He liked her around all the time and she knew that she loved him. She could have given a dozen rational reasons for loving him but she knew that none of them was the real reason. She didn't know what the real reason was. But for her he was a rock, caring and affectionate and never devious. Reliable.

Chapter 25

He was lying on a bed against the stone wall, his head raised up by several pillows, and he could see the shadows of leaves on the curtains at the small high window. He tried not to breathe deeply because of the pain in his chest. He tried desperately to stay awake but he couldn't, and he slid into a kind of dream world where he was half awake and half a long way away. He could hear traffic on the street but he knew there was no such traffic at any time in that part of Brantôme. There was a slow trickle of tears down his cheeks and he felt someone wiping his face very gently. It was the noise of the traffic in Paris outside the Fresnes prison.

'I shouldn't have trusted them,' he said through swollen lips and she said softly, '*Dors ma mignon, dors.*' He sighed as he slipped away into that limbo again.

'How long have I been out?'

'Nine days not counting the journey down from Paris.'

'What happened?'

'What do you remember?'

'I was supposed to meet Réne by the Orangerie. He was late and I remember cursing him because I was so exposed . . .' he shrugged '. . . that's about it. So tell me what I missed.'

'Drink your soup up first.'

'What is it?'

'Chicken soup. Cures everything from broken ribs to broken hearts.'

He spooned it up slowly, his hand shaking as he lifted the spoon to his mouth. She watched him carefully and wondered how much she should tell him. He was so English that he'd barely understand the intrigue that had gone on for him to end up as a Gestapo prisoner in Fresnes. The English never cared enough about politics to betray anyone, especially a friend and ally. The vicious rivalries between RF Paris and the Communists with their *maquis* were bitter and real. Without rationale and without mercy. Both sides could claim '*vive la France*' as their war-cry.

She had guessed that Paris would be a problem but not even her instincts had prepared her for how deep the rifts and rivalries were. She had tried to persuade him to pull out but even she hadn't realised how far good Frenchmen would go to put down their markers for how France would be if they ever were liberated. Jamie Frazer had not taken sides. He had listened but hadn't always understood the underlying tensions. Both sides actually liked him for his fairness and attempts at peace-making. But they still saw him as an attempt by F Section to control the Free French RF organisation. The English in London may be Francophiles or even French nationals but they had different scenarios for how the war would end. De Gaulle may have promoted himself to General but to London he was still a colonel from a tank regiment. Bloody-minded, uncooperative and what was worse, ungrateful for all the help he had been given. And a self-importance that was bordering on mania. He quarrelled with Churchill, and Roosevelt despised him and had his own candidate for taking over after it all ended.

She knew they would cause trouble of some kind for Frazer but she could never have imagined that they'd betray an ally for the sake of teaching London a lesson.

When she had heard that Frazer had been picked up by the Gestapo she still couldn't bring herself to accept that they had thrown him away just to make a political point. She had contacted Brantôme that night and ignoring security had told them over the phone what had happened. She had insisted on speaking only to the network commander, Henri Ravel. He had cursed the RF and sworn that they would take immediate action to release Frazer. They too had games they could play in Paris. He warned her not to let Paris know that she had contacted him.

She never found out what pressure had been applied by Brantôme and London. She knew that it was a combination of money and threats of exposure that ended with her, Henri Ravel and two others picking up an unconscious Frazer from the prison and driving him back to Brantôme lying on bales of straw in an empty horse-box. When the *maquis* had been told of what had happened they willingly provided protection and clearances for the whole journey.

It had taken four weeks of care and doctoring before the broken bones and cracked ribs had healed sufficiently for Sabine and Henri to arrange with London for a Westland Lysander pick-up for Jamie Frazer.

When she had given him her version about what had happened in Paris, she implied that it was errors and misunderstanding that had caused him to be picked up by the Gestapo. But she realised as she went through her story that Jamie Frazer knew all too well the real facts. He seemed to bear no grudge or apportion any blame but she knew that he was much shrewder and aware than she had imagined. When she told him that she was not going back to London but was staying on as radio operator for Henri in Brantôme, he raised no objections so long as she cleared it with Scott in London.

When they lit the flares in the meadow near Puy de dôme, she sat with him in the darkness of the hedge and remembered him comforting her on the journey out when they were dropped. It seemed a long, long time ago.

As the Lysander came over the treetops they had two minutes from touch-down to take-off and they only just made it as Jamie Frazer clambered awkwardly up the short ladder on the fuselage.

She waved to him as the plane gathered speed into the wind for take-off. But he didn't wave back. For months she wondered if maybe he didn't see her waving. But beneath the wishful-thinking she knew instinctively that to him she was part of the French. And not to be trusted.

Chapter 26

To: Major Scott I.C.   *Date:* October 1943

From: Capt. Frazer I.C.

Field report on certain SOE networks in German Occupied France.

This report is a summary of the information given during a number of debriefing interviews which took place at 54 Broadway and at the Royal Free Hospital, Hampstead.

1.   **Brantôme (SITA)**
This network was my main base for this operation. HR was in charge and had spent time in training his team and at the same time carefully recruited locals at two levels, (a) actual participators and (b) people in responsible positions who could provide invaluable information on local conditions.

HR heeded advice from Baker Street to avoid premature action against the Germans which would gain nothing and lead to German retaliation. This will be a significant unit when Allied operations in Europe take place.

HR. Much respected by his own people and by the locals. He is not political in any way.

2.   **Clermont-Ferrand (SABA)**
JF who commands this network is essentially a soldier rather than an intelligence officer. Most of his efforts were concentrated on liaising

with the local 'maquis'. His requests to Baker Street were always for weapons and explosives. He was well aware that the local maquis leaders were Communists but was not concerned with their policies or politics. If he is called on in the future to give support to Allied troop movements he will be ruthless and efficient. Not enamoured of the French or France.

3.   Nantes (NANE)
TF-G in charge of network. Too much involved in local politics. Would not collaborate with Communists. More French than British and a constant critic of SOE London. Bitterly resents not being accepted by Free French and RF Section. He is both admired and disliked by many influential locals who see him as trying to be an alternative authority. Is in touch with the Gaullists locally and through them with RF Section in London. Despite all this, his reports to London are accurate and wide-ranging. He provides a mass of information on German troop movements and communications. His team are efficient news-gatherers but morale is poor.

4.   Chartres (TISA)
FMcC in charge. The most all-round efficient network I visited. Well trained. Good morale. Good local support. Emphasis on planning, for future operations rather than petty harassment of local Germans. Adheres to most instructions from Baker Street. Needs another radio operator urgently and would benefit by a short break in UK.

Note. There are three pages of this report missing and only the single page of the following summary is available.

Summary
Bearing in mind the difference in character of the personnel concerned and the wide range of activities available, it is fair to say that all the networks visited are carrying out successfully at least some of the functions required of them.

From my experience with the RF Section in Paris, I think we are missing opportunities of getting alongside the Free French Sections. It is undoubtedly a fact that at the moment the Communists are the most active group in the maquis and are intent on taking control of France if and when it is liberated. However I feel we have under-estimated the appeal of de Gaulle amongst the population. He is seen as a leader already despite his dependence on London's goodwill. If we allowed him to return to France still angry or resentful of his dependence on us, I feel we should be making a grave error. After he and his entourage are back in France, the opportunity for co-operation will have been lost. He is undoubtedly, for the average Frenchman, their Winston Churchill. And my experience on this operation convinces me that we have to accept that despite the work that has been done by SOE and will undoubtedly be done in future, SOE makes the intelligence-gathering function of SIS in France both more difficult and more dangerous.

Signed: James Frazer, Capt. I.C

London

Chapter 27

During the four months before the case came to court the press had stepped very carefully around any comments on what was in the book and gradually the case had fallen into the background for the media. But on the opening morning of the case there were three TV crews and over a hundred photographers and reporters outside the court. Questions were shouted at counsel and their clerks but none of them responded. A clerk from his solicitor's office had acted as 'minder' for Al Pinto who was longing to get at a microphone. Bowman had felt it was his duty to give some sort of response to his fellow-journalists' questions even if his response had to be a series of 'no comments'. Jamie Frazer had smiled and waved as he struggled past thrust-out microphones. Healey's clerk had reported that the reporters were all on Frazer's side. Elderly ladies grabbed for 'vox-pops' said they thought it was disgusting that such a lovely man should be insulted by a tabloid rag. A representative from Age Concern had been disgusted by the harassment of an elderly gentleman at the hands of a rich newspaper group, a third-rate publisher and a sleazy American journalist.

It was nearly two hours later before counsel and their entourages were assembled in the court. All stood as Lord Justice Hooper swept in and bowed, before seating himself and nodding towards the jury.

When the Clerk to the Court had read out the brief description of the complaint it was Howard Rowe who adjusted his wig as he stood up to address the court.

'My Lord, in this case I appear for the plaintiff, Sir James Frazer, and the defendants are represented by my learned friend, Sir Graham Pollock. The defendants being the publisher of the book in question,

Primrose Publications, the author, an American citizen Albert Jefferson Pinto, who describes himself as a freelance journalist, and finally, Sidney Francis Bowman, the editor and member of the board of the *Daily Bulletin*, a tabloid newspaper which is owned by a media group which has major or controlling interests in other newspapers, Satellite TV, a dozen or so magazines and two commercial TV channels.'

Howard Rowe paused for a moment like a parson waiting to see if anyone was going to protest at the marriage, and then, tucking his hands behind his back as the Duke of Edinburgh does, he went on, 'In most libel cases, my Lord, there are sentences or pages which are the source of the plaintiff's complaint. However, in this case the whole book is objected to. The book purports to be, and is advertised as, an exposé of the alleged unlawful and unauthorised misdeeds of SIS, the Secret Intelligence Service, or, as some people call it, MI6. These events are centred around the character and career of the plaintiff, Sir James Frazer, who was at one time Director-General of the SIS but has been retired for a number of years.' He paused. 'My Lord, the whole tenor of the book is a malicious attack on Sir James and the organisation. No proof offered for any of the allegations. Just Albert Pinto's statements. A man about whom we know very little, and that little, may I say, does not show him to be one of the United States great commentators.

'Because our complaints cover the whole of the book and its serialisation in the newspaper, the court is faced with a problem. My client does not have to disprove any – I repeat any – of the allegations made. The defence has to prove that the allegations are true. It is on their shoulders to produce factual evidence to convince the jury that the book is not just a farrago of unfounded spite. And I want to remind the author and the publisher and the newspaper that their testimony will be questioned by me in vigorous terms.' He shifted the papers on the desk in front of him. 'However, I find no mention of independent witnesses in the defendant's notes.'

Sir Graham Pollock stood up as Howard Rowe sat down.

'My Lord, my learned friend has, as is his wont, touched on the crux of the matter. Which leads me to a point that I had hoped to raise a little later. I had hoped that the plaintiffs might agree to Sir James being questioned by me on a few of the more salient points . . .'

Howard Rowe stood up with a clatter of box files. 'My Lord, what my learned friend is suggesting is that we, the plaintiffs, should be party to a fishing expedition by the defence in the hope that they might come up with something they haven't yet mentioned.' Rowe fiddled with the ribbons at the back of the collar of his gown. 'I do ask my Lord for the defence to be told that we are not required to make concessions just because they cannot prove that any of their accusations in this book have a shred of truth in them.' Having picked up Pinto's book Rowe tossed it onto the desk in disdain.

Lord Justice Hooper looked across at Sir Graham.

'Sir Graham, do you want to comment?'

Sir Graham rose slowly and reluctantly. 'Yes, my Lord. I do. My mind goes to the members of the jury who it seems the plaintiffs would like to prevent from learning the truth of these matters because the only person involved – Sir James – is not prepared to give them his version of the facts.'

'Sir Graham. You have an alternative course of action available to you, have you not?'

'You mean subpoenaing Sir James as an unfriendly witness?'

'That's available to you if you so wished.'

'Thank you, my Lord. But I wonder if that might not confuse the jury even more. One witness merely contradicting the other. Unfortunately science has not yet discovered a litmus paper that identifies the truth.'

'Sir Graham. Methinks you do protest too much. Juries are frequently capable of deciding who they think is telling the truth.' He had just the ghost of a smile on his lips as he went on. 'They can often tell a liar more easily than we lawyers can.' Lord Justice Hooper nodded to Howard Rowe. 'Could I suggest that we adjourn for the lunch break now and return at 2 p.m. Meantime I suggest that both counsel assemble in my chambers to see if we can come upon some more constructive solution.'

Hooper pointed at the two vacant chairs and looked at the plates on his desk.

'Beef, smoked salmon and tongue. Help yourselves.'

As they helped themselves, Hooper took a good bite out of a beef sandwich.

'OK. What is it you two bastards want?'

Howard Rowe looked at Sir Graham who nodded. Rowe looked across at his Lordship and said, 'We reckoned that if we played it by the book the case could drag on for at least two months. We worked out a compromise.'

'Go on,' his Lordship said, but he was rearranging the beef in his second sandwich as he spoke.

'The basis was that Sir James would go in the box for questions chosen from the highlighted passages that Howard has marked in the books for the jury.'

'And your witnesses?'

'Unlimited questions.'

'And what about the bloody jury? Aren't they entitled to know whatever there is to know?'

He smiled at their obvious embarrassment at his jibe at their ethics. Then he said, 'You know the jury will find for Sir James, don't you?'

Sir Graham said, 'It has seemed to be heading that way.'

'It's just a question of *quantum* and I shall make that clear in my summing up.' He paused. 'How long will you need?'

'A week, maybe ten days.'

'Tell me,' his Lordship said, 'Didn't any one of these idiots have the book checked by a libel lawyer?'

'No. The contracts were made to shift libel liability from one to the other. From the tabloid to the book publisher who relied on a contract clause that put total responsibility for libel and defamation on the author.'

'Incredible.' His Lordship was fiddling with a pen on his desk. 'Have you worked out an apology that satisfies the plaintiff?'

'Yes.'

'What's it like?'

'Grovelling.'

His Lordship leaned back in his chair and looked at Howard Rowe. 'Did you get any idea if there was any substance in what this idiot wrote?'

'I didn't ask. I don't want to know. Most of it's been kicked around in other books and news stories over the years. But they never centred their so-called revelations on one individual. MI5 and MI6 never take any overt action against them.'

'That sounds ominous.'

Rowe shrugged. 'I gather that it's all quite gentlemanly. The Inland Revenue just happen to drop on you for a real good look at your last ten years' declarations. And of course, wherever you park your car it gets a wheel-clamp.'

His Lordship smiled. 'Bastards.' He stood up. 'You'd better get back in court.'

His Lordship turned in his chair to look at the jury.

'Ladies and Gentlemen of the jury. I have had a meeting with the counsel of both sides in an attempt to reduce the length of their case from what could be several months to a week or so. Counsel for the plaintiff has agreed that his client will answer a limited number of questions from the defence side provided that he has written details in advance. I emphasise that this is a gesture of co-operation from the plaintiff that he need not have accepted. When a man's character is at stake he is entitled to force the other side to subpoena him as a hostile witness if they want to question him and that would have extended this trial very substantially. Any justifiable action that can save jury time and public money is to be welcomed.' He looked at his watch. 'The court will adjourn now and reassemble tomorrow at 10 a.m. Thank you.'

His Lordship looked at his watch as he swept out of court. With a bit of luck and a taxi he might get an hour at Lord's watching the Australians.

Chapter 28

When the rituals of swearing-in and establishing identity were over,
Howard Rowe stood up and took over.

'Mr Pinto. How would you describe the way you earn a living?'

Pinto shrugged. 'I don't understand.'

'What is your job?'

'I'm a freelance journalist.'

'And what do you write about?'

'Politics and current affairs.'

Rowe held up a copy of the book. 'Did you write this book, entitled
"*Who Goes There*"?'

'Yes.'

'It's a book in which you allege a number of defects in the British
intelligence service known as MI6?'

'Yes.'

'Did you have to do research to write the book?'

'Yeah. Of course.'

'Could you describe your research for this book? How you went
about it?'

'I read up previous books on the subject. Newspaper records and
magazine articles.' He shrugged. 'That sort of thing.'

'Did you check whether this material was authentic or not?'

'No. It's in print already. Public domain.'

'So what you really did was assemble a lot of other people's published material? None of it was your own original work?'

'Some of it was.'

'Like the interviews you describe with Sir James Frazer?'

'Yeah.'

'Mr Pinto, you describe these interviews or meetings you had with Sir James. One starts on page thirteen and continues for six pages, another is ten pages starting on page one hundred and four. And the third is the whole of chapter thirteen.' Rowe looked at Pinto. 'Would you tell the jury where those meetings took place?'

'Which one?'

'Any one of them, Mr Pinto. Any one of them.'

'I don't remember where they took place.'

'You are telling the jury that you can't remember where any one or all of those meetings took place when you alleged that you established that Sir James was a card-carrying member of the Communist Party, was indulging in, or ordering others to take part in, illegal activities, was a womaniser and an adulterer. But you don't remember where the meetings took place?'

'No. I don't remember.'

'Were those meetings in this country or elsewhere?'

'Here.'

'In London?'

'Yeah.'

'In a hotel?'

'I don't remember.'

Rowe stood silent and turned slowly to look at the jury as if he were checking that they were still there.

'Mr Pinto,' he said slowly and clearly, 'would I be right in suggesting that you have not only never interviewed Sir James but you have never even met him? Anywhere or at any time.'

'I told you. I don't remember.'

A few moments silence so that the jury could absorb the situation and then, smiling amiably, Rowe said, 'Tell the jury, Mr Pinto, why did you write this book?'

Pinto shrugged. 'It's my job. Exposing what politicians and governments get up to that the public never hear about.'

'So if I suggested that you just cobbled together a pile of old press-cuttings to earn a quick buck, I'd be wrong, would I?'

'Yeah. You would.'

'So how much have you earned from the book so far?'

'Just the advance.'

'And how much was the advance?'

'About a hundred grand.'

'Dollars or pounds?'

'Pounds.'

'A hundred thousand pounds. I see.' He paused and then went on, 'You realised of course that you'd get more for the book if you could make it appear that with your alleged interviews and phone-calls to Sir James it made the book more saleable. Am I right?'

'I guess so.'

'I suggest to you, Mr Pinto, that you have never met or interviewed Sir James Frazer, nor spoken to him on the telephone, nor in fact ever seen him in the flesh until in this court.'

Pinto stood without responding.

Lord Justice Hooper said sharply, 'Please answer counsel's question, Mr Pinto.'

Pinto shrugged. 'I don't understand the question.'

'I am suggesting to you, Mr Pinto, that you have never met Sir James Frazer, never interviewed him and never spoken to him either on the telephone or by any other means. Am I correct, Mr Pinto? Yes or no?'

Pinto shrugged. 'It's up to you if that's what you want to say.'

'Mr Pinto, I am suggesting that the material in your book where you describe and quote from so-called interviews and telephone conversations are all, I repeat all, a figment of your imagination.'

'I can't stop you saying it, mister.'

'Mr Pinto, I'd like to turn to the subject of libel. I am sure your legal advisers have explained to you the definition of libel and defamation. Am I right?'

'I guess so.'

'And you are aware that from time to time authors and publishers and even booksellers are sued on the grounds of libel and defamation?'

'Yes.'

'And you know that quite frequently newspapers are also sued for libel?'

'Yes.'

'So you know that these people who could be sued for such offences usually take legal advice before they publish potentially damaging material.'

'Yeah.'

Rowe paused and then said, 'Have you, Mr Pinto, ever had one of your books turned down by a publisher on the grounds that it was libellous?'

'Not that I know of.'

'Let me refresh your memory, Mr Pinto. In March nineteen eighty nine you offered the manuscript of a book entitled "*Hands in the Till*" to several New York publishers including Gordon Luckhurst Press who turned it down on the grounds that it was, I quote "full of libel" unquote. You went on offering it to other publishers who all refused it on the same grounds. You remember this, Mr Pinto?'

'Vaguely.'

'Yes or no, Mr Pinto.'

'Would you repeat the question.'

'Yes or no, Mr Pinto.'

Pinto shrugged. 'If you say so.'

'When you drew up the contract with your co-defendants, Primrose Publications, it included a clause which gave you sole responsibility for any libel accusations that might arise. Including any legal costs and responsibilities. You remember that?'

'I do.'

'So did you take the precaution of having your manuscript read by a libel lawyer?'

'No way. Whatever you write a lawyer can turn it into a libel if you pay him enough. It's a waste of time.'

'So you decided that Primrose Publications and the newspaper could sink or swim with you if you were all sued for libel and lost?'

'We ain't lost yet, mister, or we wouldn't all be sitting here in court. Innocent until found guilty and all that.'

'Do you regret not having taken legal advice?'

'No way.'

'Do you regret anything of what you wrote in this book?'

'No. Not a thing.'

Lord Justice Hooper intervened. 'Gentlemen, I think this would be a good time to adjourn. We'll reassemble at 1.45 p.m.'

* * *

Bowman and Pinto had gone to the Groucho and Rowe, Healey and Frazer had gone for a sandwich at the Wig and Pen across the Strand.

As Rowe sipped a Guinness, Frazer said, 'Looks to me as if the judge is on the other side.'

Rowe put his glass down on the bar and stared at Frazer.

'What on earth makes you think that?'

'When you try to make Pinto give a yes or no answer and he dodges your question, Hooper lets him get away with it. Dozens of times you tried to pin him down but he got away without answering.'

Rowe looked at Healey and then at his Guinness as he said to his colleague, 'Tell him, Francis.'

Healey said quietly, 'He's deliberately letting the other side get away with it so that they can't come back when they lose, with an appeal based on the judge having put undue and unfair pressure on their main witness.' Healey shrugged. 'It's part of the game, Jamie. The judge will be pointing out all the weaving and dodging when he comes to sum up at the end.'

'How can you be so sure?' Frazer looked at Healey.

Healey smiled and leaned forward and said quietly, 'When Howard and I used to play for the Wasps it was our duty to drag our friend Joe into a taxi and escort him home to his sweet young wife. If we won of course, we'd never get him that far and we'd put him to bed at the pub. Now that he's Lord Joseph he hasn't forgotten it. *Noblesse oblige* and all that.' He stood up. 'We'd better go across. I've got a longish session this afternoon. And I expect that Graham Pollock will ask for leave to counter some of the points that I raised this morning.'

As they crossed the Strand Frazer asked Healey, 'Does Pollock know about you two and the judge?'

Healey laughed. 'I imagine so. Pollock played for the Barbarians and they had to drag home half their team on Saturday nights.' He smiled. 'Fortunately most of the top rugby teams had at least one copper and a couple of doctors playing for them.'

Jamie Frazer was not amused. Being working-class wasn't only about leaving lights on in empty rooms.

'How long would you need, Sir Graham?'

153

'Twenty minutes or so, your Lordship.'

'And you have no objection, Mr Rowe?'

'No, milord.'

'Go ahead then, Sir Graham.'

Sir Graham adjusted the neckline of his gown, picked up a bundle of papers and then put them down to look at Al Pinto still in the box.

'Mr Pinto. You realise that you're still under oath don't you?'

'Yes.'

'Mr Pinto,' Sir Graham said quietly, 'where were you born?'

'In the Bronx, New York City.'

'At what age did your education finish?'

'About twelve years old. I didn't go no more.'

'What did you do for a job?'

'I sold newspapers. I had a place by the County Court House.'

Howard Rowe stood up but Pollock remained standing looking in appeal at His Lordship.

Rowe said, 'I'll be happy to concede that Mr Pinto was born in a tough area of New York City and worked hard to earn a living. But none of that is relevant to what we are discussing here today. If a tough childhood absolved one from breaking the law of the land then we should all be claiming that we had gone barefoot to school.'

Rowe sat down and His Lordship nodded to Sir Graham. 'Do go on, Sir Graham. Perhaps we could skip a year or two.'

'When were you first employed on any kind of work that could reasonably be described as writing or journalism?'

'I did reports on local junior baseball matches. Amateurs. Then I worked on a local paper doing funerals and weddings. After that, I got assignments covering local committees and politics.' He shrugged. 'I did that when I was twenty-five and I've done that sort of stuff ever since. And one or two books. This one was the first that got published.'

'Would it be fair to say that you were rather an innocent abroad when it came to the legal side of writing and publishing books?'

'I guess so.'

Sir Graham sat down and Rowe stood up.

'But you had already had very practical experience of slander when your previous attempt at exposing the misdeeds of Washington was refused publication by at least four reputable publishers on the grounds that it was full of libels. Yes?'

'They were scared of the FBI and the White House.'

Rowe smiled dismissively, said, 'Thank you, Mr Pinto,' and sat down.

like their mothers and grandmothers? It was going to take some time for both sides to sort themselves out. And, as always, the edicts of non-combatants in Westminster and Whitehall were ignored because of their crass ignorance of what conditions were like on the ground.

Jamie Frazer was back in uniform again, still a captain in the Intelligence Corps. He was sent down to command a Field Security Unit at the extreme south of the British Zone, that called for particularly acute judgment. Germany had been divided into four occupation zones. The Russian, United States, French and British Zones. The FS unit lay on the border of all three of the other zones and as post-war tensions began to rise it would be easy to create situations that could develop into threatening incidents. Germans fleeing from the Russian Zone into the British Zone came over the border in large numbers. This not only created vast problems for the local administration responsible for accommodation and feeding the refugees. But it gave the Russians a perfect cover for infiltrating people employed by the KGB to spy on the British military. Checking identities of hundreds of people whose documents had been lost or destroyed in the last weeks of the war was beginning to take up the whole resources of Frazer's FS unit. Diverting them from their real task of hunting down war criminals and members of the Nazi intelligence organisations like the Gestapo and the Sicherheitsdeinst. 21 Army Group sent him a second FS unit and he used that for the border checking so that his main unit could carry on with their more important tasks. For three months Frazer ran the two FS units and he realised that although from a point of view of pro-secutions for war crimes his original FS unit was important, in real intelligence terms the unit checking refugees from the Russian Zone was far more important. They came with up-to-date knowledge of what the Soviet military were actually doing behind their bit of the Iron Curtain. Giving them their due 21 Army Group and Intelligence HQ in Bad Salzuflen noticed it too. Frazer's analysis of interrogations was providing more information than all other sources put together. There were only two problems. The first was that the information they got was random and uncontrolled. The second problem was that the infor-mation came from untrained civilians who couldn't tell the difference between an infantry unit and an artillery or tank regiment. It was Bad Salzuflen's thinking on the subject that prompted Major Renshaw's visit to Frazer in Hildesheim. He arrived unannounced in a confiscated Mercedes. An apparently easy-going man whose appearance was deceptive, John Renshaw was a shrewd, observant and experienced assessor of men who could learn more about a man's character and potential in half an hour's discussion of rugby or modern art, whichever was appropriate, than all the newfangled tests of Rorschach blots and hypnotherapy could reveal. On arrival he had announced that he just wanted a day or two away from desks and meetings. He brought with him the military equivalent of a civilian guest's bunch of flowers – the copy of Part 2 Orders that announced that Captain Frazer was now Major Frazer. There is a subtle difference in standing when an officer moves up into Field rank and Renshaw was aware that Jamie Frazer's old working-class background would recognise the promotion as a kind of marker in his career and in his life in general. He probably wouldn't admit it, even to himself, but he had been around long enough to know that he had been noticed and revalued.

Frazer and his units were located in two large mansions that had survived the US bombers who had destroyed the old town in just over twenty minutes. Frazer's quarters were his office as well as his living space and both buildings were still furnished with the fine furniture and belongings of their previous wealthy owners. Both of them had been employers of slave labour but the wife of one of them had been a professional musician and it was her Bechstein grand that took up one corner of Frazer's sitting-room. At a small party that first evening he had played all the current ballads from 'Lovely Weekend' to his own version of 'Rhapsody in Blue' to his visitor and several acquaintances from Military Government and local units.

The others had long gone when Renshaw edged into the prime purpose of his visit.

'Do you ever analyse the stuff you send us from the Russian Zone?'

'No. I don't have the time.'

'We've got a six-man team trying to evaluate all we get. From you and from others.' He shrugged. 'But we're not very good at it. And we're a bit worried about what it seems to add up to. Doesn't look too good.'

'In what way?'

'They've got masses of troops right across the zone border from you. To Magdeburg and beyond. Infantry divisions. At least twenty. Artillery regiments, pioneers, signals and engineers.' He paused. 'And if you add to all that the present political situation between the Americans and the Soviets, people are wondering if the Soviets aren't thinking of trying their luck.'

'Surely they've had a bellyful of war by now.'

'The brass asked us to do an exercise on where and how the Russians might attack the West.'

'And?'

'And the estimate was that they could be at the Channel ports in six weeks.'

'But why now?'

Renshaw shrugged. 'We've got our politicians, and the general public too for that matter, all hollering for our chaps to be sent home. There won't be much left of the army in our zone in a couple of month's time. There's nobody but us and the Americans to even hold them up for more than a couple of weeks as they swarm across Germany. And as for the French . . .' he shrugged '. . . your guess is as good as mine. They won't fight and even if they wanted to they don't have the troops.'

Frazer looked at his guest. 'I've got the feeling that you came here for a reason. Am I right?'

'Of course you're right. We've been working out what kind of chap we need to find out what's really going on and how he'd go about it.' He paused. 'Your name kept coming up again and again.'

'Tell me more.'

'It's full of snags, Jamie. It's unofficial and if anything went wrong the brass at 21 AG would swear it was not only unauthorised but that they knew nothing about it. It could have diplomatic repercussions at high level. And it's dangerous.' He paused. 'There could be a promotion if it works out – but no medals. And you'd sign that piece of paper – the Official Secrets Act.'

'Sounds like it's already all worked out.'

'Far from it. The general idea is worked out but it would be up to you how you tackled it.'

'Tell me the general idea.'

'We train a group of men to do a line-crossing operation. Go over the other side and actively look for the kind of information we need.'

'Information we need to do what?'

It was long moments before Renshaw replied and then he said quietly, 'To call it a day and let Europe look after itself without us, or show the Soviets that they'll have to fight a long bitter battle if they cross the zone border anywhere between here and Hamburg.'

'Are the Americans involved in this idea?'

'No. Just us.'

'Who's us?'

'21 AG and Bad Salzuflen. Not even London at this stage. Not until it's over, one way or another.'

'What's the budget?'

'Whatever you need.'

'And people?'

'We reckoned between six and ten. More than ten you wouldn't be able to control 'em.'

'How long would the operation run?'

'As long as you and we thought it necessary. You to be the only one who could vote on a personal basis with no reason necessary.'

'What kind of guy is going to risk his life on something like this?' He paused. 'He's got to be at least bilingual German–English. And crazy with it.' His voice was raised. 'And how do I motivate him?'

'I've got twenty men who could do the job. Most of them are German or from the Baltic States. All of them are tough. And they all have all the motivation they need.'

'Like what?'

'Like not being hanged.'

Frazer shook his head slowly in disbelief.

'How could you trust them?'

'Not me, Jamie. Just you. You'll be the judge. Your word will be final.'

'What if I don't trust any one of them?'

'It's not a question of trust, my friend. Just – are they capable of doing it? Tough enough, intelligent enough? They don't have to love us. Just do the job, get paid well and given immunity against prosecution for whatever they did in the past. New identities and backgrounds if they want it.' He looked at Frazer and said, 'You don't have to do it, Jamie. Just say no and we'll all forget it.'

'I'll do it if you agree to one condition. No, two conditions. First, I'm in sole command. Nobody can overrule me on anything. Second, if it isn't done in nine months we call it a day and the people in my network have all the benefits they've been promised.'

Renshaw noticed the 'my' network and said, 'No problem. Both agreed.'

'Who'll take over here?'

'Nobody. The two FSOs go on, each with his own unit. You're still in command but you won't be around very often. OK?'

'OK. Let's see how it fits in.' He paused. 'When do you want me to start?'

'Come back to Bad Salzuflen tomorrow with me and I'll brief you and then you'll need time to choose your men and train them. Soon as you can, Jamie. We're desperate for an answer but we don't want you to skimp any preparations.' He paused. 'Sleep on it. We can talk again tomorrow.'

'What do we tell my people here?'

'Nothing. You just won't be around so much.' He smiled. 'It's up to you what you tell your girl-friends.'

Frazer was silent for a few moments and then he said, 'I'll go back with you tomorrow and we'd better get started or we could find the answer comes too late.'

'Good man.' Renshaw smiled. 'It's going to be our first close look at what the Russians are doing over there. A piece of history maybe.'

'Or a cock-up that everyone will swear they had nothing to do with.'

Chapter 30

Bowman had almost given up his hunt for someone who could get him alongside somebody senior inside SIS when he realised that he had just the right person on his board of directors. Lord Roper had been put on the board to give the paper a bit of substance. And, of course, because his Lordship desperately needed the money.

When Bowman phoned Lord Roper he was his usual amiable self. One of the Tory squires from the backwoods of East Anglia. No problem he said, Sir Hugo Platt, the current D-G was the man to speak to and he was a member of his Lordship's club. He'd come back to Bowman as soon as he'd fixed a meeting.

When Lord Roper called back an hour later the meeting had been arranged. Lunch the next day in a private room at the Reform Club.

The two old boys were already there when Bowman arrived. They made him comfortable and pointed at the food on the long low table before continuing their discussion on the economics of Aberdeen Angus versus Charolais cattle. They got to the coffee before his Lordship stepped onto what he knew must be rather thin ice.

'Are your people a bit pissed-off with this wretched libel case that we're heading for?'

'Not really, Charlie,' Sir Hugo said, waving a hand dismissively. 'We're not involved. It's purely a private thing with Jamie Frazer not liking what your people said about him.'

'The problem we have, Hugo, is that inevitably we have to criticise the organisation that he controlled. You can't disentangle them, and if we tried we'd be putting ourselves at a real disadvantage.'

'Who've you got acting for you?' His Lordship asked, well aware of who it was.

'Sir Graham Pollock.'

'A good chap. I'm sure he'll put up a good fight for your chaps.'

'Would your people mind if we subpoenaed one or two of your people to be questioned about various episodes?'

'Who have you got in mind?' Sir Hugo didn't care who they had in mind but he wanted a few moments to work out how to react.

'Naming no names of course, we had in mind whoever was in charge at the Soviet desk about ten years ago. And whoever Sir James reported to when he was in Germany. Particularly his time in Berlin.'

Sir Hugo tried to cast his mind back through the years but he hadn't been in SIS in those days. But it seemed they thought they were onto something.

'You've got something specific in mind then?'

'Several things, Hugo.' His Lordship looked across at Bowman. 'We couldn't say more than that could we?'

Bowman had no idea of what his Lordship was on about but he recognised a lob when he saw one.

'Maybe we could compromise on one or two of our points.' He shrugged. 'But Sir James would have to compromise too.'

Sir Hugo said, 'Jamie doesn't look like a compromiser to me.'

Bowman said, 'What about SIS, they've got a lot to lose?'

Sir Hugo smiled benignly. 'They're used to this sort of thing. Water off a duck's back.'

'Nobody's going to convince me, Sir Hugo, that SIS haven't got up to some pretty dirty tricks in their time.'

Sir Hugo's eyebrows lifted. 'That'd have to be proved, Mr Bowman. And SIS aren't on trial.'

'They'll be drawn into it one way or another. I'll see to that.'

That was going too far.

Sir Hugo stood up slowly, holding out his hand to his Lordship, his face turned to look at Bowman.

'Mr Bowman, SIS have taken on the Nazis and the Russians in their time and I don't think they're going to quake in their shoes at threats from a tabloid newspaper.' He looked back at his Lordship. 'If you don't have a ticket for Wimbledon, old chap, give me a ring next week.'

When they were alone his Lordship said, 'Well, Sidney. You had your meeting.' He shrugged. 'I guess that's about it.'

'Typical of those stuck-up bastards. They think they're God and nobody can touch 'em.' He stood up. 'But I ain't finished yet, believe me.'

'A drink before you go?'

'No thanks.' Bowman knew he was being dismissed and looked at his Lordship. 'You think I've blown it, don't you?'

'You forgot the basic essentials of doing a deal.'

'Like what?'

'Like not offering something the other guy wanted in exchange for what you wanted. And what you wanted was never available.'

'And what was that?'

'You wanted him to throw in his lot with you. In a fight where everybody except you knows you're going to lose.'

Bowman opened his mouth to say something and then changed his mind. 'Thanks for your efforts anyway.'

Chapter 31

They had gone over to the Healeys and Frazer had gone off alone to meet someone who was coming to check the boat's compasses. Adele and Helen Healey were sitting on cane chairs under a striped canvas sunshade, cans of Coke and coffee in a thermos jug on the grass between them.

'Did you ever meet any of Jamie's wives?'

'I met Laura, the one who now lives in Scotland. And I met Patsy. The one who died.'

'What were they like?'

'Laura was very pretty and very bright. Patsy was beautiful. That wasn't her real name. She was Russian or Polish. I'm not sure which. Very sophisticated, well-educated and stinking rich. She'd been married before to some very rich guy who'd died in a plane crash. I think he was German but I'm not sure. She was always a bit of a mystery. But she was special. And it seems she was crazy about Jamie. She was killed in some kind of accident.'

'And Laura?'

'Oh Laura. She was one of those little-girl-lost types like Marilyn Monroe. Long legs, big boobs and quite a lot of fun.'

'What happened with her?'

'She went off with a golf-pro. A big, dumb, handsome hunk. Jamie and she were divorced and shortly afterwards the hunk went off with somebody else. She was pretty, but I don't know what else she had. Mind you, I'd guess she was very good in bed.' She sighed. 'I never met Joanna. She's in a nursing-home in Switzerland.'

'What's the matter with her?'

'I don't know the proper medical description but in plain words she's mad.'

'Does he ever visit her?'

'No. The doctors have forbidden it. They say it would damage her. He never talks about her. That's not quite true. He talked about her to me once but he was very guarded. Sympathetic but there was nothing he could do apart from paying for her nursing.'

'How did he come to marry her?'

'I don't know. She came after Patsy, or whatever her name was, died, and I think she was already unbalanced. Francis hinted that it was booze and drugs. I think Jamie thought he had the magic touch. It lasted about six months. According to Francis it was a real nightmare time for Jamie.'

'What were their relationships like with Jamie?'

'With Joanna it was pity on his part, I'm sure. Caring for a lost soul. But you can't play God for long. With Laura I think she loved him as much as that kind of girl can and they seemed happy together, not that I saw much of them. Patsy was the only one who really counted. For her he could do no wrong. She adored him. And as for him, I've never seen him so calm and contented. They were a pair.'

'And what happened?'

'I don't know. I know she died, somewhere in Germany I think. Jamie was working there for SIS at the time. Francis thinks she killed herself for some reason but he's only guessing. Jamie stayed there in Germany for quite a time before he came back. Nobody seems to know what he was up to. He was a very different chap the first time I saw him after he came back. Still looked much the same but strained around the eyes. Bought the cottage and the boat. Had several lady-friends but nothing serious.' She smiled. 'And then he met you and we were all very relieved.' She paused. 'And in case you're wondering, so far as I know there's never been anyone else since you came along.'

'He doesn't love me but I've got used to that.' She paused. 'I think.'

'Love's a big word, sweetie. Easy said but the proof's in what's done. He cares about you and loves being with you. He's told me so. You've got all of Jamie Frazer that's there to be had.'

'I'm not complaining. But it's hard to love someone who doesn't love you back.'

'Remember what Shakespeare said.'

'Tell me.'

' "*Love is not love that alters when it alteration finds* – something, something – *oh no, it is an ever fixed mark that looks on tempests and is never shaken* – something, something – *love alters not with his brief hours and weeks, but bears it out even to the edge of doom. If this be error and upon me proved, I never writ, nor no man ever loved.*" '

Adele was silent for long moments and then she looked at Helen Healey.

'You're a good friend, Nellie. To both of us.'

'I'd better go and load the dish-washer. Coming?'

Chapter 32

At Bad Salzuflen they had allocated him a house on the edge of the town, a car and an RASC driver.

For a week he read, analysed and made notes on the dozen or so files of possible recruits for his network. All the existing information indicated that the Russians' main HQ across the zone border was based near Magdeburg. None of the potential recruits had been told what their mission concerned or what they would have to do. They were told only that it was extremely dangerous and given an outline of the rewards that would come their way if the mission was successful. They were already aware of their likely fates as war criminals and there had been no refusals. Frazer interviewed each one of them individually, concentrating on how they had been recruited, their training and their experience. He only ruled out two of them on the initial interviews. Both of them were SS who had been concerned with the administration of concentration camps. One at Auschwitz, the other at Belsen-Bergen. Of the others he gave top priority to three men who had been Sicherheitsdienst officers. Three others were ex-Kripo officers and the rest from various sections of the SS.

Frazer concentrated on looking for good observers, physical fitness, and the potential for blending in with the general civilian population the other side of the zone border. The dangers they risked were not from being involved in any kind of subversion or sabotage but merely from being caught in some routine check and imprisoned by the KGB. There were two extremes of attitudes that he eliminated. The over-enthusiastic and the uncommitted who might be tempted to accept escaping from their present captivity as reward enough, and disappear as soon as they were on the other side.

Eventually Frazer settled for seven men. One to be held in reserve. He didn't have enough time to make their training individual and although it was poor security he decided that they had to be a team and therefore aware of who the other agents were.

The training was mainly on the organisation of the Soviet forces. The different services, uniforms, ranks, and equipment. They were all used to absorbing that type of information and training. The next step was to provide them with cover stories and documentation. This also meant that the background had to allow them to exercise any skills they had that could help them earn a living. They had to merge into the civilian population without being noticed.

Frazer's old FS Section in Hildesheim had provided them with a suitable meeting place, a small farm west of Magdeburg with an owner who was already co-operating with the FS Section.

The crossing of the zone border at that time was quite simple with the border barely defined apart from printed warnings on posts hammered into the ground at 200-metre intervals. There were random checks along the border by Russian border-guards with dogs but no wire and no land-mines.

Throughout their training he emphasised that all they had to do was observe and report. One of them would act as a courier and would meet Frazer at the farmhouse. Once every ten days they would have the chance of a short meeting with Frazer himself at some prearranged place and time.

At the end of the fifth week Frazer drove them in a civilian truck to a spot about half a mile from the zone border and waited with them as they crossed the border at hourly intervals. The first ten days brought little useful information but by the fourth week not only was the operation working smoothly, but hard information was forthcoming about Soviet army dispositions and identification of many of the army units involved, their commanders and their apparent roles. One man had disappeared in the third week but there was no indication that he had been picked up by the KGB or the German police. In week seven Frazer had given them new targets regarding local supplies to the Soviet forces. Frazer was beginning to form a conclusion that he could put to the evaluators at Bad Salzuflen. He estimated that another three weeks of the operation would provide conclusive information.

His meeting that week had been moved to Sunday to suit his agent, and Frazer's driver had dropped him at the usual place at the edge of the woods. The sun was going down and the woods were wet from a sharp summer rainstorm. He stood at the edge of the far side of the wood and checked that both fields were empty. The lambs and the ewes had probably gone to market or, more likely, been confiscated by the Russians. As darkness fell he moved off slowly along the ditch that separated the two fields. There was a trickle of water from the rainstorm. When he was in sight of the farm-buildings he saw that the light was on as usual in the kitchen and another dim light over the door. The old fool had obviously forgotten the security routine that they had been using. He kept to the shadows as he edged slowly around the barn and waited for a moment before he crossed the twenty yards or so to the kitchen door. He knocked with the Morse V sign on the door and then he was blinded by the light from a powerful torch as the door was flung open. The first blow cracked against the side of his head and he was barely conscious as more blows rained down on his head and shoulders. When he came to he was already in a cell in the old Gestapo HQ in Magdeburg that had been taken over by the KGB. His shirt was covered with blood and vomit and he groaned with pain as he tried to sit up, falling back helplessly, before he passed out again.

The rules of the game were that you did your best to stay silent for forty-eight hours so that the others in your network could get away. After that there was no need to be heroic. Say as little as you can but if you talk there's no come-back.

He was barely aware of what went on the first day but in their session with him on the following day he realised that they thought he was a German. They spoke Russian amongst themselves but when they questioned him it was in almost unrecognisable German. It was easy to behave as if he couldn't understand what they were saying. That night they started the beating. Using solid black rubber truncheons they pounded his naked body as he lay fastened down on the cement slab. But when they untied him and bundled him into the old-fashioned cast-iron bath filled with cold water he lost consciousness as they held his head under water. From time to time as he came to he was conscious of the terrible noise he was making as his lungs fought frantically for breath. He was aware of their voices as they shouted questions at him. With his lungs and mouth filled with water he would have been unable to answer even if he had wanted to. They were like animals as they brought him to near-asphyxiation. Then alternate sessions on the slab and in the bath for days on end until they suddenly seemed to have tired of him. He tried desperately to stay conscious but even when he was unconscious it would be that awful heaving, echoing noise as he struggled to breathe that would arouse him. That struggle and that pain put him beyond thinking into a nightmare world of its own.

Chapter 33

After Jamie Frazer had taken the oath, Sir Graham smiled at him amiably. 'Do sit down, Sir James, if you would be more comfortable.'

Pollock waited as Frazer settled himself on the chair in the witness stand. When he seemed comfortable Sir Graham continued. 'Sir James, there are one or two sections that you have highlighted in the book, sections you said you found offensive, yes?'

'Yes.'

'I'd like to ask you about the piece that starts on page thirty-seven and continues over the page. It refers to you having been a member of the Communist Party, yes?'

'Yes.'

'So I ask you, Sir James, yes or no, have you ever been a member of the Communist Party?'

'In the sense that . . .'

Sir Graham intervened. 'Yes or no, Sir James. Have you ever been a member of the Communist Party?'

For a moment Frazer hesitated and then he shrugged and said, 'Yes. I suppose you could say that.'

There was an audible stir in the court as Sir Graham let Frazer's answer sink in. He paused for a moment and then said, 'Thank you, Sir James,' and sat down.

Howard Rowe stood up slowly and said, 'Could you explain to the court why you objected to this item in the book?'

'I objected for two reasons. The book described me as a "committed" member of the Communist Party and in fact I joined the CP as part of my job.'

'Why was that necessary, Sir James?'

'Because we needed inside information on how the CP here and in Germany were financed. And what their plans were.'

'How were they financed, Sir James?'

'From Moscow through the Soviet Embassy here in London and in Germany directly from the Kremlin.'

'And why were you the person who had to do this job?'

'Because I knew the background of how the Communists worked. I spoke German and I was used to their methods of operating.'

'In fact your official duties consisted of working actively against the Soviet Union and its front organisations both here and in Europe?'

Frazer nodded. 'That's a fair description.'

'And being described as a committed Communist was not only untrue but a reverse of the truth that could lead to your being despised by your associates in both your business and private life. If they were stupid enough to believe the blatant lies in this infamous book.'

'I've had anonymous letters threatening me on that score. Suggesting that I'm a traitor.'

'Thank you, Sir James.'

And Rowe sat down looking toward the jury and then his Lordship who took the hint.

'We'll adjourn for just half an hour today.' He stood up, gave a perfunctory all-embracing nod and swept through the door to his chambers.

As Rowe took Healey's arm as they walked to the corridor, he said, 'The old bastard wants to get to Epsom for a couple of races.' He smiled. 'I don't know whether you know it but his Lordship was a member of the CP when he was up at Cambridge. Everybody was.' He laughed. 'The old crook didn't bat an eyelid when I was questioning Frazer.'

Chapter 34

When he saw Schenk unlocking the cell door, Frazer thought he was having hallucinations but Schenk was carrying his bowl of watery soup. As Schenk bent over him the German said, 'Don't know me for God's sake. I work here. Ask me if you can have exercise. Go on. Ask me.'

His heart pounding in his chest Frazer whispered, 'Exercise. I need exercise. How did they get you?'

'They haven't. I work here as a cleaner. They haven't got any of the others.' He sniffed loudly. 'Got to go now.' He snatched the bowl away from Frazer's hand and walked to the door, turning the key in both old-fashioned locks.

It was two days before Frazer was taken up into the small back-yard by Schenk. He could hardly walk and as he leaned breathless against the brick wall he listened intently to what Schenk said.

'I got all the money from the others. I got it changed to cigarettes and I got enough to get you out. They're not interested in you no more. They say you got nothing to say.'

'How do I get out?'

'Be ready all the time. Maybe next Sunday.'

'What day is it?'

'Wednesday. You got to go back in. Keep resting.'

'How many days have I been here?'

'Nearly a month. Now shut up.'

Royal Army Service Corps' driver, Private Lewis, had gone to Frazer's crossing- point day after day. Sitting there reading *No Orchids for Miss Blandish* and smoking Woodbines. Nobody had ordered him to go and wait but nobody had stopped him and he rather liked Major Frazer. It was a Sunday when Frazer hadn't come back and it was a Sunday when an unkempt man in a faded blue shirt and dark slacks appeared on the edge of the woods. Private Lewis put his paperback down on the seat beside him and tossed his fag-end onto the gravel path.

As he got to the man he said, 'You lookin' for somebody, mate?'

'I look for officers from Bad Salzuflen.'

'That's a long way away. Why them in particular?'

'I got one of them here. In the woods. He needs help.'

'Show me.'

The bruises on his face and the awkward shape of his body as it lay between two bushes made him barely recognisable. But Driver Lewis recognised him all right. He looked at Schenk. 'Are you one of his men?'

Schenk shrugged and then nodded his head. Driver Lewis sighed and said, 'Help me carry him to the jeep. And you'd better come with me.'

Renshaw was perched on the edge of the hospital bed and a captain with a stethoscope and the insignia of the Royal Army Medical Corps was fixing a safety-pin into the wide bandage wrapped round Frazer's ribs.

'What d'you think, doc?'

'Two broken ribs, both little fingers broken and probably unrepairable, multiple severe bruising and a fine selection of minor contusions. He ain't gonna die but he needs a lot of rest and nursing.'

'How long before we can start talking to him?'

'What kind of talking, skipper? Chatting or interrogation?'

'A bit of both I guess.'

'Give him a couple of days and then you'll have to see how it goes. You'll just have to play it by ear. Has his next of kin been informed?'

'No. That's not possible.'

'Why not?'

'Security.'

The doctor looked at Renshaw with eyebrows raised. 'I don't get it. He'll have to have leave before going back to whatever he does.'

Renshaw nodded. 'We'll see what he wants.'

When the doctor had left, Renshaw stood by the side of the bed looking at Frazer's bruised face and the splinted fingers of both hands. The X-ray had said that his fingers had been broken sideways and that there was no way to reset them to give any real articulation. But it wasn't the bruises and broken bones that mattered. What mattered was how Frazer had got back. Had he done some deal with the Russians? If not, how the hell did he escape? He'd have to interrogate the German, Schenk, on how he featured in it. And Schenk had been one of Frazer's team. How did he get in on the act? But most of all he needed to know what the Russians had wanted in return for Frazer's release.

As the days went by Renshaw put his carefully phrased questions to Frazer and became convinced that he was telling the truth. One fact was always in his mind. If a deal had been done with the Russians there would have been no need for Frazer to have been so severely beaten up. A few token bruises maybe but not broken bones. A man whose main pleasure is playing jazz piano doesn't voluntarily agree to have his little fingers broken so that he can never encompass a full octave again.

There were others on the intelligence staff who found it hard to believe that the KGB men had been so stupid that they never even realised that Frazer was a Brit and not a German. But the questions that Frazer said they had put to him showed that they had no idea what they were looking for, beyond the fact that he had regularly crossed the zone border. But Frazer's written conclusions about the Russian military in the Soviet Zone showed that the evaluators at Bad Salzuflen hadn't seen the facts that were staring them in the face. It had taken Frazer and his network to provide the facts that made his evaluations totally credible.

It had taken several days of Renshaw's cautious questioning before Frazer realised that he was actually under suspicion of having been 'turned' by the Russians. It was in the middle of one of these sessions that Frazer said, 'I want to see the DDMI, John.'

'Why?'

'Because it's become obvious to me that you and probably others think that I am suspect. I'm not sure of what but I've had enough of the pussyfooting around that's going on.'

'This isn't DDMI level, Jamie.'

'It was enough for a bunch of men to be put at risk of what I got, to find out what the Soviet army was doing in the Magdeburg area.' His voice was tight with anger. 'You haven't even asked me what I decided they were doing. Two months ago 21 Army Group was considering whether to pull out of the British Zone if the Russians crossed the border.' He paused and then went on angrily, 'Have they decided yet what to do and what the Russians intend doing? Have they?'

'Calm down, Jamie. I'm just trying to get things back on the rails. I'm just doing my job.'

'Don't give me that bullshit. If you believed what I've told you you wouldn't be still asking bloody stupid questions. If those KGB idiots wanted me on their side why am I lying here in a hospital bed? They thought I was a German who'd crossed the border to get cigarettes and nylons to sell on the black market. My chap Schenk worked there, he's told you what they said to him.'

'I've raised all these points, Jamie. I've pretty well convinced every-one concerned.'

'Did your people search my quarters when I went missing?'

'Only superficially.'

'Did they pick up my report?'

'They didn't pick up anything.'

'You'd better find it and make it your bedtime reading tonight. 21 Army Group might be interested too. I only went over the border to bring my men back.'

'Don't take all this badly, Jamie. You've been in the business long enough to know that this is just standard procedure for anybody in these circumstances. Not just you.'

Frazer sighed deeply and let his head fall back against the pillows.

Major Renshaw unlocked the door, opened it, switched on the light, and looked around the small room. He found the report lying quite obviously on the desk by the telephone and a standard-issue army report-pad with pale-blue, squared pages. There were several separate sheets pinned together. He read the main pages twice before reaching for the telephone. It was 23.00 hours.

Report on Operation Orion
by Major Frazer J. I. Corps.

The task was to evaluate the strength and purpose of Soviet military dispositions in the Magdeburg area. Concern had been expressed that the strength and number of units was far beyond what was needed for the administration of this occupied area. Concern was also expressed that the units deployed were all attack units rather than defence, and that this might indicate aggressive intentions.

Attached is a virtually complete Order of Battle for the area. The Soviet HQ is on an estate ten miles north of Magdeburg. More than half of the military strength consists of attack forces, including tank units, artillery and support services. There is no doubt that they represent a vast superiority in numbers over Allied forces in this area.

But careful probing elicited that none of the attack units nor the normal units were armed. All appropriate ammunition is stored and under the control of Berlin and it is estimated that it would take at least three weeks to supply even token ammunition for such a large and spread-out command.

It is also significant that in mounting this operation there have been few problems in crossing and recrossing the zone border. If any kind of attack was being planned I suggest that the border would be strictly controlled. Another significant factor is that Soviet troops are able to take leave locally and in Berlin but leave is not granted for visits to the Soviet Union.

It was the details I received from the network concerning local German morale and attitudes to the Russians that provided an answer to the anomalies above. Both German officials and the general population had no problem in explaining the odd situation. Their view is cynical but I believe it is true. The huge numbers of high-class Soviet troops in the area are there almost solely because they live at the expense of the local German population. They have complete control over all food supplies and exercise it rigorously. German rations are barely above starvation levels. Visits to the Soviet Union would expose the poor conditions prevailing there. An indication of the validity of this theory is that it is estimated that 75% of all Soviet forces are stationed in occupied countries. Those troops are all paid in Occupation

Marks and Zlotys . . . which have no actual worth. They are just paper.

In conversations with local people my agents confirm that the local Soviet troops are establishing facilities and relationships that indicate a long stay.

On my next crossing I intend recalling all my men and request that the various rewards and facilities which were promised shall be dealt with promptly.

Signed: James Frazer

Neither Bad Salzuflen nor 21 Army Group were much impressed by the report but other intelligence sources had confirmed Frazer's conclusion. The Red Army was not preparing to roll its tanks over the border at the moment. The money, the documentation and the new identities that had been promised had been taken care of and new lives had been started in Sao Paulo, Philadelphia, Ottawa and less well-known places.

Jamie Frazer had recovered, more or less, from his crude battering. But his treatment by Renshaw and the others still rankled. On reflection he accepted that it was just routine precautionary security, nevertheless he still resented the fact that he wasn't made an exception.

He had been approached by both MI5 and MI6 and was given a month's leave to think it over. He spent a week with his grandparents in Birmingham. Still in the same Victorian house. Nothing had changed there. His small bedroom at the back of the house overlooking the bowling-green of the Workman's Club still had the etching on the wall of two floating angels entitled 'Easter Morn'. And in a wooden case were the eight bound copies of Dickens' works that Grandpa got when he agreed to take the *Daily Herald* for twenty-one weeks. But 67 Mere Road was the only thing that hadn't altered. It was strange being an outcast because of his uniform and the crowns on his shoulders. When he had been a sergeant that was OK but it seemed now as if he had crossed some line that everyone could see except him. It wasn't that they suddenly disliked him, not even that they were envious or resentful. When he joined them in a pub or checked out the tennis-club they were simply embarrassed. He had become a stranger, a foreigner. Conversations and chatter stopped and he had nothing to say. Grandma had warned him what it would be like but he had thought she was just being old-fashioned. But it seemed she knew his old school-friends and work-mates better than he did. He took a train to London on the Sunday and found a room in Paddington near the station.

He had one more offer of employment during his leave. He spent hours of each day and every night at a basement jazz club called Joe's Place and by the end of the first week there were people coming from every part of London to hear Jamie Frazer and the seven-piece band playing all the old favourites from blues to rags, and Joe Klein, who ran the club and played tenor sax, was begging him to join the band permanently. His injured little fingers were a hindrance but a doctor who frequented the club had shown him how to tape both joints on his little fingers so that although the fingers were completely stiff they could still strike a note when they had to. But shaking hands was always going to be really painful, any sideways pressure had to be avoided.

Jamie Frazer loved his time playing at the club but he had seen too much and experienced too much to think that it was anything other than a relaxation. The others in the band were dedicated, much older than he was, and although they had survived the bombs and destruction, the war to them was just an unpleasant background instinctively ignored. Their lives were devoted to jazz and nothing else.

In the third week of his leave he had informal talks with his contacts at both intelligence organisations and it became obvious that his languages and field experience would not be used much in MI5, whose field of operation was the security of the United Kingdom, so he negotiated a deal with his contact at MI6. They made clear that both his languages and his experience would be put to good use. They had arranged with the Ministry of Defence and the War Office that he should retain his commission in the Intelligence Corps with the rank of Lieutenant-Colonel so that he could wear uniform where it would provide suitable cover. He enjoyed the thought of evening the score with the military in Addis Ababa who wouldn't even let him keep his local rank of captain.

There was going to be a couple of months of initiation into the workings of MI6 and its methods of operation, and Frazer found himself a large one-room flat that was only a ten-minute walk from 54 Broadway.

His old friend, Tom Scott, from SOE days, was appointed as his mentor, and Frazer found that what he had heard or read about MI6 was nothing like the facts. MI5 was responsible for preventing foreign intelligence agencies, friends or foes, from obtaining information that was highly confidential. It was controlled by the Home Office and operated only in the UK. MI6, which was controlled by the Foreign Office, operated all over the world and its rôle was the collection, active or passive, of information that gave a picture of what policies or activities of other states could do harm to Britain.

A specialist, who had been a history professor before the war, spent a week describing the intelligence organisations, both official and covert, of those countries which were current MI6 targets. It was a long list. Frazer spent a week with the organisation responsible for monitoring radio and telephone links all over the world. He spent several days with the section responsible for providing false passports and documentation of all kinds and some time with the archive section. A lawyer instructed him on the legal aspects of what he could do but made quite clear that both internal and external laws were there to be ignored when necessary. There was a specialist team which assessed and evaluated documents that had been surreptitiously obtained, to check not only their significance but the possibility that they had been fed into the system for disinformation. The people he found least appealing were the desk men, senior men each responsible for all MI6's intelligence operations in one particular country. They tended to be either from Cambridge or Oxford and Frazer got the impression that they found him amusing because of his lack of sophistication. They were the kind of men who could spend the whole of a mid-morning lunch-break arguing about the shades of difference between a participle and a gerund. He disliked intensely their air of superiority. When he had mentioned this in a conversation with Tom Scott, Scott had smiled.

'I've noticed you bristling a bit when talking with them, but you're missing the point, and it's a vitally important point.'

'What is it?'

'When you're talking to them they listen, they listen very intently, they are interested. Like you they recognise that you're very different from them but they don't resent it or find it devalues you or your opinions. But your resentment of their attitude annoys you and it shows.'

'Is it all that obvious, Tom?'

'I'm afraid so.' He paused. 'You're letting the thinking of working-class Birmingham get in the way. If I was stuck in a dark alleyway facing a couple of thugs I'd rather have you with me than one of our desk people. But when it comes to thinking and analysis I'd put my money on them.' He smiled to soften his words. 'You're very bright. Very intuitive but those chaps are brighter. You must have shone very brightly with your Brummie contemporaries but those desk chaps are brighter than you are. That's what going to university did for them. It pitted them against other bright minds. Opinion and prejudice always took a back-seat to facts.' He paused and smiled again. 'Here endeth today's sermon.'

It had become obvious that he was going to be posted to Germany and he spent a week with the SIS man from the Bonn office learning about the current relationships with Germans who were being encouraged to take over the administration of their defeated country.

Unfortunately there were others whose political aims were subversive. It was over a year since the three western zones had amalgamated to form the German Federal Republic and the Russians set up their zone as the German Democratic Republic. There were undercover Nazis, undercover Communists and a growing number of agents sent over the border by the KGB to spy on both the Germans and the occupying forces of France, the United States and Britain. It was identifying and penetrating these agents that was to be Jamie Frazer's responsibility.

Chapter 35

They were sitting around in the Healeys' garden. Making the most of the last of the sun. Jamie Frazer was carrying out a cafetière and coffee cups despite the fact that it wasn't his home and he wasn't the host.

Healey leaned forward to make a space for the tray on the low table. As he moved aside the Sunday papers he looked up at Frazer. 'We were just talking about what motivates people and it made me think of you wanting to be a fighter pilot. Why, for God's sake? Why that? Why not a lawyer or a surveyor or something else useful?'

Frazer looked around at the three faces. 'All take with? One no sugar, yes?'

Without waiting for confirmation he poured the coffees out, handed them around, before sitting in the cane chair and leaning back, cup in hand.

He smiled. 'Philosophising are we? Well forget it. It wasn't patriotism for a start.'

Helen smiled. 'Don't dodge, Jamie. We want to know what motivated you, not what it wasn't.'

'You won't ever understand. None of you.'

'How do you know we can't understand?'

'Because you asked the question.'

Healey laughed. 'Don't dodge the question, Jamie. Just tell us the answer. You're worse than we lawyers are.'

Frazer frowned, smiling. 'OK. Let me try. I wanted to be a fighter pilot because it was glamorous. I'd no idea of what it meant but I fancied wearing a uniform that made me different from my pals.' He shrugged. 'It was just what we would have called *swank* in those days. Today we'd call it *ego*. A need to be more important than others.'

Healey nodded. 'And when that didn't work what made you go on and join the army when the war started? Wearing battledress wasn't anything like as glamorous.'

'This is the part you won't understand. For me it *was* glamorous. I'd be a soldier. Something definite. Not just one of the mob.'

'And were you disappointed once you were in the army?'

'No way. I loved it.' He laughed. 'Girls like chaps in battledress. I was mixing with bright people. Making friends. It was the best year of my life that first year.'

'So what went wrong?'

'Nothing. I just got used to it, that's all.' He smiled. 'And I liked being liked. That was the best part.'

'Who were your role models?'

'Churchill – and later on – Montgomery.'

'Why them?'

'Montgomery was in a hurry. He wanted to win. But he had the strength of character to plan in advance. And Churchill I admired for his big mind. A real statesman. We haven't had once since. Imaginative. Generous-minded but nobody's fool.'

Helen Healey said, 'You said you liked being liked. Why?'

Frazer laughed. 'I'd never had that before. I lapped it up.'

'But it must have made you very vulnerable in some ways.'

'I don't understand.'

'I suspect that if some pretty girl said she loved those beautiful blue eyes of yours you'd have tended to want to marry her so that you could have her approval every day.'

Frazer looked at Helen Healey who had said it and then looked away, obviously thinking. He was silent for long moments and then he said quietly, 'I guess that could explain a lot.' Then he smiled, as if dismissing it all. 'Anyone want more coffee? And now I've been psychoanalysed don't mention how well I made the coffee.'

Adele sensed that there could be an awkward silence and she stood up. 'Let's go inside, it's getting too warm in the sun.' She smiled at Frazer. 'Play me "As time goes by" and "Goodnight Sweetheart".' And she reached out a hand for Frazer and pulled him up out of his chair. She followed him inside the house and the others followed as Frazer lifted the lid on the Healeys' upright piano. He played for nearly an hour as they called out what they wanted.

Chapter 36

Frazer had rented a quite extensive flat in a side street off Kant Strasse that he could use as his operational base as well as a home. Everyone concerned had been strongly for him not to operate out of the Olympia Stadion which was the base for most British intelligence operations in the Berlin area. His cover was as a photo-journalist with a press-pass from a well-known New York agency. He had an office in the flat with three telephones. The red phone was a secure dedicated line to 54 Broadway. One was a private number. There was also an old Olivetti portable typewriter and a metal filing cabinet.

Frazer had put down a marker as a freelance but agency-backed photo-journalist at the British, American and French HQs in Berlin, Bonn, Dusseldorf and Hanover. There had been no problems. The airlift to break the Soviet blockade was over, so most foreign journalists had moved on.

London and the political research sections had provided him with a list of names and addresses for potential informants. Being on the list did not mean that they were necessarily going to be co-operative. He found that many people seemed to have no inhibitions about talking quite freely to a journalist. By the end of the first month he had five or six contacts deeply involved in party politics. Even the two Communists talked openly of when the Soviets would take over both Germanys and turn them into a socialist state that would be a model for the rest of Europe.

Frazer was taking a photograph of bombed houses that had been partly restored and were now used as a meeting-place for Berlin communists.

He was using a Leica IIIb with a standard Elmar lens that he had bought on the black market. When he had taken six or seven shots he turned to walk back towards the Ku-damm when he saw a man wave to him from a car that had pulled up. An expensive-looking car. When he didn't respond the car door opened and a smartly-dressed man got out and walked towards him.

Frazer knew he had seen him somewhere before but couldn't place him.

The man smiled up at him. 'It's been a long time.' He paused. 'Otto Schenk. How are you?'

'My God, Schenk. I didn't recognise you. I'm sorry.'

Schenk smiled. 'I don't want to be recognised, Mr Frazer.'

'Did they give you what we had agreed?'

'Yeah. Everything. Documents. Money, and best of all, permits.'

'What sort of permits?'

'To make whisky, gin, vodka and schnapps. Permits to open clubs. Permits to make radios.'

'Let's find somewhere where we can talk.'

'I got a nice place in Grunewald, why don't we go there?'

The 'nice place in Grunewald' was a villa not far from the lake. Well cared-for and handsome. Inside, the rooms were large and expensively furnished, but furnished in good taste. Schenk took Frazer's arm and led him through the open door. A maid in uniform was waiting in the living room but Schenk told her that they'd help themselves to drinks.

When they were sitting, Frazer said, 'Tell me what happened when you and the driver got me back to Bad Salzuflen.'

Schenk laughed. 'They arrested me. Interrogated me day after day, trying to get me to say you'd done a deal with the Russians. After about ten days they seemed satisfied that I'd bribed one of those KGB bastards to turn a blind eye.' He shrugged. 'Like I said, they did what they'd promised to do.' He grinned. 'I don't think they saw much value in permits.'

'You saved my life, Otto. You could have just left me there to rot and walked off yourself.'

'All our team gave money for the bribe.'

'Do you know what happened to them?'

'No. I never heard anything,'

'How did you manage to get Berlin residency?'

Schenk laughed and shrugged. 'Just another permit.'

'Have you got a family?'

'I've got a beautiful daughter, two years old, Anna. My wife's Jewish and she found out about my background and walked out on me. She divorced me a year ago.'

'Is there anything I could do to help her change her mind and come back?'

Schenk thought for a moment and then shook his head.

'Thanks, but no. She didn't want me, nor the child. Said she'd made a mistake. Wanted her freedom.' He shrugged. 'I hear she's making the same mistake with some other guy.'

'Who looks after your daughter?'

Schenk smiled. 'A good old-fashioned nanny. She's great.' He laughed. 'She mothers me too.'

'Are you a rich man now, Otto?'

'Yeah, more or less. By the way, the name's Schmidt. But I kept the Otto.'

'You must be a very shrewd businessman, Otto.'

'Not really. If you've got the permits you can't go wrong.' He paused. 'I suppose I shouldn't ask but what are you doing these days?'

Frazer smiled. 'Let's just say I'm a freelance journalist.'

Otto smiled. 'OK. Let's leave it at that.' He paused. 'Can you stay for a meal?'

'I'd enjoy that.'

Schenk had driven Frazer back into the city himself and as the German drove off, Frazer realised that despite the wealth and the business interests Schenk was a lonely man. The only phone calls that evening had been business calls. It seemed from what Schenk had said that when his wife was around there had been a lot of socialising but now Otto Schenk had retreated into his villa by the lake with a two-year-old daughter and an elderly nanny. A strange ending for a man who had been a rather ruthless SS officer.

He wondered what had motivated Schenk to organise his escape. If it had gone wrong the least he would have had was a lifetime in a labour camp. Schenk had seemed eager to keep in touch and it hadn't escaped Frazer's thinking that Schenk could be a very useful contact in areas where he himself had no background.

Chapter 37

They were lying on the slope of the hill that led up to Goodwood racecourse, looking up at the clear blue sky. Frazer was chewing the sweet stalk of a long blade of grass.

'Penny for your thoughts, Jamie.'

'As a matter of fact I was thinking about my grandparents and regretting that I'd never told them how grateful I was for the way they cared for me. It made me wish that they could come back just for a few minutes so that I could tell them how much I loved them in my own peculiar way.'

'Have you ever been back there since they died?'

'I went there once about seven or eight years ago. The BBC did a TV thing about me and they had me walking around all my old haunts and talking about them.'

'Has it changed a lot?'

'It had hardly changed at all. Everything looked much the same but smaller. It was I who had changed. Everything seemed to have gone on in the same old way. It made me slightly ashamed.'

'Ashamed? Ashamed of what?'

'Those people had carried on just as they always had. Reasonably contented with their lot and not much interest in what went on in London or the world in general. They had been bombed night after night, women had done men's jobs in factories, and after the war they survived rationing and depression without too much complaint. They're a community. You go next door for a bit of sugar and if the old man is ill they'll bring you soup. And if the old man dies they'll keep an eye on his widow and kids. They're good people.' He sighed. 'But I don't belong there any more.'

'Do you regret that?'

Frazer sat up slowly, stretching his arms. 'No. I never did belong there. But if it wasn't for the war I'd still be there.' He looked at her. 'There are hundreds of young men whose only escape was the war. It was our university. May seem unpleasant but that's how it was, sweetie. A fact of life if you were working-class. But nobody wants to admit it.'

'The other night we were going to listen to the radio but when you turned it on and you heard what they were playing you switched it off, and you looked upset. Do you remember?'

'Yes.'

'Can you remember what the piece of music was?'

'Yes.'

'What was it?'

'Mendelssohn's Violin Concerto.'

'It sounded rather sad music, was it?'

'I guess so.'

He stood up and reached for her hand to pull her to her feet. Then, making an effort to smile, he said, 'What would you like for your birthday?'

She smiled and said softly, 'Just to be with you.'

As they strolled back to the car she knew that she'd been stupid to rake over those memories of his young days. They always seemed to put his nerves on edge and despite his apparent unconcern about the law case it was obvious that the need to rake over the past was disturbing him and upsetting his simple routine with the boat and the Rolls and fiddling with the Austin Healey 3000 in the garage. But there was so much she didn't know about him and his past life and she wanted desperately to understand and do and say the right things to comfort him.

Jamie Frazer felt a growing resentment at being questioned just because he was taking action against people who were peddling lies and distortions about his life and character. He realised that people were trying to help, to show that they were on his side, but their questions all too often pushed him unwillingly back into a past that he wanted to forget. None of it really mattered but looking back made him aware of how naïve he had been. And how juvenile. Always ready to have a go. Some had seen it as courage and others had seen it as ego. It was too late now for him to be made to decide which it really was. But hearing those few bars of the Mendelssohn had brought those days back so vividly. Like the poet said, 'His days of wine and roses', his days of delight and happiness. When just seeing her was enough. It was a long time ago. But it wasn't over. It never would be over.

Chapter 38

Sir Graham Pollock QC had decided that it was time that Jamie Frazer's apparently impeccable past ought to be probed. He had taken Al Pinto aside and questioned him again before they went into court.

'You say you were told about this episode in Rome by someone who was there at the time. How reliable was your informant?'

'He was there in Rome at the time. He saw it going on.'

'So why won't he come to court as a witness?'

'Doesn't want to be involved.' Pinto grinned at Pollock. 'The Brits don't like to be seen as sneaks. They pass the dirt to *Private Eye* or the *News of the World.*'

There was enough truth in what Pinto said for Pollock to risk venturing a cautious step onto the thin ice of moral values.

Half an hour later he was looking at Frazer in the witness box.

'Sir James. You have admitted to having close and friendly relationships with Italian prisoners-of-war during your sojourn in Addis Ababa. Is that correct?'

'I wouldn't use the word "admitted". I stated the facts.'

Sir Graham smiled back at the witness who had just shown that he could rise to the bait if it was cast out cunningly.

'You say that you were particularly incensed and humiliated by the episode in chapter six in the book. Am I right?'

'Yes.'

'You objected, I understand, to it being pointed out that you shared the sexual favours of a young woman who at the same time – the same time, Sir James – was the mistress of an Italian officer who you had arrested.' He paused. 'Surely those were the bare facts, Sir James. A matter of record, however one may deplore them, or however one may regret them.'

Howard Rowe rose and interposed. 'Counsel is asking the witness to condemn himself on facts which are a travesty of the truth, my Lord. May I cover with the witness the real facts so that the court is not being used as a cover for publishing once more the libels already perpetrated by the other side in the offending book?'

His Lordship noticed that Pollock had sat down and after a moment's reflection nodded at Howard Rowe.

'All right, Mr Rowe, carry on.'

Howard Rowe looked across at his client.

'Sir James. We are talking about a certain Capitano Simonini, are we not?'

'Yes.'

'Who was he?'

'He was the Italian officer of their intelligence services in Rome who controlled and directed the Italian underground organisations in Ethiopia.'

'And it was your responsibility to penetrate and destroy such organisations?'

'Yes.'

'So what was your business with Capitano Simonini?'

'To interrogate him about his organisation and its current functions when we went in to Rome.'

'So you interrogated him?'

'Yes.'

'On London's orders?'

'Yes.'

'Was it a lengthy interrogation?'

'About three days.'

'And was Capitano Simonini co-operative?'

'Absolutely.'

'You established a friendly relationship with him, yes?'

'Yes. I liked the man.'

'Despite his rôle in organising the resistance in Ethiopia?'

'He was just doing his job.'

'Just as you were doing your job?'

'Yes.'

'Where did this lengthy interrogation take place?'

'At Simonini's flat in Rome.'

'Am I right in suggesting that a good interrogator aims to achieve a friendly relationship with his subject?'

'Yes.'

'And you had established such a relationship with Simonini?'

'Yes. It was a friendly relationship.'

'And when the interrogation was finished what happened?'

'Simonini went to a POW camp in Naples.'

'Was Simonini a prisoner while you were interrogating him?'

'Formally, yes. But I didn't treat him as such.'

'Before Simonini left for the camp he gave you the keys to his flat.'

'Yes.'

'Tell the court about that?'

'He told me the flat was paid for for another four months and I was welcome to use it. He also gave me the keys to his small car, a Fiat Topolino.'

'Did you take advantage of his offers?'

'I used his flat as my HQ for about two months. Rome was very crowded in that time. And I used the car until I got an official car.'

'Have you ever heard from Simonini since those days?'

'Yes. We correspond regularly and we've met a couple of times when I've been passing through Milan where he lives.'

'What does he do now?'

'He's chief justice at the Regional Court of Milan.'

'One last question on the subject. Did Capitano Simonini have a mistress?'

'I've no idea but I should think he might have. He was very handsome and very charming.'

'But you aren't sure?'

'No.'

'Thank you, Sir James.'

Rowe sat down and his Lordship nodded to Sir Graham who stood up, said, 'No further questions, m'Lord,' and sat down again.

When the court adjourned about 4.15 p.m. Howard Rowe took Healey and Sir James across the road to the Wig and Pen.

As Howard Rowe put the drinks on the table in front of them, he sat down and raised his pint to Jamie Frazer. 'Tell me, Jamie. *Did* the Italian guy have a mistress?'

'I've always assumed that a mistress was a woman who was financed full-time by the man. Simonini just had lots of girl-friends and when I sent him down to Naples for deep interrogation he left me a dozen telephone numbers.' He smiled. 'We had two great nights in Rome before I put him in the bag and after that I carried on Simonini's good work and loved them all.'

It was Otto Schenk who had persuaded him to go to a cocktail party at the French Mission. Schenk did a lot of business with the French in Berlin. And inevitably Jamie had been pressed into a session at the piano. All the old ballads by Charles Trenet, Jean Sablon and Tino Rossi. He was playing the third repeat of 'J'ai deux amours' when he noticed the girl in the wheelchair sitting alongside him, listening intently. When he looked round at her she was smiling as she said, 'Will you play "*Sag beim Abschied*" for me?' When he hesitated for a moment she said, 'Please.' He played the old Viennese song for her and then when he had finished he turned to look at her. 'Why that old song?'

She smiled. 'It's a lovely melody and I love the words. A song about not saying goodbye.'

And that was it. She was very beautiful but what he remembered later was her voice. Soft and husky and a little bit breathless. He had fetched her a drink, a Coke, and they'd sat talking about the words of songs. She spoke good English and reasonable German, and French with a Paris accent. Otto Schenk knew her father well. A very rich man Schenk said. Tough and devoted to his paralysed daughter. The mother had died giving birth to the girl.

Schenk smiled as they sat there in Jamie's place, talking.

'Why all the questions?' Then not waiting for an answer he said, 'You've fallen for her, haven't you?'

Jamie smiled. 'She's very beautiful.' He paused. 'How do I get to see her again?'

'It won't be easy. Her father keeps everyone away from her. Doesn't want her to be involved and then dropped when they find out that there's never going to be any sex.'

'So how do I get to see her again?'

'I'll invite her and her old man for dinner and a couple of other people. See how it goes.'

'Will he let her come?'

'Only if he's with her.' He grinned. 'I'll keep him occupied and you can play her songs for her. How about Sunday?'

'Fine by me, Otto. Thanks.'

'Take good care of her.'

'I will.'

The evening had gone quite smoothly and Jamie had been surprised to find that the girl's father was rather different from what he had expected. He was undoubtedly a very shrewd, tough man but behind the aloofness was a wide-ranging mind. Jean-Paul Corot had a touch of Montaigne in his seeming isolation. He was very friendly with Schenk and rather formal with Jamie Frazer.

After the others had left Schenk said, 'You seem to have made a hit with Marie-Claire. Couldn't take her eyes off you. And her father obviously enjoyed an Englishman who could speak French and German.'

'A bit cool towards me I thought.'

'Not cool. Neutral maybe. But you've got to remember that he's been over these hurdles many times before. He isn't going to let her get hurt if he can possibly help it. But what about your side of the equation?'

'What d'you mean?'

'Do you want to be emotionally involved with a young woman who's very beautiful but who you can never make love to and who lives from day to day with a prognosis that says she'll be lucky to live another two years?'

'Is there nothing that can be done to help her?'

'If there were Jean-Paul would have done it.'

'Maybe I can help her just by being around.'

'I'm sure you can. But is that enough for you?'

'I'll make it enough if her father will let me.'

'I'll put a word in, Jamie. But it'll take time for him to relax about it.'

203

* * *

For several weeks Frazer had taken the girl in her wheelchair to the zoo and to the usual beauty spots and it was after he had returned her to her home after a visit to a concert that Jean-Paul Corot had taken him into his study. He stood with his back to the window as he looked at Jamie Frazer. He didn't beat around the bush.

'I want to ask you, Mr Frazer, what your interest is in my daughter.'

Frazer shrugged. 'I'm very fond of her. I find her a very pleasant companion.'

'You know that there's no possibility of any physical relationship with her?'

'I assumed that was the situation. I wasn't sure.'

'So where does your relationship with her go from here?'

'Mr Corot. I don't want to be either rude or antagonistic because I am well aware of your devotion to Marie-Claire, but you're turning what is a close and caring relationship into some kind of obstacle race.' He paused. 'I love your daughter very dearly and she seems to be very happy with me. Why don't we just leave it at that?'

'Would you be so interested if she wasn't an heiress?'

Frazer laughed. 'I wasn't aware that she was an heiress.' He stood up. 'I think this conversation should stop or you might say something that really annoys me.'

'What if she wanted to marry you?'

'Jean-Paul. Just relax.'

'Answer my question then.'

'Marie-Claire and I are quite content with our present relationship. If she wanted to marry me the answer would be that I'd be delighted and flattered. And your daughter knows that.' He paused for a moment and then said, 'You must get out of your mind that I'm fond of Marie-Claire out of pity because she is paralysed.' He paused and said quietly, 'Her mind is not paralysed, it's only her body that is frail.'

As the weeks went by Jean-Paul Corot's attitude had changed. Jamie Frazer was treated almost like a favourite son. Always made welcome at his home and no longer the watchful eye.

Frazer was already asleep when the phone rang and he reached for it in the dark.

'Yes. Who is it?'

'It's Otto. I need to see you, Jamie. It's urgent.'

'Where are you?'

'I'm at the Savoy in Fasanenstrasse.'

'Come on round.'

They sat in the small kitchen with a thermos of coffee between them on the table. As Frazer pushed across the basin of sugar cubes, he looked across at Schenk.

'What's the problem, Otto?'

'They're going to build a wall to cut off West Berlin from East Berlin.'

'Who's going to do this?'

'The Russians and the East Germans.'

'What makes you think that?'

'I do business in East Berlin. They've hired all my dumpers and lorries for six months. That's fifty vehicles. Then they want concrete-mixers and all the breeze-blocks I can lay my hands on for them. At least four other companies in construction have been given similar contracts. And their contracts and mine are with the Russian military.' He sighed. 'I've seen the marked-up maps. They mean business, Jamie. Your people should be warned.'

'How long before they start?'

'Everything's got to be on site in two weeks' time. Say another two weeks to get started, roughly the beginning of August.'

'Anything else?'

'Yes. It seems that Soviet troops are being brought in by the bus-load and they're in a barracks just outside the city. My contact said that Soviet army people will be in charge of the building operation. There are tanks and carriers parked in the streets in Pankow.'

'Do you think the Americans and the French know about this?'

'I'm sure they don't.'

'Thanks, Otto. I'll let London know. But God knows what they can do. It's a breach of the treaty.'

'And the start of the next war.'

'Why are they doing this?'

'Because people are leaving the Russian Zone in their thousands. Anyone with a skill is moving out. And those that are left are ready to riot.'

'Any idea of where they'll start building?'

'Yes. At Brandenburger Tor across Unter den Linden.'

'They really are asking for trouble.'

Frazer used the scrambler line to contact London but felt that they weren't understanding the significance of what he had to say. He booked himself onto a flight and asked Scott to meet him at the airport.

They sat in the coffee bar at Gatwick and Frazer gave Scott all that Schenk had told him. Scott listened carefully but Frazer got the impression that Scott saw it as so unlikely as to be not more than a rumour or some Moscow propaganda to keep down the East Berliners.

'If they really did this, Jamie, it would virtually be an act of war. I think at most they're bluffing. Just trying us out to see how we react.'

'And if it's not a bluff and they go ahead and do it, what do we do in reply?'

'God knows. We could either send our tanks in or do nothing. Shit or bust to put it bluntly.'

'Have you heard anything from our diplomats?'

'No.'

'From the Americans or the French?'

'Not a thing.'

At 5 a.m. on the morning of 13th August Frazer got a phone call from Schenk. He just said, 'They've started.'

Frazer stood in a group of people watching what was going on at Brandenburger Tor. The tanks were there already with guns capped but pointing in an arc from the zoo to Potsdamer Platz. There were Russian officers carrying side-arms and light machine-guns, busy giving shouted orders to the workmen unloading the breeze-blocks from the trucks while other men were busy mixing cement for the footings.

Frazer watched for an hour and then went back to his flat and phoned Scott to tell him the news. There was nothing on the German radio news about the building going on. He walked back to the Brandenburg Gate and by now there was a large crowd watching the operation, with people shouting insults and obscenities at the Russians who ignored it all.

It seemed incongruous to Frazer to see the Russians throwing down the gauntlet to the Western powers. It was a warm sunny day and Frazer remembered that the Sunday when Chamberlain declared war on Germany was also a warm sunny day. There was a theory that you didn't start a war until the harvest was in. Like everyone else in the crowd of onlookers Frazer wondered how it was going to end.

He heard on the mid-day news that there was to be a meeting that afternoon of the Joint Control Committee. He phoned Marie-Claire and took her out to the lake at Grunewald and called in at Schenk's house for a lemonade. That evening they were there again at a dinner-party Schenk was giving for his daughter's seventh birthday. Nobody mentioned anything about what was going on at the bottom of Unter den Linden but the men there talked together as they stood later in the garden. They all wondered what the Allies would do in response. The cynics said they'd do nothing and the others phoned relatives in Cologne, Hanover and Dusseldorf. Just checking in case of need.

London called him back for a couple of days to quiz him on who his informant had been but he had insisted on giving them no details.

When he got back to Tegel the following evening Jean-Paul was waiting for him at the airport. Marie-Claire was in hospital and was seriously ill. She had been asking for him all day.

The doctor said that there was no hope for her. She was terminally ill. Jamie and her father sat with her for three days and nights taking turns on a camp-bed the hospital staff had rigged up for them. She died peacefully in her sleep in the evening. Jean-Paul was beside himself with grief and Jamie had offered to move in with him for a few days and deal with the formalities of the funeral. It was a time that he knew he would never forget. Coping with the distraught man and his own sadness. Eventually he had agreed to stay permanently and even when Jean-Paul was beginning to come to terms with his loss he begged Jamie to stay on.

Chapter 39

'Is that you Graham?'

'Yeah.'

'You in chambers tomorrow?'

'Nine until ten-thirty.'

'I'll pop in and see you on my way.'

'OK. You all right?'

'Yeah. Fine.'

Kegan put the file on Graham Pollock's desk.

'This stuff you asked me to look at. Tell me again what it's for.'

'It's for this bloody libel case.'

'Why did you ask me to read it?'

Pollock looked surprised. 'Just a routine precaution. Why?'

'D'you pay for it?'

'No. Got it from my client.'

'Did he pay for it?'

'No idea. He could have. He's that kind of chap.'

'Good job you showed it to me.'

'Why?'

'It's a load of crap and it's so obviously crap that it would have made you a laughing-stock.'

'Go on. Tell me.'

'First of all the material itself. It's taken straight out of the *Spycatcher* book and a few others. Stuff cobbled together with titles like *The Truth about British Intelligence*. There isn't a single item that hasn't been published half a dozen times in one book or another. Most of it is figments of the imagination of some disgruntled chap who was once a clerk in the Home Office or something.' He paused. 'And that brings me to another thing. This chap who wrote it and signed it. He was a minor body in MI5.'

'So?'

'Sir James Frazer never had anything to do with MI5. He was Director-General of MI6. So even if the rubbish this chap wrote was true, it would still be nothing to do with Sir James Frazer.'

'But they're both to do with espionage.'

'About as far apart as you could get they are. MI5 operates in the UK to clobber our friends and enemies who try to spy on us. MI6 does the opposite and mainly overseas. Spying for our benefit on our friends and enemies. It's about like saying that the Prison Service and the High Court are the same because they're both to do with the law.' He smiled, pointing at the file. 'That cheeky bastard has taken your client for a ride.'

'Don't gloat, Micky. It doesn't become you.'

Kegan stood up. 'Can you really imagine Sir James Frazer clambering over backyard fences in the dark to bug Harold Wilson's phone?'

Graham Pollock sighed. 'I owe you one, Micky. I'll handle your next divorce for you.'

Kegan laughed. 'Spoken like a true Etonian, my boy.'

He looked again at the note before he put it back in his wallet. It was all he wanted to remember about Berlin. Well almost all.

It was hand-written in brown ink.

Dear Jamie,

Just a note to say thank you for everything. For two years of happiness for Marie-Claire. Happiness that she had never known before you came into our lives. It was wonderful to have a man I could trust with her without worrying. Always knowing that you would do and say the right thing.

And thank you too for staying with me when I so desperately needed help. I shall never forget it. No son could have been kinder, and for me you will always be my son.

If you ever need me I shall always be here for you.
All the love of Marie-Claire and Jean-Paul Corot.

Chapter 40

Healey had noticed that despite Frazer's self-assurance in answering the defendant's questions in court, he was beginning to be depressed in private. When Healey had questioned him tactfully about this, Frazer had said something that made Healey realise that there was so much that none of them really knew about Jamie Frazer.

'You won't understand, Francis. You can't. Nobody will understand. What depresses me is that after all the things that I have seen or experienced that are dreadful beyond belief and description, I should end up having to defend my life for such petty and tawdry reasons.' He paused. 'Just think of it. There's you and Pollock and Judge Hooper and all the panoply of the law and the courts to argue that those bastards have tried to make a quick buck out of blackening my whole life. This is nothing to do with justice. It's just an elaborate game. A charade. It's kind of sick.'

'The bank holiday will give us all a week off and we can forget all this for a bit.'

But Healey was aware of how banal his comment sounded against his friend's angry outburst.

Healey had taken a party of friends including Jamie and Adele to the races at Goodwood. They had picnicked in the sunshine and when the racing was over they had all gone down to Rose Cottage for drinks. There were a dozen of them sitting around on the lawn and Adele had persuaded them to play the game she called Favourites, where somebody had to suggest a subject such as music, books or films, and the others had to say what their favourite was. The books had ranged through *The Great Gatsby*, *Catcher in the Rye* to *Rebecca* and current novels. There was some surprise when Jamie chose Palgrave's *Golden Treasury*.

Helen Healey had suggested they each chose what nationality they would choose to be if they weren't Brits and give their reasons for the choice.

Three of them chose New Zealand, two chose France, the Healeys both chose Sweden, Adele and another woman opted for Canada and Jamie said nothing until he was pressed by Adele.

'I'd choose to be Italian.'

'Why, Jamie? Why on earth Italian?'

Someone laughed and said, 'Just the sunshine and pretty girls.'

Frazer shrugged and smiled. 'Those too.' He paused. 'There are so many reasons and some of them are just vague instincts. But I like Italians. They're the only really civilised people in Europe.'

Francis Healey smiled. 'What do you mean by civilised?'

'I mean that ordinary working-class people, not just rich people, go to the opera and have opinions about the performance. They care about painting and sculpture and music and writing. And . . .' he paused '. . . they like kids and families, they welcome them in cafes and restaurants. Loving people is OK and hating politicians is universal.'

Healey said, 'Is that all that being civilised amounts to, Jamie?'

'More or less.' He paused. 'But of course they also didn't have an Italian equivalent to Dachau and Belsen like the Germans had. Nor did they rape and pillage in Berlin like the Russians did.' He turned away impatiently and looked across at Adele. 'I think it's time to call it a day.'

She watched him walking in the garden when the others had gone. It was a clear night with a full moon that was bright enough to show the tension in his shoulders and the grim lines on his face. It was obvious that something had upset him but she had no idea what it was. Nobody had said anything provocative and he had seemed calm enough as he said his piece about the Italians. When he came in he smiled at her.

'How about a night-cap, honey?'

As he poured the drinks, she summoned up her courage.

'What was it upset you?'

He hesitated for a moment and then handed her her glass.

'Talking to those people and the stuff in court makes me feel like a monster. We're from different worlds and . . .' he shrugged hopelessly '. . . I can't explain it.'

'Try. For my sake. I want to help.'

'Nobody can help, honey, that's for sure.'

'Try me. Jamie. Give me a chance.'

He took a deep breath and then started talking as if he were talking to himself.

'They've never seen a man's face blown to pieces with his brains hanging out. They don't know how heavy a head or a leg is when it isn't attached to a body. They've never seen starving people fighting like animals over a crust of bread. They've never seen a woman breast-feeding a child that is long dead. They've never had to tell a woman that her husband isn't ever coming back again and lie about how he died trying not to talk as they beat him to death.'

He looked at her as if he didn't remember who she was and she took his hand.

'Let's go to bed, Jamie. Tomorrow we'll go to the boat.'

She wasn't sure what had woken her but she could hear the noise and it frightened her.

'What is it, Jamie? The noise?'

When there was no reply, she switched on the bedside lamp and turned to wake him up but his side of the bed was empty. The noise seemed to be coming from downstairs. She slipped on her dressing-gown and went downstairs. The lights were on in the hall and Jamie was standing there, his head back, trembling as he made desperate efforts to draw breath.

She rushed over to him, patting his back, but he impatiently brushed her hand away and she just stood there. She realised what the noise reminded her of. It was the noise the sea-lions made at feeding-time at the zoo. And then she saw Charlie Bates in his pyjamas and a torch in his hand.

'What's happening, Charlie? Has anyone called a doctor?'

'He won't have doctors, miss. Just leave him be. It goes as the stress goes. If it doesn't he'll pass out and that'll probably stop it.'

215

'Has he swallowed something?'

'No. It's something that happens from time to time. It just comes when he's under stress from something or other. I've seen this one coming for days. You just go and make us all a cuppa and I'll stay with him and settle him in a chair when it goes.'

'I don't like leaving him like this, Charlie.'

'There's nothing you can do, miss. I'll do whatever needs to be done. He generally beats it without passing out.'

Reluctantly she left them and headed for the kitchen.

He was sitting in the armchair, his bathrobe draped around his shoulders as she used a wet towel to wipe the sweat from his face and forehead. She could feel him trembling as he breathed slowly and cautiously.

Charlie Bates had said it was something to do with the war but he advised her not to talk about it or ask any questions. He'd be fine later that day but she should keep the windows open wherever he went.

An hour later he seemed to have completely recovered and as she sat beside his armchair he stroked her hair. 'I'll be OK now. Don't worry.'

'Is there anything I can do or anything you need? What about a paracetamol tablet?'

He smiled. 'I don't need anything, honey. How about you put me on a Fats Waller CD and then we'll go back to bed.'

After a while he had switched off the CD and walked with her in the garden. It was getting light and the birds were singing. He made her sleep in the guest bedroom so that she wouldn't be disturbed if he got up and had breakfast when Maggie Bates came in at 7.30.

She sat on the edge of the bed wondering what kind of thing in a war could cause the episode she had just witnessed. He had seemed so vulnerable, so wounded. And she wondered how it was that Fats Waller could seemingly do without trying what she couldn't do. She wondered too if Francis Healey knew about the attacks. As she switched out the light she wondered if just loving him was enough. Could you really love someone if you didn't understand them? She didn't wake until Jamie brought her her breakfast tray with a rose from the garden in a glass.

Chapter 41

When Le Tissier called him, Frazer had arranged to meet him at the Spread Eagle at Midhurst. The Frenchman was waiting for him in the lounge and took him upstairs to his room. Frazer smiled at all the papers and files laid out on the double bed.

As Frazer took over one of the cane chairs beside the bed, the Frenchman poured them each a glass of wine. As he held up his glass he said, 'Thanks for seeing me at such short notice. It gives me a chance of taking a holiday next month.' He waved towards the papers on the bed. 'It has to be in and registered in the next ten days.'

'So let me sign what I have to sign and you can fly back tonight to Paris.'

Le Tissier smiled. 'It's not as easy as all that, Jamie.'

'Why? What's the problem?'

'There's no problem but this is a lot of money and taking care of it is a big responsibility.'

Frazer shrugged. 'It's in your good hands, Pierre.'

Le Tissier sighed and took a deep breath. 'This money was a man's life. The reward for hard work and shrewd and inspired investment. Like you he lived very modestly. He had only one concern in his life and that was for Marie-Claire. When she died his life was virtually over. He had nothing to do. No aim. No hope even. He never stopped talking about your kindness and care for Marie-Claire.' He paused. 'When he made his will he left everything to you. It was all he had to give. So to me it's not just a lot of money I'm controlling but a man's life and his last wish.'

For long moments Frazer was silent and then he looked at Le Tissier.

217

'You're right, Pierre. I'm ashamed not to have seen it the way you saw it. So. Let's get on with what has to be done.'

'Briefly we've made almost 14 per cent gross profit before tax. That will bring it down to about 9 per cent net. It's spread very widely and I've had the whole trust computerised. The non-trust records and income are at your entire disposal. No restrictions, no accountability, the income and capital are yours to save or spend as you choose.'

'Sounds OK to me.' He paused. 'Do we pay you enough, Pierre?'

'Yes, thank you. Our agreement covers that. But there's one favour I'd like to ask for.'

'Tell me.'

'Could I have a free day every week to look after another account rather like this one?'

'In what way is it like this one?'

'It has to be handled with tact and kindness.'

'Can you tell me about it?'

'No. It's confidential but I can give you a rough idea. It's to administer the estate of a Frenchman who was in the Resistance in France and he fell in love with a girl who saved his life, hiding him from the Germans. They had a child but never got around to getting married. They're both dead and the estate is for the benefit of the daughter who's an alcoholic.'

There were several moments of silence before Frazer stood up and said, 'Take all the time it needs.' He looked at his watch. 'Have we finished?'

Le Tissier smiled. 'Just two copies of the accounts to sign.' He handed Frazer a biro and after he had signed both copies he handed back the pen and looked at the Frenchman. 'Does it depress you, all this clearing-up of people's lives?'

'No. The people matter to me.' He paused and smiled. 'And you matter to me too.'

Chapter 42

The morning news on the radio had said that it was going to be the hottest day of the summer so far and they had packed a hamper and a cold-box and gone down to the boat. There was an hour before they would be able to ease their way through the small Birdham lock that led into the main Chichester Channel and Frazer had spent the time checking the instruments and running the engines.

There were four boats ahead of them for locking-out and it was midday when they finally got through. There was a pleasant cool breeze as they headed down the channel and Adele sat on a canvas chair on the aft-deck. There were a lot of boats mainly heading back to Chichester Marina and they were on their own as they turned north into the Bosham channel. By the time they got to Bosham it was almost high-tide and they anchored in sight of the old church. But the small village was crowded with visitors and they dropped anchor so that the boat was kept steady by the flow. They decided to eat on board.

By the time they got back to Birdham the breeze had dropped and the red ensign at the stern hung down rather forlornly. It was beginning to get dark as Frazer unfurled the ensign and checked the mooring-lines and fenders. As Adele tidied the hamper and the cold-box he called out to her.

'Let's go to the Ship and have dinner.'

'Fine by me, Jamie. Can we go to the cottage first so that I can freshen up and change?'

He smiled. 'You don't need freshening up, honey. But OK if that's what you want.'

As always they had a good meal and as they sat over their coffee she said, 'How is it you always come to the Ship and never the Dolphin and Anchor?'

He shrugged. 'I guess I'm just used to this place. The D & A always seems to be full of hearty men drinking gallons of beer and talking loudly. The kind of men who snap their fingers at waiters and send the wine back swearing it's corked to show they're connoisseurs of Cabernet Sauvignon or whatever.' He smiled. 'We can always go to the Anchor if you'd like a change.'

'No. I like it here.' She smiled. 'And it's very you.'

He laughed. 'Dull and rather boring.'

'Not at all. Modest, friendly, and always reliable.'

He smiled. 'Thanks. How about we walk down to the cathedral and have a look at the new floodlighting?'

'Yes. I'd love that.'

North Street was quite busy with late-night strollers as they made their way down to the cross and turned into West Street past the Dolphin and Anchor, standing to look across the street at the cathedral.

'It's beautiful, isn't it?'

He took her arm. 'Let's cross over and walk around the outside.'

There were bright lights inside as they stood at the open door and a man hurried over to them.

'I'm afraid the cathedral's closed, perhaps . . . Sir James . . . my apologies. I didn't recognise you in this hazy light. How are you?'

'I'm fine. The new lighting of the building is wonderful.'

'Yes it is. I'm on duty this evening. I could give you a quick look around if you wish. The cleaners will be another hour yet but I have to keep on the move.'

'Let me introduce my companion – Adele Burton – the Reverend Mortimer.'

They shook hands and said the usual things.

'Let's go. Follow me.' As they went inside the Reverend turned to Adele. 'You know this man read the lesson here in the cathedral at Sunday service way back in 1940, when he was doing his training up at the Royal Sussex barracks.' He sighed. 'I was in the congregation that day and I remember feeling rather sad. That young man in his battle-dress reading out the lesson. I wondered what was going to happen to him. So many of them didn't come back.' He waved his arm impatiently as if to brush away his thoughts. 'Let's get on with the quick tour.'

He had shown them Graham Sutherland's tapestry in the chapel and John Piper's vivid tapestry hanging from a sixteenth-century oak screen. Then what is called the Sailors' Chapel, a memorial to Sussex men who died at sea in the war and had no known graves. Finally he led them to the Chapel of St George, the chapel of the Royal Sussex Regiment.

'You show Adele the bits and pieces, Jamie, and I'll go and check the cleaners. If I'm not back to escort you, just go back the way we came.'

She sat down on an upholstered bench as they looked at the long list of the names of the Royal Sussex dead from the two wars. The regimental standards looked tattered but imposing.

'Do you remember this chapel, Jamie?'

'Not really. I wasn't religious, it was just another parade so far as I was concerned. But I loved reading the lesson.' He smiled. 'Made me feel important.'

She didn't smile. 'I can't bear to think of you then. So young and so defenceless. Nobody to fall back on. Nobody to rely on.' She sighed. 'I wish I'd been around in those days.'

He smiled. 'You'd be a beautiful old lady now, my dear.'

'So what. At least I'd have been able to stick up for you.'

He was silent for several moments and then he said, 'You know. What you just said is the nicest thing anyone has said to me for a long, long time.'

'More's the pity, my love. More's the pity.' And she burst into tears, her face in her hands. For a moment he was taken aback and then he sat down beside her on the bench and put his arm around her.

'Don't be sad, sweetie. I've survived and I've got you to take care of me now.'

She turned to look at him, her cheeks wet with tears. 'Do I take care of you, Jamie?' She sighed. 'I love you so much.' As he stroked her hair she looked at his face. 'Tell me you care about me too, Jamie. Please.'

'I think there are at least two kinds of love. One is steady and true and reliable. It just goes on and on. It passes no judgment on the person loved. They are just themselves.' He paused. 'And then there is what the French would call love "*à la folie*". A kind of madness. Nothing else matters. No other person matters. It's very often obsessive. It's waiting for a telephone to ring that doesn't ring. It's hanging about in the rain in the hope of seeing that other person. It can be selfish, and you can get hurt. Both of you. Whatever happens it stays with you for the rest of your life.'

'Have you ever loved anyone "*à la folie*"?'

'Yes.'

'How does one know which love is real?'

'That's easy to define but very hard to do. Real love is loving the other person more than you love yourself. Being ready and willing to sacrifice your own happiness for the sake of theirs.'

She had watched his face intently as he spoke the words slowly and she shivered as babies do when they have been crying.

'I couldn't want more than just you caring, Jamie. And that's all that I'll ever look for. I count myself very lucky.' For a moment she glanced at the names on the plaque and the draped regimental flags and then she stood up, smiling as she wiped her eyes with the back of her hand.

'If ever I get down, Jamie, this is where I'll come. I feel I belong here.' She smiled a watery smile. 'You, me and the Royal Sussex.' She paused. 'There's your friend the Reverend, waving to us, I think he wants us to go.'

Chapter 43

Frazer spent most of his free time at Schenk's house and Anna had become part of his life. It had been a chance meeting that had changed all that. He had been browsing in the bookshop near the Europa Centre when he saw the pretty girl smiling and waving to him from the street. When he realised who it was he'd put down the book he was holding and walked out of the shop.

'How nice to see you. Have you got time to have a coffee with me?'

She laughed. 'Of course I have. I'm glad I saw you because I need to check something with you.' She paused. 'It's your birthday next week, isn't it? The twenty-fourth?'

He smiled. 'Yes it is. I'd forgotten about it.'

'I've just bought your birthday present and I want to make sure it's all right with you.'

'I'm sure it will be. What is it? I can't wait.'

'It's some tickets for us to go that night to the concert.' She paused as she looked up at his face. 'It's the Mendelssohn Violin Concerto. Karajan and Ann-Sophie Mutter and the Max Bruch as well.' She was smiling up at him. 'Will you come with me?'

For once Frazer was at a loss for words. He stood looking past her at the people in the square, unaware of the noise of the traffic and life going on around them.

'Are you all right, Jamie?'

He shook his head like a dog coming out of the water and put his hands gently on her shoulders as he looked at her face.

'Why did you bother?'

'Because I wanted to please you.'

223

'Why should you want to please me?'

'Because I care about you.'

For a moment his arms went around her and he bent his head so that his forehead was touching hers. Then he lifted his head and looked at her and she saw the tears on his face.

She said very quietly, 'I love you, Jamie. I always have. Even when I was a little girl.' She smiled. 'You'd better get used to it.'

They spent all Frazer's free time together and Otto Schenk seemed to take it all in his stride. As a father he found the difference in their ages a disadvantage but as a man he had experienced enough of the world's evils to be glad that at least his daughter had found a man who really was a man. Lonely himself he was aware of the difference that the girl had made to that man. They were obviously happy together and that was all he could hope for.

As the weeks and months went by he found some peace himself despite his loneliness.

Schenk didn't recognise the man who approached him as he got out of his car.

'Herr Schmidt?'

'That's me.'

The man smiled. 'Or should I say Herr Schenk?'

'You can say what you like but my name's Schmidt.'

'And my name's Weber. Hans Weber. Your new partner.'

Schenk stared at the man. 'Are you crazy? I don't have partners. Old or new.'

'We'd better talk about it, Herr Schenk. It would be crazy to ruin a very successful business for want of listening. How about we go for a cup of coffee and talk about it?'

'Look, mister, if you don't piss off I'll call the police.' And Schenk waved the cell-phone in his hand.

The man smiled. 'And then you could watch your business go down the pan. You wouldn't sound too good answering questions in the bankruptcy court about false documents and other things.'

Schenk shook his head in disbelief and turned to walk to the steps leading into his office building, but the man caught his arm and held him back. He said quietly, 'Otto Schenk. Or should I say Sturmbannfuhrer Otto Schenk, Waffen SS. Special Group 390 attached to Leibstandarte Adolf Hitler. War criminal and black-marketeer. Wanted for trial by the Russians for crimes committed in the Ukraine and elsewhere.'

For a moment Schenk felt as if he were going to faint. He was aware of the distant hum of traffic and found it difficult to breathe. Slowly his surroundings came into focus again but as he stared at the man he was lost for words. Then the man said, 'Let's walk down to the Savoy and have a coffee.'

Schenk was silent but he turned and walked with the man who was still holding his arm. He walked slowly, his eyes on the pavement in front of him as he desperately tried to gather his thoughts. He was barely aware of them going into the Savoy and heading for the leather armchairs in the small bar-lounge. He heard the man order coffees for them and then turn to him.

'Let's start all over again, Otto. My name's Weber. Hans Weber. We've no need to make a song and dance out of this situation. Neither of us benefits from that.' He smiled and patted Schenk's leg. 'Here's the coffee coming. Have a drink and it'll help you settle down.'

Schenk took a deep breath and said, 'What's this all about? Who are you?'

'I'm a private investigator, Otto. And quite by chance I came across some old records. Operation Orion wasn't it? Very naughty of the Brits to use people who were wanted as war criminals. And very careless to leave the records hanging around in the vaults of the Stadion.'

'How were you able to have access to such records? And why were you interested in me?'

Weber laughed softly. 'I wasn't interested in you, Otto, I was interested in something very different – a Brit intelligence officer who'd used his job to smuggle very valuable paintings that had been stored in a salt-mine near Hanover. I just came on your stuff by accident.'

'But how did you get access to such files?'

'I was hired by the British themselves. They wanted to trace the paintings as part of some deal with the government in Bonn.' He smiled. 'I didn't find what I was looking for but I found your stuff. I was sure we could do a deal.'

'Why should I do a deal?'

'Saves standing trial as a war criminal. False papers. False identity. The Russians would probably ask for you to be extradited.'

'Blackmail, yes?'

'Yes.'

Schenk was beginning to get back into the world and he knew that it was trouble. Real trouble. And young Anna would inevitably be heart-broken. He looked at Weber. He guessed he was about forty or so. Cool, calm and ruthless.

'And what's your idea of a deal?'

'Ten per cent off the top. Everything.'

Weber reached inside his jacket pocket and pulled out a bunch of papers folded in half and held with a rubber band. He handed them to Schenk.

'I've done a summary of all your business, Otto. Those are the details I'll be working to so that there's no misunderstanding.' He nodded. 'Have a look at them.'

Schenk slid off the elastic band and unfolded the papers. There were about a dozen A4 pages and he looked at each one carefully. He wasn't in a fit state to absorb the details but he recognised that most of the figures were accurate and only one aspect of his wealth was not included, a deposit of bonds in the vaults of a bank in Brunswick. He folded the papers slowly and put on the elastic band before offering them back to Weber.

Weber shrugged and said, 'Keep them if you want. They're only copies.'

'How do you expect the money to be paid? I'll have to show it in my accounts and tax returns.'

Weber smiled. 'You hire me as a consultant. And I get a cheque on the first of the month.' He paused. 'There'll be a separate payment for the documents themselves. Just your file.'

'How much?'

'Let's say half a million D-Marks in US dollars or pounds sterling.' Schenk did a quick calculation. It would be about £75,000.

'I'll think about it, Herr Weber.'

Weber shook his head slowly. 'Don't let's play games, Otto. You just give me a contract as a consultant. The fee. Four lines of typing should do it and I'll bring you the file tonight at your office.' He paused. 'Don't try playing games. It's you who'd go down the pan, not me. Remember that.'

'What time?'

'Seven OK?'

'Yes. I'll need your full name, address, bank.'

'No problem.' Weber stood up. 'Take it easy, Otto. At least you'll know it's the end of that particular story.'

It was only two blocks to Schenk's office but he took a taxi. He sat at his desk for about an hour. Trying to absorb what had happened. But his mind wouldn't cope with his thoughts of defiance and anger and disbelief. It didn't seem real. But what a fool he'd been to trust the Brits and to trust Frazer. Never a word of warning from the man whose life he'd saved. But life was about learning lessons. An expensive lesson for him but he would ride with it.

He had been busy for the rest of the day. Arranging the security guards at the house. Working out the words of the contract for his secretary to type. But the part he dreaded was telling Anna. Forbidding her any contact ever again with Frazer. At twenty-one she'd never had eyes for any man apart from Jamie Frazer. And what was more he couldn't tell her why. His last job was to draw half the so-called introductory payment to Weber. He already had the balance in his office safe. He had bought two small Sony recorders and set the timers to cover those hours from 7 p.m. before he put them underneath his desk. He wasn't sure why he wanted to record the meeting with Weber but it seemed like it might be some sort of insurance. He'd checked again with the security service and they confirmed that one of their men was already at his house.

Frazer parked at the main gate and walked across the grass verge to where the man was standing, and as Frazer went to go past him he held out his arm.

'Are you Herr Frazer, sir?'

'Yes. What's going on?'

'I've got a message from the owner of the property for you. He's ordered me to tell you that you are no longer welcome at his home and

227

he does not want any further contact with you.'

'You're kidding.'

'I'm not, sir.'

'Will you tell Fraulein Anna that I'm here?'

'The same applies to her, sir.'

'What are you for Christ's sake? You're not a police officer.'

'I work for Sanger Security, sir.'

'Has something happened? Is Otto OK?'

'I'm not allowed to discuss anything with you.'

'Will you tell him I called please?'

'He knows you've called, sir.'

'You mean he's in the house?'

'No comment, sir. It would be better if you just left.'

For a few moments Frazer hesitated in disbelief and then he walked slowly back to his car.

Back at the flat he dialled Schenk's phone number and a recorded woman's voice informed him that the number was not available. The next day he phoned Schenk's office numbers, both the public number and a direct line. There was no response from either of them. For two days he made no attempt to contact Schenk and then he went through the telephoning process again, but with the same result. That day he wrote and posted a letter to Schenk but there was no reply in the next few days. This prompted Frazer to go to Schenk's offices but found another guard standing impassively in front of the elevator doors. He obviously recognised Frazer and shook his head.

'I'm afraid not, sir. And this is private property and I must ask you to leave.'

'Is Herr Schenk here?'

The guard just shook his head without replying. Frazer turned and left. As he walked back to his flat he realised that possibly the only way he could find out what was going on was to hire somebody to do a surveillance job on Schenk. But what really puzzled him was what was Anna's part in this strange scenario. He knew also that he would never be able to bring himself to have her put under surveillance.

The phone on the bedside table rang and Frazer, still with his eyes shut, reached for the phone.

'Yeah.'

'Jamie, are you all right?'

He sat up quickly. 'Anna, what the hell's been going on?'

'I don't know, Jamie. He's been like a mad thing. Something's terribly wrong but I've no idea what it is. He had to have the doctor because he had a minor heart problem and the doctor warned me not to let him get worked up or he'd probably have a stroke. I don't want to upset him but I'm longing to see you. How can we meet? I think he's having your flat watched.'

'Does he let you go out?'

'Not at first but I told him I'd move out if he didn't leave me alone. He eventually agreed so long as I didn't contact you.'

'Tomorrow at the zoo. By the lions. Can you make that?'

'What time?'

'You say.'

'11 a.m.'

'OK.'

'I love you, Jamie.'

'I love you too.'

It was a sunny day but she was sitting on a bench by the lion enclosure in a black coat with a fur collar fastened up to hide most of her face. He nodded to her and walked slowly past. She followed him to the flower gardens and he turned and hugged her.

'It's lovely to see you. Are you being followed?'

'I don't know. I thought I'd better act as if I was being followed.'

'D'you know *Theater des Westens*?'

'Yes.'

'Take a taxi there and wait for me by the booking office.'

They ended up in an ice-cream parlour in Charlottenburg sitting at a table away from the windows.

'I just don't know, Jamie. He came home very late that night. I was in bed but I heard him shouting on the telephone. When I got downstairs he could hardly speak. I asked him what was the matter and he calmed down and said he'd been betrayed and then went on to say that I was forbidden to ever see you again or contact you in any way. Then the first guard arrived and I went back to bed. When I tried to telephone you the next day the operator said I could only receive calls on our new line. Father had a mobile. About ten days later I had to call the doctor for the pains in his chest. The doctor said he had a heart condition. He gave him drugs and told me he mustn't be excited or scared and the condition would settle down.'

'How did you get to phone me?'

'I bought myself a mobile and kept it hidden.'

'And he still hasn't told you what it was all about?'

'He never talks about it and I don't ask in case he gets upset.'

'Are you allowed out?'

'I am now that he seems to assume that I wouldn't disobey him about you.'

'Is there any surveillance on you?'

'I'm pretty sure there isn't. Maybe for the first week but not after it had settled down.'

'And he's given no hint of what it's all about?'

'Not the slightest. But it's changed him a lot whatever it was.'

'In what way?'

She thought for a moment. 'He's lost his self-assurance. He's almost a different man. And I think his heart is worse than they say it is.'

'How is he with you?'

'A bit guarded but loving and caring as always. It makes me feel a bit of a traitor even eating an ice-cream with you.'

He smiled. 'Don't feel like that. Whatever the reason he's not being reasonable. If I've said or done something that's offended him he should just tackle me about it, not change two people's lives without even an explanation or an attempt to put it right.'

'There's nothing that you can think of that's made him like this?'

'Not a thing. I've tried to contact him but I'm turned away by his wretched guards. I wrote him a letter but had no reply. I can't get through on the phone.' He paused. 'It's irrational, honey, by any standards.'

'What can we do, Jamie?'

'What do you want to do?'

She shrugged. 'Just get back to how things were.' She paused and looked at him. 'Are you offended by all this?'

'No. Of course not. Puzzled, irritated, but that's with him not us.'

'Tell me what to do?'

'Do you want us to carry on? Or would it give you more peace of mind if we waited until enough time had gone by?'

'I want us to be like we were. Why should we stop caring for one another because of something we don't even know about? He's being unreasonable and I can't confront him because he's a sick man.'

'Is it OK for me to call you on your mobile?'

'Yes. But if he's around I'll pretend you're one of my girl-friends.'

'OK. Let me think about what we should do and I'll phone you tomorrow and we'll meet here again.'

'I wish I could just move in with you today but I can't bear to think of what would happen to him.'

'Don't worry. We'll find a compromise.'

Chapter 44

The flat was furnished. A living room, bedroom, bathroom and kitchen. It was old-fashioned but the furnishings were well-made, most of them pre-war. All they had to provide was linen, cutlery and crockery. It had its own entrance from the street up a flight of stairs to the first floor. Its old-fashionedness gave it an air of solidity. Thomas Mann would have recognised it even though it wasn't in Hamburg.

She sat on the edge of the bed looking up at him. 'I'll feel terrible about deceiving him but there's no other way, is there?'

'Not that I can think of at the moment. We could just go on meeting at odd places a couple of times a week.'

She shook her head slowly. 'That's no way for us to live, Jamie. And it's all so crazy anyway that we don't even know what it's all about. I've asked him again and again but he just won't discuss it. It's not us that's the problem. It's him.' She sighed. 'But he's been such a good father to me, Jamie. I hate having to deceive him.'

'What about telling him what we're going to do.'

'The doctor said he must avoid any stress or he'll end up in hospital.'

'How about you think about it for a couple of days?'

'I don't need to think about it. I want to see you every day.' She shrugged. 'And if this is how we do it, so be it.' She smiled up at him. 'I like this place already. It's ours.'

They were sitting on a bench in the Tiergarten. The area that had once been the embassy quarter was now being developed with new buildings and with an emphasis on culture with open-air concerts and even a memorial to the German Resistance and the men who were so mercilessly executed on 20th July 1944. The Tiergarten, despite the museums and new buildings, had been taken over by ordinary Berliners. The diplomats had given way to family picnics. A hundred yards from the bench where they were sitting were statues of Lessing, Goethe, Wagner and Lortzing. They had survived the war and now nobody had the heart to remove them.

It was six months since they had taken the apartment near Savigny Platz and Anna's guilt had receded so that their rather strange life had become normality.

She was looking at a tape that he had bought her. Von Karajan and Ann-Sophie Mutter and the Mendelssohn Violin Concerto.

'I can remember the first time I heard this.' She turned to look at him, smiling. 'It was on the radio at home and you made everyone stop talking and listen to it. You were sitting on a chair alongside Marie-Claire. Holding her hand. And I was madly in love with you, wishing that it was my hand you were holding.' She laughed. 'I'd have settled for you holding both our hands.'

He smiled. 'I was nearly the same age as your father.'

'That's got nothing to do with it. I wanted to be loved like you loved Marie-Claire.' She smiled. 'I still do.'

'When this is all settled, where would you like to live?'

She frowned, thinking, and then she looked at his face, smiling as she said, 'I'll say what Ruth said – "whither thou goest, I will go, and where thou lodgest I will lodge".'

Jamie Frazer laughed. 'But Ruth was saying that to her mother-in-law, Naomi.'

She shook her head in disbelief. 'How is it you always know these things?'

He stood up slowly and held out his hand to help her up alongside him. 'I've got a small thing for you back at our place.'

'What is it?'

'You'll have to wait and see.'

She sat perched on the edge of the bed as she unwrapped the small packet and then carefully opened the little box. She gasped as she saw the silver ring with its intertwined hearts and looked up at him. 'It's so beautiful, Jamie.'

'Try it on.'

She slid it onto her finger and it was, of course, a perfect fit. At the bottom of the box was a folded piece of paper which she opened. In Jamie's neat writing it said, 'This is for you, my lovely girl. Remember the song by Chaminade: *"This little silver ring which once you gave to me, keeps in its narrow band, every promise of ours."* Jamie.'

Jamie Frazer at that time had been fully occupied in building up archives on ex-Nazis who had worked their way back into positions of influence in government and industry. London's instinct was to hinder their progress or put pressure on Bonn to throw them out. But Frazer had been involved in German life far too long not to be aware that being a member of the Nazi party could stem from a variety of pressures and temptations. In those days most official jobs required you to be a party member. It included most jobs from teaching to driving heavy goods vehicles. But it was the date when they joined that mattered. Joining in 1938/9 was not significant. But if the joining date was 1932/5 the man was classed as a 'premature Nazi'. The problem for the German government in Bonn was that anyone with experience in administration of any kind was almost certainly a party member from the early days. The Germans resented the intervention of Military Government deciding who could or could not be employed in even local government and it led to a strange anomaly where men who had been anti-Nazi or apolitical were being cold-shouldered by those who had thrived in Hitler times.

It was apparent that Frazer's cover as a journalist worked very well. He was classified as a 'foreign correspondent' so that there was no need for his name to appear on a by-line. His role was the broad panorama of German affairs. The work also allowed him to assess potential recruits and contacts for SIS. Not only from Germans but from other foreign members of the press corps. There was talk from time to time of it being more useful if he were based in Bonn but his relationship with Anna and the tension in his life with her father made him against the move. And quite genuinely Berlin was where anything happened. Bonn was the Federal capital but it was a city for time-servers and paper-pushers.

As a couple they didn't socialise but Frazer found it irksome that she couldn't take any part in his official life and he was aware that she was often lonely when he had to attend social occasions at the various consulates. It seemed to him senseless that they had to go through this charade just because of her father's inexplicable attitude. They didn't actually avoid the places where Schenk was likely to be and the man was now virtually a recluse in the house in Grunewald. He went to his office two or three days a week but he no longer talked with Anna about his business affairs. Neither did he ask her any longer where she spent her time or talked about how she lived.

Their love and affection for each other was their compensation for the restrictions on having a normal life. It was a time that made him aware that he had no friend close enough to talk about his circumstances. And he was constantly concerned that for a young girl it was a complete distortion of what her life should be. The underlying tensions, the guilt about disobeying her father and her awareness of their strange relationship. She never complained but needed constant reassurance that he loved her despite the restrictions. By any normal standards their lives were grotesque and an unnecessary strain on both of them and their emotions. So many unspoken evasions and so many heart-breaking partings that put a burden on love that others could take for granted. Twice Frazer had seriously considered confronting Schenk but there was always that threat of bringing on a serious heart attack. Frazer wasn't a religious man but he believed that the Good Lord sometimes sent you signs. Signs to do something – or to forget it. Without giving it much thought he reckoned that this was one of those situations where you waited for a sign from God. No matter how long it took.

Frazer had had lunch that day at the Savoy with one of the SPD's senior people. The SPD man obviously knew a lot about Frazer's time in the early days after the German surrender, especially Frazer's close relationship with the man who was then the leader of the SPD, Erich Schumacher.

'I was told that you knew Schumacher very well. What was he like?'

'When I knew him he was just out of a concentration camp. He was a very sick man, and very tired. Tired of politics and tired of life. He'd survived the camps as an act of defiance but now that pressure had gone the fighting spirit had gone too.'

'How often did you see him?'

'About once a week.' Frazer smiled. 'He smoked at least two packs a day and I was able to keep him supplied.'

'Was he disillusioned about socialism?'

'No. His disillusion was about mankind in general. He'd suffered too much and seen too much to care any longer about inter-party fighting, either locally or nationally. He let them use him, his name and his reputation but he knew he was dying.' Frazer paused. 'Why's the SPD in such a mess today?'

'The old, old story. Too many contenders for the leadership. All fighting one another instead of the CDU.'

'Who's going to come out on top?'

The man smiled. 'The CDU and Deutsche Bank.'

Frazer had chosen the Savoy for lunch because it gave him time to pick up the anniversary present for Anna on his way to his own place and then on to their flat at Savigny Platz. It would be two years of their relationship the next day.

At the jewellers in Fasanen Strasse he had checked the work they had done putting their initials on the linked hearts of the gold chain bracelet. They wrapped it in tissue-paper and arranged it with his message card in the velvet-lined box.

Back at his place Frazer checked the machine but there were no recorded messages. He looked at his watch. It was 4 p.m. and they were due to meet at their place at 5 p.m.

He sat at his desk and wrote his notes on the meeting with the SPD man. It looked as if London were backing the wrong horse in Bonn. He tried Anna's mobile number but there was just the woman's voice saying that 'the number was unavailable, please try later'. He guessed she was probably already on her way. There was time to get her some flowers from the stall by Zoo Bahnhof. He chose a bunch of early chrysanthemums and a single red rose.

He was still early as he slid his key into the lock of the street-door and walked up the stairs to their place on the first floor. As he opened the door he had a strange feeling. Everything was in its usual place but the room seemed oddly silent. The kind of silence that said that nobody lived there anymore.

He walked into their bedroom to put her present on her pillow and saw the envelope on his pillow. There was a moment's pleasure as he realised that she had remembered the day. There was just his name – Jamie – on the envelope. He opened it and took out the two pages of her handwriting and stood there reading it in disbelief. When he had finished he sat down on the edge of the bed and read the note again.

The day following their last meeting she had confronted her father and told him that their relationship was more important than whatever his objections were. He had collapsed as he tried to reply and he had been taken to a private hospital. The consultant said that it was a severe stroke but he would recover after a few weeks' nursing. He had asked if there was any stress and she had told him the truth. She had decided that she was the root of the problem and that she was making it impossible for the three of them to live normal lives. There seemed to be only one solution. She was going away and would not be coming back to Berlin. She said it was the saddest day of her life but she could no longer cope with the situation. She knew he would be sad too but she wanted him to have the chance of a normal life. She had added a postscript.

P.S.

You gave me a book of English poems a long time ago and there was a verse that says what I feel so much better than I can say it myself. It's by a poet named de la Mare.
> Like truthless dreams
> So are my joys expired.
> Beyond recall are
> all my dandled days.

P.P.S.

I love you so much, dear Jamie, and I'll always be your loving, loving Anna.

He sat there for a long time. Trying to absorb the contents of the note. Part of him wanting to make phone calls to try and trace where she had gone but he knew in his heart that it would be unfair to her. She must have been desperately unhappy to take this step and she had probably worked out that this was the only way she could deal with the situation. But it *wasn't* the only way. This way two people were unhappy for the sake of that fool Schenk who would suffer as well because he had lost his daughter. He wished that he was a drinker so that he could get blind drunk just to get through the night.

He moved about the place for an hour or so seeing if there was anything she had taken as a souvenir. But nothing had gone. They were the same rooms. Except that they never would be the same again.

As he walked back to his own place he was aware again that he had no friend, nobody to talk to about what had happened. But that was the job. That was the way he had survived for so long. Just him and the signs from God.

Chapter 45

It had been a miserable weekend of rain and winds despite the fact that it was the second week in June, and in court there was an air of discontent. Counsel discontented with their juniors, juniors with managing clerks and managing clerks with their clients, the solicitors.

Sir Graham Pollock straightened his wig, fiddled with his gown and moved a pile of papers in front of him. He realised that they were the wrong papers but he looked up to Sir James in the witness stand.

'Sir James, you took strong objection to references in the book to your attitude to the Communist party.'

'That's correct.'

'But isn't it true that you had a lot of contact with Communists?'

'I arrested and interrogated a lot of Communists if that's what you mean.'

'But you had a reputation for being rather friendly, if I can put it that way, with those people who you arrested.'

'Being friendly, or seeming to be friendly is one of the aspects of successful interrogation.'

'So your friendliness was calculated. A ploy. A deception?'

'Not always.'

'When was it something else?'

'I very often found that I had a lot in common with the man concerned.'

'Were these men Communists?'

'Most of them were. At least nominally. They were like members of most political parties. They joined and were members but they were not interested in politics.'

'So why did they become Party members?'

'To gain promotion, maybe, or even just to keep their jobs.'

'And you found you had a fellow-feeling for these unfortunates?'

'No. Not exactly. All I recognised was that we had a lot in common. We were recruited the same way, trained the same way and we carried out similar tasks.'

'When you were on *Desert Island Discs* you said that you had more Christmas cards from people you'd arrested or interrogated than from other people. Was that a joke?'

'No. It was true for a number of years.'

'You were also on a BBC programme called *Start the Week* several times, yes?'

Frazer shrugged. 'Yes.'

Sir Graham picked up a piece of paper and seemed to read it. It was actually a letter from his bank but he behaved as if he were reading from some piece of evidence.

'On one of these programmes. The second appearance I believe, you said', and he glanced at the paper as if checking the words, 'you said words to the effect that there was no difference between Communism and Christianity.' He paused and frowned at Sir James. 'Is that really your opinion, Sir James?'

'Well, first of all that isn't what I said.'

'What did you say? Pray tell us in your own words.'

'I said that Communism and Christianity both suffered from the same disadvantage. They didn't work because nobody had ever actually tried them. The Soviet Union was far from Marx's manifesto and western civilisation gave similar lip-service to Christianity but never actually got around to trying it.'

Pollock smiled as one smiles at a child's babbling. 'An interesting insight into how the intelligence man's mind works.' He looked up sharply at Sir James. 'Are you political, Sir James?'

'I'm not a member of any political party. Nor have I ever been.'

'Tell the court about your membership of the Left Book Club, Sir James.'

'It was just a book club. You paid half-a-crown a month and they sent you a book.'

'A book on politics?'

'Not always.'

'Tell me one that wasn't about politics.'

'Marriage and Birth Control by Dr Griffith.'

'Sir James, let me read to you a sentence or two from a leaflet enclosed with the books. I quote – "There are now over 1,100 local Left Book Club groups . . . these groups are often the activising element in the local political life." ' He looked up. 'And it also says that the Club is designed as a piece of machinery. End of quote.' He let the paper fall to the desk as he looked at Frazer. 'A bit more than just a book club, Sir James.'

'So far as I was concerned it was just a book club. Nothing more.'

'Were some of the books written by well-known leftist extremists?'

'Four or five of them became ministers in the 1945 government under Mr Attlee. Another became Attorney-General if I remember rightly. And another was the Dean of Canterbury.'

'Did you ever attend Communist Party meetings, Sir James?'

'Yes. Quite frequently at one time when it was part of my job to penetrate various groups.'

'How come that you were accepted in such meetings? Surely a serving officer in British Intelligence would be less than welcome.'

'I used a false identity and forged documentation.'

'It is claimed in the book that you were for several years the official supervising all penetration operations against the Soviet Union and the Warsaw Pact. Is that a fair description?'

'I guess so. In lay terms.'

'So you had a very long and close interest in Communist affairs.'

'Yes.'

'Shortly after you were appointed Director-General of MI6 there was a scare that there was what intelligence people call a "mole" operating inside MI6 on behalf of the Soviets.'

'It certainly wasn't a scare. There was a suspicion that somebody was leaking information to the Soviets. But it was part of our normal operations to be concerned about the possibility that there was a mole inside the organisation. It was the main aim of the KGB to establish a mole.'

'Somebody in a senior position. Like Philby, Burgess and Maclean for instance.'

'There was no particular profile. It could be anybody.'

Sir Graham paused. 'Even somebody like you?'

'Like I said, it could be anybody.'

'Is it not the case that you yourself were interrogated and investigated as a possible mole soon after you took over as D-G?'

'Every person above a certain grade was interrogated by a special team. I was no exception.'

'And were you cleared of that suspicion?'

'I was cleared but there was no suspicion involved. It was a general check not a personal one.'

Sir Graham turned to look at Lord Justice Hooper. 'Thank you, milord.'

Hooper looked at Howard Rowe with lifted eyebrows.

'Anything further Mr Rowe?'

'Just one question, milord.' Rowe turned to look at Frazer. 'Roughly how many MI6 officers were investigated by that committee, Sir James?'

'Between forty and fifty.'

'And did they find a so-called "mole"?'

'No.'

Lord Justice Hooper interrupted. 'Right. I think this is an appropriate moment to adjourn. We'll continue at 2 p.m.'

He stood up, bowed cursorily at the court in general and swept out to his room and sandwiches with his wife. She wasn't impressed with the sandwiches. She felt the smoked salmon was too bland even with a squeeze of lemon.

'That Jamie's no more a Commie than you are. What rubbish.'

'How do you know these things, Sadie?'

'I can tell by looking at their faces. He's far too handsome to be a Commie.'

'What do you reckon Commies look like?'

'They wear glasses and they have beards and they're bald on the front.'

'That describes about a third of the male population. I've seen Sean Connery in a film looking like that. It was set in Moscow.'

'Don't you dare say a word about Sean Connery. He's a real lovely man. That other one, your friend Graham Pollock, looks like a Commie to me as well.'

Lord Justice Hooper wiped his mouth and fingers on the statutory paper napkin and stood up.

'Are you staying this afternoon?'

'No. I'm meeting Joanna. She's getting me tickets for Wimbledon.'

He bent and kissed the top of her head.

'I'm going for a pee and then into court. I'll get the official driver to drive me home. Take care.'

'And you my boy.'

She patted his backside as he put on his wig and arranged what she called his 'bib and tucker'. Despite what they said, she thought that men were just as vain as women and rather childish with it.

Sir Graham had planned to bring up the question of wives as late as possible so that it would be in Judge Hooper's mind overnight. Lord Justice Hooper had been married to the same lady for over thirty years. But Sir Graham's efforts at trying to date various markers in Frazer's career had not taken as long as he had hoped. So there was nothing left but to get on with it. He took a deep breath.

'Sir James. One of the pieces in the book that you highlighted as being grossly offensive were the references to the fact that you had been married several times.' He paused. 'How many times *have* you been married, Sir James?'

'Three times.'

'And three times divorced, yes?'

'No. One of my wives died while we were still married.'

Sir Graham paused. 'Doesn't three marriages and two divorces indicate an unusual interest in women?'

'I hardly think that three relationships in fifty years indicates anything other than a respect for the institution of marriage.'

'Sir James. Could you tell the court what went wrong in these marriages?'

'I could, Sir Graham. But I have no intention of doing so.'

Howard Rowe stood up but Lord Justice Hooper waved him down and looked at Sir Graham.

'I will not allow you fishing expeditions, Sir Graham. Nor any further questions on this subject. They are totally irrelevant. And I advise you that if your clients wish to prove the facts they have stated in the book you should call them now.'

'Thank you, milord. I've no more questions in that area.' He moved over another pile of papers and then turned to Frazer again.

'Sir James. I understand you found the suggestion that you were a snob was neither true nor were there grounds for the suggestion.' He picked up a newspaper. 'I have here a page from the *Daily Telegraph*. It's quite old. There's a photograph on the page of you and a lady sitting in the Royal box at Wimbledon. The lady was a Miss Barbara Hutton and in the interview alongside the picture she claims that you are one of her best friends.' He paused. 'Do you remember that occasion?'

'I remember the occasion but I don't recall the interview. It was a long time ago.'

'Were you a good friend of hers as she claims?'

'I think she was being rather generous but I gladly accept her description.'

'You have often fended off enquiries into your background by saying – and I quote – I'm just a boy from the back streets of Birmingham. Which is the phoney Sir James? The boy from the back streets of Birmingham or the man sitting with a woman described as the richest woman in the world in the Royal box at Wimbledon?'

'I'd say that that's for other people to judge.'

'I also have a press photograph of you with the then Attorney-General. The caption said you were old friends.' He paused. 'What did you have in common?'

'During the war he was, as I was, an officer in the Intelligence Corps. He was at one time one of my junior officers. And very good he was too.' He paused. 'And, as a matter of fact, he came from the back streets of Sheffield.'

'One last question, Sir James. What car do you drive?'

'A Rolls Silver Shadow Mark I. It's twenty-six years old and you could buy one for about the same price as a new Ford Escort.'

Lord Justice Hooper barely concealed his impatience.

'If you have no more questions on this aspect, Sir Graham, we'll adjourn until our usual time tomorrow morning.'

'I have finished, milord.'

Healey and Frazer had travelled together on the train to Chichester where Charlie Bates had left the Rolls at the station after taking Adele to the Healeys' cottage where they were all having dinner that night.

Francis Healey was thinking of buying a boat and the conversation as they ate had been on the virtues and economies of sail and the convenience but expense of power. And of course the perennial assessment of GRP against good, honest wood.

Helen Healey had asked the question that was so interesting to both women.

'Tell us about Barbara Hutton, Jamie. What was she like and how did you come to meet her?'

Frazer smiled. 'She was small, I guess you could describe her as petite if you wanted to. Rather fragile, sort of china-doll and didn't trust a soul. Desperately unhappy. Been taken for a ride by every man she ever fell for.'

'How did you meet her?'

'It's a longish story Nellie. You could be bored.'

'No way.' Both women spoke together, laughing.

'On your head be it. I knew her because of a friend of mine. A German. An international tennis-player named Gottfried von Cramm.'

Adele burst out. 'I've seen him on an old Pathé News. He was playing Fred Perry. Good-looking. Still wearing long white trousers. A great smile.'

Frazer laughed. 'That great smile and a lot of genuine charm made him a very famous man. The silver coffee tray at Rose Cottage was a trophy from when he played tennis for Germany at the Blau-Weiss Club in Berlin.' He paused, frowning, for a moment and then said, 'The problem is how far back to go. Let's say I start by saying that Gottfried was not only a very good friend of mine. But we really liked one another. I was running a unit in Lower-Saxony and Gottfried lived a few miles out from my HQ town of Hildesheim. So I was a Brit intelligence officer and he was one of the Germans who had recently surrendered. I met him when I had to interrogate him because he was an important local guy. He'd never been in the armed forces. Never been a Nazi Party member, and had no interest in politics whatsoever.' He paused. 'He also gave me an insight into what the local population felt about what we were doing. His advice helped both sides from being too stupid.'

Helen Healey said, 'Get to the bit about Barbara Hutton.'

'Right. In those days no German was allowed to travel outside the *kreis*, the county, where he lived. It was part punishment and partly to help us control movement. So when Gottfried told me that he was desperate to go to Paris I wanted to know why. He was in love with an American girl, he said, name of Barbara Hutton, the Woolworth heiress. And to round things off she was madly in love with him, and had moved to Paris and taken rooms at the Ritz to be near to him.' He smiled. 'Americans' idea of "near" is a bit flexible.' He paused. 'I felt that with my backing 21 Army Group might be prepared to bend the rules a bit. But no. Under no circumstances. He had the same restrictions as any other German. I even tried the American Ambassador but he couldn't help. The law was the law.' He laughed. 'So I had a bright idea. I could get Barbara on the phone and then hand her over to Gottfried. I phoned her for him two or three times a week but instead of making it easier for them it made them more desperate.

'That made me even more determined to arrange a meeting. Barbara would not be allowed entry to Germany so the meeting would have to be outside the country. When 21 AG notified me that I was to be the British delegate to a Joint Intelligence meeting of the Allies that was to be held in Paris in two weeks' time I pressed the button. With Gottfried kitted out in battle-dress and with forged documents done by my own chaps we set off for Paris in a jeep.

'We arrived in the early hours of the morning and I booked us both in at the Scribe Hotel which was a transit mess for officers. Gottfried was Lieutenant Matthew White, Intelligence Corps, inevitably "Chalky" White. And he was my ADC and general dogs-body. I phoned Barbara and told her I'd brought a parcel for her and she took the point immediately and insisted that I took it round at once. It wasn't just a suite she had taken but the whole of one floor. They were both delighted. She asked me if there was something I'd like to celebrate the trip and I said I'd love a piece of real old-fashioned chocolate cake. I took the hint and went into the sitting-room and left them to themselves. When the cake came it was enormous and a man came in a few minutes later and sat on a sofa across the room. I offered him a slice of cake but he smiled and declined.

'The next thing was a captain in the US Army who said he was B's attorney and what did I want as a reward for what I'd done. A house, money, whatever it was he'd do it now. It was a standard formula. I was a rank above him and I was very rude and sent him packing. When he'd left, the guy on the sofa came over and sat alongside me at the table. He said there were a lot of people who would have paid good money to have watched the lawyer being sent packing. Then he asked me if I had brought over the "person" that night. I said I didn't know what he was talking about. He smiled and asked me if I knew who he was. I said I didn't and he held out his hand and said, "Let me introduce myself. My name's Cary Grant and I'm Miss Hutton's husband." When he saw how embarrassed I was he smiled and said, "There's no problem, fella. I'm only here to finalise the divorce." And that's how I met the millionairess.'

Adele said eagerly. 'What happened to them?'

'They got married. She and I watched Gottfried beaten by Drobny at Wimbledon. They parted up quite amicably some years later. Gottfried died in a car crash in Cairo and Barbara died in 1979.'

Helen Healey broke the silence and said quietly, 'And Graham Pollock tries to turn your good deed into you being a snob.'

Her husband chipped in. 'That's unfair. First of all he didn't know the background and secondly that's his job. That's what he's being paid to do.'

His wife shook her head. 'Rubbish. He's a creep.'

Francis Healey laughed. 'Actually he rather admires our Jamie but he has to serve his clients the best way he can.'

She shrugged. 'He's the snob, not Jamie.'

They watched Sky News at eleven and there was a short piece at the end showing Jamie, Francis and Howard Rowe waving down a taxi outside the court. The commentary was friendly.

When it was time to leave Frazer had driven them both back to Rose Cottage and they sat in the car after he had pulled up, listening to the last few bars of Ella Fitzgerald singing 'Long ago and far away'.

When the cassette clicked off Adele said, 'How shall we celebrate when all this libel business is over?'

He looked at her and smiled. 'Is it getting you down?'

'Only inasmuch as I hate you having to be questioned by those creeps acting for the book and the newspaper.'

'They've offered me a lot of money on two occasions to let them back off. I guess they've had nastier questions to answer than I have.'

'Have you ever wished you hadn't started it?'

'Yeah. A couple of times when it's made me feel old.'

'You aren't old, Jamie. And you never will be.'

'But like tonight. Talking about Barbara. I could only tell half the story. Suddenly I'm made aware of how long my life is. A lot of the incidents that I am asked about now are things that I've almost forgotten. Before the year when I was DG I was occupied continuously with one operation or another. Planning and thinking about what our enemies were up to, or might get up to. It's non-stop. The world won't stop while you take a holiday.'

'That's probably why you had problems in your marriages.'

'I don't think so. The mistakes I made in those were in-built. I'd have ended up doing those same fool things if I'd been a train driver.'

'Can I ask you a very personal question?'

He looked at her, her face caught in the pale, white light of the moon.

'You can ask but I don't guarantee to answer.' He paused. 'If it's about me I may not even know the answer. But go ahead.'

'Has anyone ever loved you in the way you want to be loved?'

He closed his eyes and rested his head back on the top of the leather seat of the Rolls. He was silent for a long time and then he said. 'Yes. They have.'

'What was she like?'

'It was two people.'

'Did you love them back the same way?'

'I think so.'

'Did they have problems?'

He opened his eyes and sat up, looking back at her face.

'What on earth made you ask that?'

'Because you seem to have had a tendency in your private life to subconsciously pick lame dogs, because you feel you are tough enough, capable enough, for two people.'

As if reassured he leaned his head back on the seat and closed his eyes.

'They were both young. Younger than me. And they were both very gentle and very beautiful. The first girl was French. She had a wasting illness. A kind of cancer. She was confined to a wheelchair. We had loved one another for just over two years when she died. The other girl was German. She was much younger than me. She had grown up knowing me and she knew me when I was with the French girl. They were friends.'

Chapter 46

Healey's secretary said that there was a call for him. A personal call.

'Who is it?'

'I don't know. He wouldn't say.'

'OK. Put him through.'

'Is that Mr Healey? Francis Healey?'

'Yes. Who is that?'

'My name's Henman, Patrick Henman.'

'How can I help you, Mr Henman?'

'You're Jamie Frazer's lawyer in this libel thing, aren't you?'

'Yes.'

'I think it would be wise for you and me to have a word together.' He paused. 'I phoned Jamie the day the stuff appeared in the press. Just to wish him luck. I thought maybe he mentioned my call to you.'

'He had a lot of calls that day, Mr Henman.'

'I'm sure he did.' He paused. 'I took over from Jamie in Berlin when he came back to London. But I've had some information in the last few days that maybe you should know about.'

'So why don't you ring Sir James himself?'

'You'll understand why not when we've spoken together.'

'Tell me roughly what it's about, Mr Henman.'

'It's confidential and I don't trust telephones.' He laughed softly. 'Old habits die hard.'

'When did you want to meet?'

'I'd suggest this afternoon. How about four o'clock at your chambers?'

'Let me just check.' A long pause. 'That would be OK with me.'

253

'See you at four then. Cheers.'
'OK.'

Healey had wondered if he shouldn't contact Jamie Frazer and tell him about the call but he finally decided to wait until he had heard what Henman had to say.

When Henman was shown into his office, Healey offered him a coffee which he accepted and then he looked at his visitor.

'You sounded a bit mysterious on the phone, Mr Henman.'

Henman smiled. 'Patrick.' He paused. 'Just cautious.' He looked around at Healey. 'I was in Berlin last week. I've retired but they wanted me to help sort out a problem.' He paused. 'And while I was there I came across something that worried me a little.' He paused again, looking across at Healey. 'Can I take it that we are talking in confidence – just you and me?'

Healey hesitated, then said, 'At the moment – yes. But I might want to discuss whatever it is with Sir James.'

'That's my point, Mr Healey. I'm not sure that what I'm proposing to tell you should be passed on to Jamie without we discuss the implications.'

'Mr Henman. I'm assuming that you want to help Sir James in some way but you'll have to leave it to me to decide what to do about it – if anything.'

Henman shrugged. 'Can I take it that our conversation is not being recorded?'

'Of course it's not.' He paused. 'I'm a lawyer, Mr Henman. An officer of the court. If this was being recorded it would only be with your agreement.'

Henman shrugged. 'I guess that'll have to do.' He leaned back in his chair. 'Did you know Jamie when he was in Berlin?'

'No.'

'Has he ever talked with you about a German guy named Schenk or Schmidt? Otto Schenk?'

'No.'

'Did Jamie ever mention a line-crossing operation he ran into the Russian Zone just after the war?'

'No.'

'I wasn't around in those days but I've read the files. Being a line-crosser was a very risky business so it wasn't easy to recruit people to do it. You couldn't stick to the rules on an operation like that.' He shrugged. 'Anyway, Jamie got together a group of men who were war criminals and in return for their co-operation they were promised immunity. No prosecution. New identities and all that stuff. Otto Schenk was one of those men.' He sighed. 'Cutting a long story short, Jamie was caught by the Russians and beaten up pretty badly. Schenk helped him escape.' He paused. 'Schenk saved his life. 21 Army Group and Intelligence kept their promises. No prosecutions et cetera. The only snag was that they didn't destroy the records. It sounds like typical intelligence duplicity but having looked at it myself I don't think it was. It was just plain inefficiency. Intelligence was grossly overworked in those days.' Henman waved a hand dismissively. 'But back to today.' He looked at Healey intently. 'I was told that the newspaper or the author of the book had commissioned somebody to look into Jamie's time in Germany. The chap they've hired is a pro. He's ex-BND, the German Intelligence Service. He's found out about Schenk's back-ground and it seems that when Jamie went back to Berlin Schenk was a close friend of his.'

'So what's the problem?'

'It won't be difficult for the other side to suggest that Jamie protected a man who he knew to be a war criminal. A man who was given immunity and a new identity. As you know we're still going through the motions of hunting down alleged war criminals today.'

'But that was in the line of duty. Other people above Jamie must have agreed to that.'

'But they didn't have a war criminal as one of their closest friends long afterwards when they were "our man in Berlin".'

Healey was silent for what seemed a long time, then he said, 'I still don't understand why you contacted me, not Jamie.'

Henman smiled. 'I think you understand very well, Mr Healey, that if anyone thought it might be a good idea to tidy things up a bit it would be better if Jamie knew nothing about it.'

'What do you mean by tidy things up?'

'Schenk's records as a war criminal and the records that he was used by Jamie still exist. The BND man your opponents are using knows the basic facts but he doesn't know that the records still exist. If he found that out and they were brought in as evidence it wouldn't look too good for Jamie. You could argue that he was acting under orders or with tacit approval, but a jury may not appreciate the difference. When the Nazis were prosecuted at Nuremburg we didn't accept that old German dictum – "*Befehl ist befehl*" – an order is an order and has to be obeyed without question.'

'Where are the records now?'

Henman hesitated. 'I don't think we should go down that road.'

'Why not?'

'Well. If the other side subpoenaed those records and you had them or knew where they were, would you have to produce them or say where they were?'

'Yes. I'd have to do one or the other. How would the records affect Jamie's case?'

'It would be disadvantageous.' Henman shrugged. 'It could raise a doubt about Jamie's judgement?'

Healey didn't reply, and Henman went on. 'That's all I wanted to know.' He stood up and held out his hand. 'Pleased to have met you, Mr Healey.'

Healey ignored the hand and said, 'How well did you know Jamie?'

'We worked alongside one another for nearly ten years.'

'What did you think of him?' When Henman hesitated Healey said, 'Can you spare the time to have lunch with me?'

Henman nodded. 'Sure I can.'

Because it was in walking distance Healey had taken Henman to the Betjeman Restaurant at the Charing Cross Hotel and later they took their coffees in the residents' lounge. They sat around a low coffee table in comfortable armchairs in the smoking area in deference to Henman being a heavy smoker. They had got on well together and Healey was satisfied that Henman was one of Jamie's hero-worshippers.

'What do you feel were his weak points? What about the women, the wives? Why were they all such failures?'

Henman leaned back in his chair and looked towards the high windows and then back at Healey.

'I wouldn't say I knew them all but I met them all at one time or another. They were all very pretty. And all quite ordinary in their own particular ways. But poor Jamie always had two strikes against him right from the start so far as women were concerned. First of all his mother. Never a good word to say for him. So when some pretty girl said what a great guy he was or praised him in some way, he wanted to marry her so he could have a permanent supply of affection. The second thing of course, and maybe it was the real loser for him, was his job, his experience.' Henman shifted in his chair. 'You know it's hard to explain to anyone who hasn't been in the business what it's really like. When you're chasing the kind of people we were after you spend a lot of time analysing their thinking, their motives and their backgrounds. And always you end up with a human being you understand better than he understands himself. They weren't born Nazis or Fascists or Commies, they were just kids who grew up with some kind of loser's gene. Some flaw in their lives, in their upbringing or environment. In other words, all too often you found that they were very like you yourself. So, nature being what it is, you sympathised. Maybe even wondered if you couldn't solve their problems for them.' He paused. 'So Jamie Frazer had a soft spot for women with flaws. And he felt that he had the strength for the two of them. And he'd got an eye for lame dogs.' Henman shrugged and smiled. 'That's my diagnosis on Jamie and his women.'

'So why did he abandon them when they didn't work out?'

'He never abandoned them. He just backed off. His job instincts took over. He was too much a realist, even a cynic, to pretend that it worked when it patently didn't.' He sighed. 'Once you switch back to the work mode you recognise the lies and the deceptions and you act accordingly.' He paused. 'You can see that working in the sub-text of Jamie and the wives. The extreme caution. Never the final commitment of children. That's been his saving from his mistakes with women.'

'What you're saying is that he never really loved any woman?'

Henman shook his head. 'No. I'm not saying that. There were two women Jamie really loved. Genuinely and completely.'

'So why didn't he marry one of them?'

'The first girl died. She was a wheelchair-bound cripple. But they lived as if they were married. He probably gave her those last two years. They really loved one another.' He paused. 'The other girl he really

257

loved had family and background problems that I won't go into that prevented them from marrying. She was stunningly beautiful and she adored him.'

'Is she still alive?'

'I don't know. She kind of disappeared.'

'Were they both English?'

'No way. The girl who died was French. The second girl was German.' He smiled. 'No. Jamie had learned his lesson about Brit girls.'

'What were his strengths as an intelligence officer?'

'A first-class interrogator. Patient and observant. He was a good planner of operations. Imaginative but not foolhardy. His chaps trusted him implicitly. He seemed to get on well with all sorts of people and was a shrewd analyst of both people and situations. He was good at assessing people's motivations. But his great operational strength was that his men knew that Jamie had done it all himself. He never gave people things to do that he couldn't have done himself.' Henman shrugged. 'That's about it.'

'What were his weaknesses?'

Henman took time to think and then he said, 'I'd say that his only weakness came from one of his strengths, his understanding of people. When you do that it's terribly easy to identify with the other guy. You're both in the same game and you realise that you've got more in common with your opponent than you have with your fellow-countrymen.'

'How did he get to be Director-General?'

Henman smiled wryly. 'A lot of people asked that at the time his appointment was announced. But in fact it was virtually a unanimous decision by the people responsible for appointing D-Gs to MI6.' He took a deep breath. 'As you probably know, both MI6 and the diplomatic service are the responsibility of the Foreign Office and the Foreign Secretary gets the most confidential information personally from the D-G. There's always been friction between MI6 and the diplomats. First of all ambassadors don't like reports on "their" country that they don't see themselves but go direct to their masters in Whitehall. Secondly they complain that the activities of people they see as "spies" sometimes cause bad feelings with "their" country's politicians.' He shrugged. 'There's something to be said for both points of view. So far as Jamie was concerned the diplomats represented the privileged chaps. Oxbridge and all that. Nevertheless he got on with them very well on the whole. They go for charm, and Jamie had lots of that. And he went out of his way to keep his ambassadors well briefed. They recognised that they didn't get everything but they appreciated the effort. So when the selection committee considered who should be the next D-G and Jamie was proposed by the intelligence representatives, everyone was happy. Or at least not antagonistic.'

'Why did the MI6 people choose him?'

'Personality, reliability and unusually wide experience. Very often the appointment goes to a non-intelligence man. A general who won't stand for any nonsense from the "spy-boys". There had been two such military compromises prior to Jamie and neither of them had turned out well. And the military representatives knew that Jamie had been in the army before he was in MI6 and all the reports on his record were extremely favourable.'

'Was he a good Director-General?'

'Not particularly. There isn't scope in the job for anything beyond keeping the organisation going. He protected the outfit's budget and extended its remit but he didn't stick his oar in just for the hell of it. He pressed for what he believed in and I guess they accepted that he knew what he was talking about and gave him what he wanted.'

'Tell me about the two girls.'

'I don't know much about either of them. The French girl was beautiful but dying and Jamie gave her the love and care she needed. When her father died a few years after the girl died, he left Jamie all his fortune.'

'What would you call a fortune?'

Henman smiled. 'Let's say several millions. Jamie's a very wealthy man although he doesn't look it or live like it. I don't think he's much interest in money.' He paused. 'The German girl was beautiful too. I never met her but I saw them around together.'

'Why didn't they marry?'

'I don't know. I seem to remember hearing that there was some problem but I don't know what kind of problem.' He paused. 'I heard that somebody had casually enquired about the girl when she had not been seen for some time and I gather that Jamie had looked as if he was going to strike the man but turned and walked away.'

'Do you still have contact with the MI6 people?'

Henman nodded but didn't reply.

'How do they feel about the libel case?'

Henman smiled and winked. 'They're strictly neutral, of course.' He paused and then went on. 'But they appreciate that for years the media have attacked people in the intelligence community and in some cases ruined their lives and reputations. People who were not able to defend themselves. Even the dead were not immune from the phoney historians and muck-rakers.' He shrugged. 'You can libel the dead without any need to substantiate what you've said. Gossip goes down as fact.' He shrugged again. 'For the first time somebody has the guts and money to strike back. And there's no doubt that the brass in MI6 are supporting Jamie.'

'Are they worried about being drawn into the case by the other side?'

Henman smiled. 'I should be surprised if contingency plans to cope with that are not already in place.' He paused. 'How did *you* get to know Jamie?'

'When he bought his cottage just outside Chichester we met at a cocktail party and he asked me to act for him on the purchase.'

'Has he got a girl-friend these days?'

'Yes. A very nice girl. Very pretty and very affectionate.'

'There's something you should bear in mind when thinking about Jamie. When somebody lets him down he never gets angry. He just withdraws into his shell. Maybe it's a failing, but I think over time he's learned that when there's a flaw in somebody's character or behaviour there's no point in trying to play God and put things right. He's found from bitter experience that it doesn't work. It's a bit defeatist but I guess that's how he's survived.'

'I'm glad we had this talk, Mr Henman. I've learned a lot and I'm grateful.'

'I'm glad to help. It was only by chance that I heard about that business with the BND.' He stood up, holding out his hand. 'I'll deal with that and thanks for a very nice lunch. I've got your phone number and it's best if you don't contact me. Take it that a nil report means everything's OK.' He paused. 'And no mention of this to Jamie.'

'If that's what you want that's OK with me.'

Healey had walked down the broad staircase with his guest to the

2

forecourt of the station, waiting with Henman until there was a taxi available. He had walked back himself to his office wondering if he should tell Howard Rowe about his talk with Henman. He decided against. If Jamie couldn't be told then neither could his counsel, but he was aware of the sound of legal thin ice crackling in the background.

Chapter 47

Every TV station in Europe and most of those in the USA and South America were showing the same pictures of people pouring through the Wall, shouting, laughing, singing and crying. It was November 9, 1989, and although the audience didn't realise it, they were watching the most significant scenes that they were ever likely to see. Men on the moon were just Star Wars games compared with the thousands of Germans released from their self-imposed tyranny and drunk with unaccustomed freedom. Only half-believing that it really was happening. Even those watching the events on their TV screens didn't yet realise that they were watching the end of an era. Not just in Germany but in the whole of Europe and then, inevitably, in the whole of the crumbling Soviet Union.

For a handful of people it involved urgent action and the MI6 detachment in Berlin had seen it all first-hand, not on TV screens. The message from London meant a lot of hard work evaluating and, where necessary, destroying old records and files. One of the problems was that there were records going back to 1947/8 and there was nobody around now who could evaluate such material. Whoever was going to decide had to have at least a recollection of the state of the game in those early days. And that was why Pat Henman had been dragged out of retirement and his kennel of prize-winning German Shepherds. He was assured that it would only take a couple of months.

Frazer and Adele had watched the fall of the Wall on the Sony portable on the boat and she had been surprised when he switched over to ITV and then, when they were showing the same shots, he switched off the set.

As they drove back to Rose Cottage, Frazer tried not to think about Berlin and its celebrations. It all seemed a lifetime ago but it was only a few years.

Otto Schenk sat in his towelling bath-robe in a wicker chair alongside his bed in the nursing home. He didn't really need much nursing but he had no great wish to get back to the villa in Grunewald. He'd been in this place for five years now. He had got over the bitterness he had felt when he had been confronted by Anna about her deception. That's what children did these days. But nothing would wipe out the double-dealing of Frazer and the Brits way back. Just holding onto the proof of things he had done that could be used as a pressure-point if they ever needed one. Bastards. Now the Wall was down Bonn would surely send them packing. The so-called Allies.

When Nurse Lilian came in she smiled and looked at him.

'You've got a visitor, Herr Schmidt. Looks very important.'

'I don't see people. You know that.'

She smiled and she was very pretty. 'He says it's very important and personal.'

'What's his name?'

'He wouldn't give a name but he said to tell you it was about Operation Orion. He said you'd know what he meant.'

For a moment Schenk hesitated, then he said quietly, 'Show him in.'

Henman realised how ill Schenk must have been just by looking at him sitting there. There wasn't all that much difference in their ages but Schenk's thin arms, the lined face and the washed-out blue eyes made him look near the end of his time. Schenk had needed to have it explained again and again until finally Henman tried to summarise the position.

'D'you mind if I call you Otto?'

'No. Of course not.' He looked at Henman. 'You weren't part of this business were you?'

'No. I was in Dusseldorf at that time.' He paused, smiling. 'Let me just go over the points.'

'OK.'

'We both agree that all the privileges – identity, permits, cash and the rest of it – were actually carried out. All except the final thing – destroying all records of the operation and the people involved, including the British.' He paused. 'Agreed?'

'Yes.'

'I've shown you the instructions that were given in writing that all the material stored be shredded and incinerated immediately. What I showed you isn't a copy, it's the actual original. And it was just pressure of work at the time that made the destruction get overlooked.'

'Why have you only contacted me?'

'Because yours was the only file that was missing. It made me suspicious but it's taken me two weeks to track you down. I asked for the log-book of anyone outside SIS who had had access to that area of our records. Only one name came up. A man named Weber, with authority from BND as a private investigator. I contacted Weber and I knew at once what he'd been up to. Intelligent, charming and greedy. I got the BND to threaten to withdraw his licence and we looked at his bank accounts. There were all these payments from an Otto Schmidt. We weren't sure that Schmidt was you but we made a few enquiries and when I found that Jamie Frazer had been a close friend of Otto Schmidt I knew that we'd solved the only remaining problem.'

'The other files?'

'I watched them shredded and incinerated, Otto. The lot. Even our internal stuff. Operation Orion never happened.' He paused. 'Except for your file. Have you still got it?'

'No. I burnt it myself long ago.' He paused and looked at Henman. 'You don't know what awful damage this affair did.'

There were tears rolling down Schenk's face and he reached for a box of Kleenex on the bed and wiped his face. He shook his head. 'I've been such a fool.'

'A quite large sum of money will be coming back to you from Weber through me.'

'How much do the BND know about me?'

'Nothing that matters. I told them that you had worked for us against the KGB and that you were under our protection.'

'Can you leave me your address and telephone number in case I need to contact you?'

'Of course.' He smiled. 'I've retired now, of course.'

'What happened to Jamie Frazer?'

'He's retired too. He was Director-General for a few years and right now he's involved in a rather stupid law case. A libel case.'

'Is he married?'

'No. He's got a very nice lady-friend but I don't think he's got marriage in mind. He's rather a lonely man.' Henman stood up. 'I'll get on my way. And remember – Operation Orion never happened. Thanks for your help in tying up this last problem.'

When Henman had gone Schenk sat in a maelstrom of thought. What *had* he done? No wonder she had accused him of being arrogant and dictatorial. The two of them must have thought he was crazy. He hadn't heard from Anna since the day she left. Not even a card on his birthdays or for New Year. And what, for God's sake, had Frazer thought he, Schenk, was doing? What could he do to try and put it right? He had been in and out of hospitals and nursing homes a dozen times in the last seven or eight years. He hadn't the physical strength to do anything. And he had no idea what he could do. He'd have to sleep on it.

Chapter 48

Despite the shaky hands the doctor had said that he was quite fit enough to go home if that was what he wanted. And Otto Schenk had headed straight for the main library and the reference section.

There was a slight problem in describing what he was looking for. Even though they had been speaking German, Henman had used the English word 'libel' when talking about Frazer and his current problems. They eventually decided that libel was '*verleumdung*' and after a fifteen-minute search the young woman came back with a small bundle of magazines and press-cuttings. At that point the only problem was, was this the right man? The name he had given was Jamie Frazer and the man in the cuttings was called Sir James Frazer. It seemed that Herr Schmidt's old friend was now a knight – '*Freiherr*' in German society.

The press-cuttings were rather crude photocopies but the copies of Spiegel and Bild were originals. There were two pieces in *Spiegel* and one of them had a picture of Frazer smiling as he stood alongside a white Rolls Royce. The caption stated that he lived in a beautiful cottage near Chichester in the county of Sussex. Schenk had no idea where Chichester and Sussex were but he bought an Automobile Association Touring Guide. He had booked himself a suite in Hotel Rempter where he had sometimes had business meetings in the old days. He didn't want to go back to the villa in Grunewald, neither did he want to go back to the nursing home. Just having something purposeful to do seemed to have revived him and given him new energy.

He sat on the edge of his bed looking at the AA guide. He slept for an hour and then phoned a couple of tour agencies about how to get to

Chichester. Plane to Gatwick and then by train or hire a car. When he asked about hiring a car with a German-speaking driver both agencies said there would be no problem.

It had been the last day in court before the New Year. The Christmas and New Year holidays seemed to have become combined into a fortnight when work came to a stop except for chain grocery-stores and retailers with winter sales.

Helen Healey had said it was a good excuse for a small party. After dinner they had descended into Favourites. They had gone through favourite flowers, favourite meals and favourite film-stars and one of the girls said, 'Can I ask about something legal?' She was looking at Healey who shrugged and said, 'Go ahead.'

'It said in the papers today that the defence counsel had asked Jamie if he had ever done anything he was ashamed of and you got up and protested and the judge agreed with you. How is it you can stop a question being asked?'

'First of all, because it's what the courts call "fishing". Asking a question in the hope that the answer might embarrass whoever was asked the question. Secondly, it was nothing to do with the case. It was for them to prove things not hope that our side might help them. And thirdly, it's an illegal attempt to get a witness to incriminate himself or commit perjury.'

Frazer laughed. 'I was grateful to Howard Rowe for intervening but I saw it coming and I had an answer ready.' He paused. 'In fact I had two.'

There were loud cries for him to tell them the answer. Frazer looked at Healey for approval who merely shrugged.

'When an officer goes to a military establishment the guard on the gate salutes him. If he's a captain or under, the guard just slaps the butt of his rifle. But if the officer is what they call Field Rank, a major or over, the guard has to "present arms", which is a quite elaborate operation.

'When I got the order promoting me to major, I asked my driver where the nearest military establishment was with guards. He said it was 5 Div and I told him to drop me there and I got the full display as I walked through the gates.' He laughed. 'If I wasn't ashamed I ought to have been.'

It was Adele who laughed and said, 'And now the second answer.'

'I had to abandon that because of the bad language involved and the bad language was an essential part of the story.'

It was Francis Healey who said, 'We can take it, Jamie. Let's hear it.'

Frazer shrugged. 'On your head, Francis.' He paused. 'When I was at the barracks here doing my infantry training, they decided to have a cricket match between the regiment and the I. Corps lot. I'd never played cricket in my life but there were twelve of us so that was OK.' He paused. 'However, one of us went sick and I was ordered to take his place. All I was told was to hit the ball if I could and as hard as I could.' He smiled. 'Let me add at this point that the umpire was the RSM, the Regimental Sergeant Major, dressed in a blood-stained white coat borrowed from the regimental butcher. He was standing just beside me as the first ball came down. I hit it smack in the middle of the bat and it soared over the boundary to where the officers' wives were sitting. It knocked the cup of tea out of the hands of the Commanding Officer's wife and the RSM tapped me on the shoulders. "You're out." I protested and asked him how I was out and he glared at me with his piggy eyes and said quietly, "You, mate, are fucking out because I say so. Get moving." '

Adele said, 'Why be ashamed of that?'

'Because I walked and I should have told him to get stuffed.'

Inevitably they ended up round the piano with Frazer playing a mixture of blues and rags and a few love songs from the war days like 'Small Hotel' and 'Lovely Weekend'.

Patrick Henman had barely settled back in his old routine when he got the telephone call from Sir Hugo. Could they meet? It was urgent. Henman protested that it was Christmas Eve but Sir Hugo had offered to drive across to Henman's place in Sanderstead and Henman had reluctantly agreed. An hour later Sir Hugo was mounting the steep flight of steps that led up to Henman's small house. The official driver made himself comfortable in the Jaguar saloon. Sir Hugo had said that it could be a longish wait. It was beginning to snow. Slowly and silently and looking as if it might last for some time.

Henman, like so many other SIS men, had ended up alone. But in his case it was from the death of his wife just before his retirement.

As he poured them each a malt whisky he said, 'What's it all about Hugo?'

'I had a visit from Bowman, the editor of the paper that Jamie is suing for libel. Telephone call at home. Secret meeting-place and all that sort of crap. Anyway, the meeting was at the Hilton coffee-shop. He was very nervous, waffled away for ten minutes before he got anywhere near the point.' Sir Hugo sighed. 'The long and short of it was that he reckons they've got information that if they bring it up in court could do us a lot of damage.'

Henman smiled. 'How much does he want?'

'It's the other way round, Paddy. He wants out from under in this bloody libel case that Jamie's brought against them. They'll pay anything and do anything if Jamie will call it a day.'

'Why the hell should he? He's obviously going to win.' He paused. 'And what in hell is the information that this chap's got that could damage us?' He paused. 'And for that matter, how am I involved in this?'

'D'you know a German named Weber?'

'Yes. I met the bastard when I was in Berlin. A blackmailer.'

'He gave your name as someone who could substantiate what he was talking about.'

'And what's he talking about?'

'A line-crossing operation into the Russian Zone just after the end of the war.'

'Is this Operation Orion we're talking about?'

'Yeah.'

'That's long gone, Hugo. I tidied that up when I was in Berlin.'

'But this chap Weber knows all about it?'

'I guess so. But he couldn't prove a thing. I witnessed all the records being shredded and incinerated.'

'Not quite all.'

'Go on.'

'The network reports from Jamie came direct to London. I did a check.' He paused. 'They still exist.'

'So get rid of them.'

'That would be tampering with or destroying evidence.' He shook his head. 'Not on, Paddy. Definitely not on.'

'Do the other side know these records exist?'

'I shouldn't think so but once they open the door on Orion with verbal evidence or a statement from this chap Weber, they could ask for whatever is still around.'

'Why should Jamie care, for God's sake? He was just doing his job.'

'At the moment I'm not thinking about Jamie but us – SIS.'

'OK, Hugo. It was more than forty years ago, the war had only just ended. The cold war had just started. Anyway, that's what SIS are for.'

'Not when we were using war criminals and offering them our protection. The media are still searching for doddery old men who live here to be put on trial. That was over forty years ago too. The media would have a field day. I can just see the headlines.'

'Too bad, Hugo. Let them do their worst. Tell the facts. Leave Jamie out. No names – national security and all that garbage.'

'He's made us an offer, Paddy.'

'What kind of offer?'

'Jamie settles out of court. Really high damages and a grovelling apology that blames the American who wrote the book.'

'And what does Jamie say?'

'I haven't told him. I know he wouldn't settle out of court.'

'So what next?'

'I don't know. We've got just over two weeks before they go back to court.' He paused. 'Have you spoken to Jamie recently?'

'No. I had a private word with Francis Healey, his solicitor, about the Orion business and I told him that I was about to clear up the whole thing. I asked him not to mention it to Jamie.'

'Why?'

Henman shrugged. 'I'm sure he's long forgotten the whole thing. Why rake it up again?'

'What are you doing for Christmas?'

'My daughter's coming here with her family.'

'Will you think about it over the holidays? You know my number. We'd all be most grateful. Maybe it would help if you contacted Jamie. Not about this stuff. Just casually.'

Henman smiled. 'You're a lovely man, Hugo, but Jamie's been in the business far too long not to rumble that I was up to something. I'll certainly think about it and I'll contact you after Christmas one way or another.'

When Sir Hugo had left, Henman set out his chess-board to do *The Times* chess problem. He had been originally recruited by GCHQ because of his science degree specialising in higher-mathematics. But life as a cryptographer had no appeal for Patrick Henman once he had been offered a transfer to a specialist SIS signals monitoring unit. It was Frazer who had decided that a keen and imaginative mind was being wasted and Henman was sent to Vienna to learn the art of surveillance and its avoidance. Four years later he was posted to the SIS detachment in Berlin. But right now Henman wasn't in the mood for solving chess problems. His thoughts were on his chats with Otto Schenk.

He had watched his words very carefully when talking to Schenk. Schenk was suspicious of all Brits, and who could blame him. So there were areas where he hadn't ventured. It was unusual for a serving SIS officer to have such a close friendship with a German, especially when the German had been involved in a clandestine operation. But the obvious explanation was there on the files. Although the Brits couldn't quite bring themselves to acknowledge it formally, there was no doubt that Schenk had saved Frazer's life. Henman didn't touch on the fact even obliquely. There had also been some gossip about Jamie having some sort of relationship with Schenk's daughter. Henman had looked at the records and it didn't look likely. Jamie was almost thirty years older than the girl. And Schenk had never mentioned his family. Then there was the odd fact that Schenk had obviously been out of touch with Jamie for a matter of years. And part of that time Jamie had still been in Berlin. Neither man had anything to gain or lose by maintaining the relationship. Or for that matter by abandoning it. Maybe they had just drifted apart.

The problem with Sir Hugo and his mates was that they would never understand a man like Jamie. You'd either have to care about him very deeply or study him as an odd human being to be able to understand Jamie Frazer. And he, Henman, was in neither category. There was nothing illogical about Sir Hugo's reasoning. Most men would have counted themselves lucky to have the chance of a grovelling public apology and a hell of a lot of money just to let their opponents off the hook. But according to Sir Hugo that sort of offer had been made unofficially twice before. And both times Jamie had turned it down. All that was different this time was that the top brass of SIS wanted him to call it a day. And only one of the top brass had ever known what it was really like doing the dirty work. And that man was Jamie Frazer.

There was no way to explain to desk officers what it was like in the field. It was nothing to do with getting beaten up or shot nor even to the possibility of ending your days floating in some Berlin canal. It was loneliness that made men like Jamie Frazer. Never having roots. Never really belonging anywhere. Knowing foreign cities inside out but not belonging. Sitting in hotel bedrooms constantly looking at your watch because you were waiting for a telephone call or because you had an RV at 2 a.m. in some back street. Never making friends so that you didn't have to explain why you were where you were or what you were doing the day after tomorrow. Never saying what you actually thought in case it was revealing, and never wishing that you had somebody waiting for you where the sun was always shining and poppies were waving in cornfields. Of course you could spend your time in night-clubs drinking and whoring at the tax-payers' expense. But you still had to go back to the room. On your own. Always. Thank God you didn't spend even five minutes thinking about all this. You just got on with the job. Subconsciously proud of being a loner because you knew what made the world tick and the others didn't. What made Jamie Frazer different was that he was a charmer. A real charmer. It wasn't faked. Jamie Frazer never complained. He got on with the job, whatever it happened to be at the time. But Henman knew that behind the charm was a very tough man. Just as lonely as the rest of them but seeming to be able to kid himself that he was a very lucky man.

When Karen and her kids had gone back north he'd see if he could contact Otto Schenk. Instinct told him that there were clues there if he could recognise them. Clues to Jamie Frazer.

Chapter 49

Otto Schenk spent Christmas Day and the following day trying to work out what he would say to Frazer. He knew what he'd got to get over to him. His terrible regrets and his guilt. But how did you start? How did you persuade a man who must hate you to listen to what you had to say? Half a dozen times he checked his air-tickets, flight details, passport, travellers cheques and 5000 DMarks in cash. He ate at a small family restaurant a couple of doors from the hotel and bought a second-hand paperback of the German translation of *Gone with the Wind* at a stall by Zoo Bahnhof. He fixed a wake-up call for 7.30 the next morning, and a taxi at 8.30.

Schenk arrived two hours before his flight-time at Tegel. He had never travelled outside Germany before apart from the war, but everybody seemed very helpful. They gave him a window seat but he sat with his head back on the headrest, his eyes closed as he wondered what Frazer's reaction would be. And then he did what he had vowed never to do, he thought about Anna. Where had she gone and what had she been doing all this time. She'd been right in what she had said about him and she'd said she'd never forgive him for ruining her life.

At Gatwick he carried his single canvas bag to the Avis counter where they took some time to find his booking. He had provisionally hired both car and driver for a week and he was surprised and pleased that the driver was a young Swiss woman who spoke fluent German. When she realised he had not booked any accommodation in Chichester she got the desk to book them rooms at the motel at the edge of the town.

The journey had taken just over an hour and he had told her that he wanted to contact Sir James Frazer who lived at Rose Cottage. She laughed and said that there must be at least fifty Rose Cottages in the Chichester area but they could check in the local phone book and the motel staff could give them directions. She said she'd heard of Sir James. He was involved in some lengthy court-case.

Maggie Bates had brought their breakfasts in bed and as she arranged the tray she said, 'There's a gent waiting to see you downstairs. Said it was a personal matter. I told him if it's to do with the case he should go to Mr Healey. He said it wasn't anything to do with the case and I told him he'd have to wait at least half an hour before you'd be available. I don't think he understands English. I reckon he's German.' She gave him a card. 'He gave me this card to give you.'

Frazer looked at the card. 'I don't believe it.' He looked at Maggie. 'What's he look like?'

'I'd say a couple of years older than you. Thin face. Not much hair and there's a driver, a young woman sitting in the car outside.'

Frazer turned to Adele. 'Carry on, honey. I'll have to see this guy. Might take some time.' Turning to Maggie he said, 'Tell him I'll be down in ten minutes.'

Schenk was standing looking out of the window at the garden and he turned quickly as he heard Frazer come in the room. Frazer was shocked at how old and fragile Schenk looked. But this was the man who had saved his life.

'Well, Otto. What brings you here?'

'I came to say how sorry I am for what I did. I know I can never put things right but I only recently discovered how wrong I was.'

'Why did you do it, Otto? I've never understood why?' He paused. 'Take off your coat and sit down. Would you like a cup of tea or coffee?'

'Maybe after we talk. Thank you.'

Schenk didn't take off his coat but he sat in one of the armchairs.

'It's a crazy story, Jamie.' He paused. 'You remember the Orion operation way back – well your people promised to destroy all our records from the war and from the operation itself. They didn't do that. It wasn't deliberate. I've seen the original letter instructing that everything should be shredded and incinerated. But all the records, not just ours, got sent up from Bad Salzuflen and 21 AG to the SIS detachment in Berlin. They had vaults a mile long where they kept stuff that was never used. Our stuff was amongst it.'

'How long have you known this, Otto?'

'I knew the records about me existed way back when I told Anna not to see you again. Foolishly I didn't tell her why but I thought that you and the others at Bad Salzuflen had kept the records in case they wanted to pressure us again some time.'

'How did you find this out?'

'An ex-BND guy who's now a private investigator came across the records accidentally. Saw the possibility of blackmail. I was the only survivor he could trace so he put the bite on me. I had to pay him a large cut of my profits month by month. Or he'd expose me to the media. War criminal, stooge for British intelligence, black-marketeer' He shrugged. 'What more do you want?'

'And you paid up?'

'Yeah. I had no choice. It would not only have ruined me and my business, but it would have ruined Anna too. Daughter of a *Sturmbann-führer* in an SS Special Duties unit.'

'Did you explain all this to her?'

'No. I couldn't bring myself to tell her. I was too ashamed of my past. And too scared of what she would think of me.' He shrugged helplessly. 'I was a coward.'

'You could have told me what you'd found out.'

'There was no reason to, Jamie. Your people had said everything would be destroyed. They didn't keep their promise.' He sighed. 'I assumed it was deliberate.'

'What's Anna doing?'

Schenk shook his head slowly. 'I've no idea. I've never heard from her since she went.'

'Have you tried to trace her?'

'No. I felt I had done enough damage.'

'When did you find out about all this?'

'About a week ago. A man named Henman came to see me. He said he knew you well. He told me what had happened.'

'How had they discovered this so long after it happened? What was their interest in it?'

'I don't know. I guess they just wanted to put things right.'

'And you've no idea where Anna is?'

'No.'

'Are there any relatives anywhere?'

'No. And she wouldn't go to them anyway.'

'Have you any objection to me trying to trace her?'

'No. None at all.'

'And no objection to her being told the truth?'

'No.'

'What are you going to do now?'

'Go back to Berlin. I was in a sort of hospice but I feel well enough to go back to my place in Grunewald. You'd always be welcome there, Jamie. You really would.'

'I'll keep in touch, Otto. I'll let you know what I'm doing to find her.'

There were tears on Otto Schenk's face as Frazer walked him down to the waiting hire-car.

Frazer looked up Henman's number in his book and dialled the number. It rang several times before there was an answer.

'Henman.'

'Patrick, it's Jamie. Jamie Frazer.'

'My God. You must be psychic. I've been meaning to give you a ring. What can I do for you?'

'I need a favour. An SIS-type favour. How do I stand with them at the moment?'

'As always, Jamie. What's the favour?'

'I want them to use their facilities to trace somebody for me.'

'D'you want me to process it for you?'

'Yes please.'

'OK. Person's name and last known address. Car registration. Occupation and Social Security number.'

'It's not one of those, Paddy. I need to talk to you about it.'

'Are you at your place in Chichester?'

'Yeah. Why don't you come over?'

'That's what I was thinking. When would be convenient?'

'Today. Soonest. It won't take more than a couple of hours so you could go back tonight or stay the night here with me.'

'OK. Expect me lunch-time. Roughly.'

As Frazer hung up the phone he saw the Rolls pulling into the drive. Charlie Bates had driven Adele back to her place in Midhurst where she said she had things to do. He phoned through to Maggie and asked her to prepare some cold bits and pieces for two, and the remains of the Christmas pudding with some of her special custard.

He tried to arrange his thoughts about his meeting with Henman but there was no need to be anything other than totally honest. He had no clues as to where she might have gone. She had her own trust fund that Otto had set up for her long ago so she had no need to work to earn a living. And she'd had no training for even the usual commercial skills. Only an organisation like SIS had the resources to start on such a wild-goose chase.

They had talked as they ate and Frazer had told Henman the whole story. As they were drinking their coffee, Henman said, 'It's hard to imagine poor Schenk here in the cottage. He looked in a pretty bad state when I talked to him in the nursing home in Berlin.' He paused. 'Tell me, Jamie, what are you going to do when you know where she is?'

'It depends on the circumstances. She may be happy in whatever she's built up as her new life.' He paused. 'She may be married.'

'And if she's not married?'

'Then we'll stay together. If she wants to.'

'It's that important is it?'

'Yes.'

'And that definite?'

'Yes.'

'May I put Sir Hugo in the picture?'

'Of course.'

'He knows about my findings concerning Operation Orion and he's very worried about it.'

'In what way?'

'He's heard on the grapevine that the other side in your case also knows the basics of Orion.'

'Which basics?'

'That SIS countenanced using German war criminals to spy on the Russians when they were still supposed to be our allies.'

'Where did the other side get the information?'

'They sent somebody pretty incompetent to look over your old hunting-ground but he was contacted by the guy who blackmailed poor old Schenk.'

'So this guy could still appear in court?'

Henman smiled. 'I'm afraid not. The Kripo and the BND have got him on a stack of charges. Sir Hugo called in a few IOUs with the BND. We shan't see him in court.'

'So how can they rake it up?'

'Just a fishing expedition by their counsel. Request for documents regarding Operation Orion.'

'But they've now been destroyed.'

'Not quite.' He looked at Frazer. 'We've still got your original reports on file in London but no mention of the operation.' He paused. 'They exist so they're evidence. We can't dispose of them or we'd be done over for tampering with evidence. Fortunately your opponents don't know that anything exists at all.'

'Is this still a problem for Hugo?'

'I'm afraid so.'

'What's he going to do about it?'

'He's hoping you'll help him.'

'How?'

'We know positively that your opponents are desperate to see the end of this. He wants you to let them settle out of court. A really grovelling apology taking all the blame, three hundred thousand pounds damages plus agreed costs and no appeal on their part.'

For long moments Frazer was silent and then he said, 'And in return you'll find my girl? No matter what it takes?'

'Yes.'

'And I agree their apology, not just the lawyers?'

'Sure.'

'OK. Can you stay the night and I'll get my lawyer over and we'll tie it up?'

'Let's do that.' Henman smiled. 'Just one other thing.'

'What's that?'

'Someone who shall be nameless told me to tell you that both SIS and 21 Army Group knew all about your little jaunt to Paris with von Cramm.'

Frazer smiled. 'No comment.'

When Francis Healey came over they had talked for two hours. He had raised no objections. If this was what Jamie wanted there was no problem. He was sure that the other side would leap at the chance. They wouldn't like the apology and taking the whole blame but they'd had enough. He was sure that Sir Graham would go along with it. They'd leave a couple of small points he could fight over and win for the sake of appearances. Frazer hadn't mentioned anything about the background to why he was letting the other side off the hook and Healey was too much the lawyer to raise the subject.

As he stood up to leave Francis Healey said, 'We're not due in court for about four weeks. It will take two weeks to settle the details with the other side and I'll see if I can get an earlier hearing in court.'

Jamie smiled. 'Thanks for all your help, Francis.'

Chapter 50

The meeting between Bowman and Sir Hugo had not been difficult. Bowman had reckoned on half a million damages against them and took it as some sort of victory that it was only £300,000. What he really objected to was the abject apology but, when contacted on the phone mid-meeting, Sir Graham had advised him to go along with whatever the plaintiff wanted.

The statement had been passed to the media as both parties went into the court and by the time it was being read out by Sir Graham Pollock it was already being knocked into shape as the page one story for the Evening Standard.

In the statement the defendants conceded that, under pressure of work, insufficient attention had been paid to checking the truth of the criticisms in the text. The defendants now withdrew all the statements objected to by the plaintiff and conceded that there was not one iota of truth in any of the allegations. The defendants deeply regretted the distress caused to the plaintiff and an agreed sum of money in damages and further sums in legal costs were to be paid into court for the plaintiff that day.

There was a piece on BBC News at midday and a couple of minutes on Sky every hour for the rest of the day. Observers noticed that Sir James had not been in court when the apology was read. Neither was Al Pinto who was already back in Washington. The US media had only given the trial brief mentions. The CIA and the FBI were their targets. Who cared what the Brits got up to.

Adele had phoned Helen Healey after she had seen the piece about the case on *News at Ten*.

'Have you seen Jamie today, Helen?'

'No. I haven't.'

'He's not at the cottage and I tried the boat number but there was no reply.' She paused. 'It's not like him to be out of touch. Does Francis know how to contact him?'

'No. He doesn't need to at the moment. They're doing all the legal washing-up from the case next week, so he's not needed until then.'

'Will you let me know if you hear from him?'

'I certainly will. Don't worry. He'll be OK.'

Helen Healey sat in the car in the parking-lot at Chichester Station listening to the news headlines at seven. A brief mention of the case and commentary at ten.

Francis's knock on the window startled her and she reached across to release the door lock and started the engine as Francis got in beside her. It was bitter cold and she could let the heater do its stuff as Francis settled himself in.

He leaned across and gave her a peck on the cheek.

'How're things?'

'OK. Have you heard from Jamie today?'

'No. Was he after me?'

'Not that I know of, but Adele phoned. Sounded a bit worried. He wasn't at the cottage. Charlie and Maggie didn't know where he was and she'd got no reply from the boat number.'

'It *is* a bit odd. I'd have thought he'd have wanted a bit of a celebration today. Maybe he's had a bellyful and wants a bit of peace.'

'But surely he'd let her know, or you, what he was up to and where he could be contacted.'

'Yes. But you know Jamie. He keeps his own counsel.' He smiled. 'Not like the rest of us, always ready for a bit of loose chat.' He paused. 'My God it's snowing again. Let's get going before it settles. Thank God it's the weekend.'

Frazer watched the lights of Berlin as the plane banked on its flight path to Tegel. He had left his number at the Savoy with Henman and Sir Hugo and Paddy Henman had confirmed that the search was already ongoing for the girl. He wasn't sure why he was heading for Berlin but some instinct drove him there. He wanted to be away from his normal life and he wanted time to think. It was strange to think that he had spent more time in his life in Berlin than anywhere else. But he knew in his heart that it was nothing so rational that drove him to Berlin. It was those rooms just off Savigny Platz. He still had that note in his wallet that she had left for him. Rather worn and crumpled now but that was when his whole life had changed.

By the time he had booked in at the Savoy and taken up his bags it was after midnight, but despite his hectic day he wasn't tired. He took the elevator down to the ground floor and walked out into Fasanen Strasse. He was tempted to turn right into Kant Strasse and on to Savigny Platz but he walked on down to the Ku-damm and turned left towards the lights in the cathedral. He put up his coat collar. There was no snow but it was a bitingly cold wind. There were plenty of lights but few people, all of them on the move.

There were the usual floodlights on the ruins of the old cathedral which stuck up starkly like a decayed tooth and as he got to the new Gedächtnis Kirche he heard the faint sound of an organ. He walked up the flat stone steps and tried the small door set in the big wooden door. There was a gush of warm air and a pleasant golden glow inside the church and he walked inside and stood looking towards the altar and the organ loft. There were at least a dozen people inside the church. A few with heads bent in prayer but most of them just listening to the organ music. As he sat down in one of the pews, he sat with his eyes closed, trying to identify the music. He could tell that it was French and he had heard it many times before. Not as a solo but with a full orchestra. Then he recognised it. It was Saint-Saëns' Symphony for Organ. He and Anna had heard it at the Konzert Halle with von Karajan conducting the Berliner Philharmonika. The organist was doing his own variation of the adagio. It had been Pierre Cochereau who had played the organ at the concert. They had not long settled all the controversy about von Karajan being a member of the Nazi party. The Allied Committee had quarrelled about whether von Karajan should be allowed to continue his career. The Brits had said that it would be as crazy to ban him as the Nazis making playing Mendelssohn's gentle fiddle concerto illegal.

He had assumed that when he retired that world of deceit and violence would be left in the past. But when that wretched book had come out it was like being dragged back into the old days. People like Bowman and Pinto and the publishers saw themselves as fearless combatants in the world of politics and espionage. In reality they were more like innocents abroad who couldn't speak the language or understand the locals. They got by playing games with politicians and their peccadilloes because they were two of a kind. The same animals in the same jungle. But when it came to what was really going on in the world they hadn't a clue. They made much ado about freedom of the press but they abused that freedom day after day and thought it was power.

He had no real plan to follow but he had vaguely decided to wait in Berlin for a month or so to see if Henman and the service had any luck in tracing Anna. Until he knew about her he wanted to be away from Chichester and that part of his life. For the first time in his life he could decide for himself what the rest of his life would be and one thing was for certain – it wouldn't just be an extension of his life so far. Not Lieutenant-Colonel Frazer, not Sir James Frazer, and not the country gentleman. He stood up slowly and walked down the aisle and through the small door into the cold of the street. As he headed back to the Savoy he was aware of something at the back of his mind. Something that he had said some months back. Something significant but he couldn't recall what it was.

It was just after midnight two days later when he got the call. He knew it must be Henman. Nobody else knew where he was.

'Frazer.'

'It's a bit late, Jamie, but I thought I'd better put you in the picture. We've located the lady in question. By the way, she's got a middle name. Anna Maria.'

'Where is she?'

'In Belgium. Bruges. Teaches German and English at a convent school. Been at the school for just over four years. Much loved by the girls and admired by the Sisters. Lives in a small flat at Dweerstraat. Has a resident's permit and is registered under her own name. Seems in good health. No social life apart from the convent. No debts. No driving licence. No police record, other than as an alien resident. Nationality, German. Seems to be in her late thirties. Something like that. I can give you the correct address of the flat and the convent and telephone numbers for both. The Mother-Superior is Sister Marie. French.' He paused. 'That's about it, Jamie. Anything else you need?'

'No. That's fantastic, Paddy. You must have called on a lot of favours.'

'Actually we didn't. Computer records save a lot of leg-work these days and when it's official to official it's pretty easy. Anyway. Let me have your new location when you've got one.' He paused. 'By the way, I had a call from your brief, Francis Healey. Nothing to do with the court case which is apparently all wrapped up. But various people have been a bit put out or concerned as to what's happened to you. Might be an idea to give Healey a ring.'

The Savoy had recommended the Central in the Markt in Bruges and had booked him a double room for the next day onwards and he'd got a seat on a Sabena flight to Brussels for mid-morning.

He had put a call through to Healey and told him that he was OK but occupied on private business which kept him on the move. He asked Healey to pass on his regards to the others but mentioned nobody by name. Healey sounded friendly but just a touch irritated.

For some reason he couldn't quite identify he took his camera and walked to their old place at Savigny Platz and took several shots of the exterior and had them printed on a one-hour deal. The wintry sun had bathed the place in a golden warmth and there was a reflection of the sun on the big windows. As he looked at them he felt the first twinge of apprehension about how it would all turn out. He bought a guide-book to Belgium and saw that her rooms were within walking distance of the hotel.

The plane landed an hour late at Brussels National and Frazer had just managed to get a seat on the last train going to Ghent and Bruges.

At Bruges he took a taxi to the hotel and he had used room service to get himself a meal. An excellent omelette and a fresh fruit salad. It was nearly 1 a.m. when he put on his coat and ventured into the square. The reception desk had given him a street guide and shown him the two streets that interested him.

It was a crisp clear night with a full moon and he recognised the famous belfry at the far side of the Markt. Every building he could see was out of the Middle Ages. He found the convent alongside a canal behind the Town Hall but he failed to find Anna's address. As he walked back to the hotel he hoped it wasn't an omen.

He was reading Irwin Shaw's *Girls in Their Summer Dresses* but it lay unopened on his chest as he lay in bed. His instinct was to go to her address and just ring the bell. But that would, in a way, be taking advantage of her surprise with no time to collect her thoughts. She wasn't in the phone book, the hotel had checked for him, but it would be an intrusion to phone her at the school. It may embarrass her. In the end he decided that the best way was to send her a note. Have it delivered by hand. Today was a Saturday and there was no school. It was just after 4 a.m. when he finally composed the note.

Chapter 51

He took a deep breath and on the second ring he picked up the phone.

'Frazer.'

'Jamie. I've just got your note. Where can we meet?'

'How about here at the hotel?'

'That's fine. When?'

'Right now.'

She laughed softly and said, 'About ten minutes.'

'Can I say something?'

'Of course.'

'I've been thinking so much about us meeting and what to say.' He paused. 'I love you, honey. I love you so much. I can't wait to see you.'

'I'll be there, Jamie. I'll be there.'

It had been as if they had never been apart. There was no reticence and no holding back. He'd shown her the colour prints of the rooms at Savigny Platz, and the crumpled note she had left on his pillow.

'Before we talk about us there are quite a few things to bring you up-to-date on.'

'Like what?'

'About your father.'

She shook her head. 'I don't want to hear about him, Jamie. I've had enough of him.'

'I wouldn't be here, my love, if it wasn't for him.'

'You mean he knows where I am?'

'No. He doesn't. It goes back long before you were born. It's quite a long story but he saved my life.'

'You'd better tell me then.'

As briefly as he could he told her about the saga of Operation Orion, the promises that were made, the documents that weren't destroyed. Her father's assumption that it was deliberate and that he was part of it.

'So why didn't he just tell me?'

'During the war he was an officer in an SS unit in the Ukraine that had a bad reputation. He could have been tried as a war criminal if we hadn't covered it up. It applied to all the men I had in Orion. He thought it might be made public and that you'd have suffered from it.'

'What's he doing now?'

Frazer told her of the old man's unhappy life and confronting him to explain what had happened and to apologise.

'Is there any more I need to know? What about you?' She paused. 'When I gave your name at the desk downstairs the girl said you were Sir James Frazer. What's it mean?'

'It's like Freiherr used to be in Germany before the war.' He smiled. 'Gets you the best table in restaurants and theatre tickets to *My Fair Lady*.' He paused. 'If you married me you'd be Lady Frazer.'

She looked at his face. 'When I was a little girl and I saw you with Marie-Claire I used to think of what it would be like to be married to you.'

'What about now that you're a young woman?'

'Still the same.'

'So. Will you marry me?'

'Of course. We've been married a long time really.'

'I'm old enough to be your father. Almost too old.'

'So maybe you'll find me boring. I've lived a very quiet life, Jamie. Not like yours.'

'So two questions. When shall we get married and where shall we live?' He paused. 'I don't have any roots, we can live wherever we want.'

'What about your friends and relations?'

'No relations and no friends I want to keep.' He paused. 'It's easier to marry in England than anywhere else apart from the United States. It would take us about two weeks if we used a registrar's office. And then we could travel around a bit. Have a look at France and Italy and Spain. Somewhere civilised.' He paused again. 'What about you and friends and the school?'

'No friends. A few acquaintances. The school's still on holiday.' She smiled. 'The Mother Superior will be delighted. Can you move in with me today?'

'No problem. But you ought to think about it.'

'Think about what?'

'About marrying an old guy like me. I seem to be offering very little compared with you.' He paused. 'Let me tell you how I feel about you and me – can I?'

She nodded. 'All right, tell me.'

'During the war when Special Operations Executive dropped people in Occupied France they had a code, solely for them. Only they knew the code. Because a poem, a short piece of verse, is easier to remember than prose the man responsible for those codes was a man named Leo Marks. He made no claim to be a poet but he was one all the same. He made up a code poem for a very beautiful young woman named Violette Szabo who was to be dropped into France. From the moment I first heard it I knew what it meant. So let me say it to you . . .

> the life that I have
> Is all that I have
> And the life that I have is yours.
>
> The love that I have
> Of the life that I have
> Is yours and yours and yours.
>
> A sleep I shall have
> A rest I shall have
> Yet death will be but a pause.
>
> For the peace of my years
> In the long green grass
> Will be yours and yours and yours.

'That's beautiful, Jamie. But you have to realise that I've been thinking about you and being married to you for years. I've had enough of thinking. I just want to do it.'

'I'm so pleased, honey. It's like I've been born again.'

She smiled and kissed him. 'Take me to lunch, Sir James. I'm hungry.'

They stayed in Bruges for two days and then moved to a service flat behind Harrods while they made the marriage arrangements.

Frazer had a rather stilted meeting with Francis Healey who naturally found it all both surprising and unwise.

He gifted the house and its contents to Charlie and Maggie Bates with a trust-fund that gave them a generous pension. The only things he was keeping were the car and the boat. Until he had settled where he would be living, the car would be looked after by a specialist Rolls garage in Goudhurst. The boat would stay on its moorings at Birdham for the moment.

There were other things for Healey to tidy up and eventually Healey said, 'Does Adele know about all this?'

'I'll be writing to her to put her in the picture.'

A meeting on finance was arranged between Healey and Pierre le Tissier who had already been briefed and instructed by Frazer.

The more Healey thought about it later the more shocked he was. And not just shocked but disapproving and rather resentful that Frazer could abandon his circle of friends without even a goodbye or a handshake.

It was his wife, Helen, who saw a little deeper into the character of the man they thought they knew so well.

'He spent a lifetime, Francis, having to be something that wasn't him. Putting a good face on it. Like that poet lady said, "Not waving, but drowning". His job, his career, his lifestyle were all part of surviving. Maybe this young woman understands him better than the rest of us.'

Frazer had taken Charlie and Maggie Bates to the Hilton with Anna and they had all enjoyed themselves.

As Charlie drove Maggie back to Rose Cottage which was now theirs, Charlie Bates delivered his own valedictory. 'Never seen him look so happy. And she obviously adores him. Good luck to the old bastard I say.'

Maggie ignored her husband's analysis. It wasn't wise to show approval of old men running off with young girls. She kept to the practicalities.

'They phoned from the Council this morning. Said it was OK to do bed and breakfasts at the cottage.'

Key House,
Midhurst,
W. Sussex.

Dear Jamie,

I heard from Francis that you'd be getting in touch with me about your new life and knowing you you'll find this embarrassing and maybe painful. So this note is to put your mind at rest. I've always known that although you were fond of me somewhere in that past life of yours was somebody who meant a lot more. I realised that when we were in the Royal Sussex chapel in the cathedral and we talked about love *á la folie*.

I've been very happy these last few years that looked so bleak when Tim died and it was you who got me back in the world again. You said that time at the cathedral that loving someone means loving them more than you love yourself. So let me wish you many happy years to come. Both of you.

Take care,

Love,

Adele.

They were married on a snowy Monday morning at Chelsea Registrar's Office with a cab-driver and a cleaning-lady as witnesses.

They spent three wonderful months following the sun in Europe. Checking on local conditions, real estate and local amenities, they decided unanimously on living in Italy. They chose a beautiful villa on the hills just on the edge of the town of Santa Margherita di Ligure. It looked down and across the beautiful bay and the marina where *Aquila* was berthed. The only other reminder of the past was the white Rolls Silver Shadow Mark 1 that was parked in its own shaded place alongside the small flat used by Angela, the housekeeper and her small daughter.

They had been there for six months when they took the bus one evening to Chiavari and Jamie had been recognised at a cafe by the elderly tenor sax who used to play in the jazz quintet at von Acker's Jazz Club in Amsterdam. Reluctantly Jamie had sat at the piano and ended up playing until the early hours of the morning. Inevitably he ended up doing this most Saturday nights. And none clapped louder than Lady Anna Frazer.

From time to time they took a trip to Paris for a week and a couple of times to New York. Her father had a permanent invitation but never took it up. His heart gave him no trouble and he wrote that he was thinking of starting up his old business again.

Primrose Publications filed for bankruptcy, Bowman was moved to a hustling job in Satellite TV and Al Pinto is now a professional lobbyist in Washington with clients ranging from a group advocating the banning of butter and substituting margarine, to a medical advocate of jojoba root as a preventative against HIV. He married a pretty young secretary who rated him as far superior to Larry King. Al Pinto was very happy in his new role and happier still when he became the father of a baby boy.

A novel with a romantic but realistic plot written by Adele with the title '*Two Kinds of Love*' has been accepted by a publisher and is expected to do well.

Francis Healey became a County Court judge and is rated as one of the outstandingly sound judges in the south of England.

On odd occasions when they hear Art Tatum or Fats Waller on the radio, Adele's and Helen Healey's thoughts go to Jamie Frazer and wonder how he's making out. Oddly enough they both wish him well.

And that's about it.

pa T.H